KAGE

THE SHADOW

Also by John Donohue…

Novels
 Sensei

 Deshi

 Tengu

Nonfiction
 The Overlook Martial Arts Reader

 Complete Kendo

 *Herding the Ox: The Martial Arts as Moral
   Metaphor*

 *Warrior Dreams: The Martial Arts and the
   American Imagination*

 The Human Condition in the Modern Age

 *The Forge of the Spirit: Structure, Motion, and
   Meaning in the Japanese Martial Tradition*

JOHN DONOHUE

KAGE

THE SHADOW

YMAA Publication Center
Wolfeboro, NH USA

JOHN DONOHUE

YMAA Publication Center, Inc.
PO Box 480
Wolfeboro, NH 03894
1-800-669-8892 • www.ymaa.com • info@ymaa.com

Paperback edition	Ebook edition
978-1-59439-210-8	978-1-59439-239-9
1-59439-210-2	1-59439-239-0

Editor: Leslie Takao
Cover Design: Axie Breen

10 9 8 7 6 5 4 3 2 1

Publisher's Cataloging in Publication

Donohue, John J., 1956-

Kage : the shadow / John Donohue. -- Wolfeboro, NH : YMAA Publication Center, c2011.

p. ; cm.

ISBN: 978-1-59439-210-8 (pbk.) ; 978-1-59439-239-9 (ebook)
"A Connor Burke martial arts thriller"--Cover.

1. Burke, Connor (Fictitious character) 2. Smuggling--Arizona--Fiction. 3. Martial artists--Fiction. 4. Arizona--Fiction. 5. Martial arts fiction. 6. Suspense fiction. I. Title.

PS3604.O565 K34 2011	2011927806
813/.6--dc22	2011

Printed in Canada.

To the Sweeney family
for welcoming me in.

PROLOGUE

Dawn. I lay for a time coming back to the world: the warmth of a blanket, the cool air of a day yet unborn touching my face. The hitch of old injuries. The tug of memory.

A Tibetan monk once told me I walked a path as narrow and dangerous as a razor's edge. As in many situations, he could see far and well. That monk wasn't just concerned with peril in the normal sense: life is, after all, suffering. He was worried, instead, about things of the spirit.

I look across the room where I have slept alone: even in the half light I can see a table against a wall. My swords rest there in a wooden rack that I made by hand. The stand is nothing fancy; merely the functional product of the whine of a saber saw, my hands' guidance, attached to the familiar aroma of cut wood. The weapons had become so much a part of me that I felt they deserved a holder that was equally personal. I've read comments about the cold steel of a blade, but they're written by people who are strangers to my art. The blade isn't cold; it is warm, a thing alive like the cycle of breath or the pulsing of blood.

The old adage is that the sword is the soul of the *samurai*. I used to dismiss it as equal parts hyperbole and mystic mumbo-jumbo. I'm no longer so sure. When you spend hours, days, years with a thing, surely a connection of some kind is shaped. The wrapped cloth of the *katana*'s handle, the nubby ray skin beneath, no longer feel like things that are external to me: they *fit*. They fill the void of my curved fingers as if my hands were shaped to hold the weapon.

It's a tool of sorts, of course; a means to an end. But there's more to it than that. Maybe I've been in the *dojo* so long that things Japanese have become part of me; form and function, beauty and utility, merged into one. The swordsman's art is a curious alchemy: a synthesis of steel and spirit where the outcome is more than the sum of its parts.

The old timers tell stories of swords that were finely wrought and yet cruel: *setsuninto*, killing swords. They were weapons whose inmost essence drove their owners mad. Other blades were as cruelly beautiful, but imbued with a spirit that inclined to do good. They sang in their scabbards to warn of danger; they were bright and clear and miraculous things and, in the right hands, could be *katsujinken*, life-giving swords.

In the right hands... how to tell and who is to judge? I've made decisions in my life and done things I am not proud of. And yet they seemed necessary. Like a pebble tossed in a pool of still water, each action sent waves in many directions. Some I anticipated. Many I did not. And I wonder.

In the half-light of each starting day, I lay in silence, alert to the swords in the rack. Hopeful. Fearful.

In the silence of dawn, will the blades moan to me or will they sing?

1
COYOTE

The *coyote* picked his way quietly over rough ground, climbing up the slope to a spot where he could watch and wait. The border smuggler, the *coyote* named Hector, settled down and listened to the faint rustling of the desert night. There was movement all around him; things hunted in the darkness, skittering and squealing, unseen. After a time he heard a different noise—the sound of men as they scraped their way over the canyon lip. Their voices were soft murmurs pulled apart by the night breeze. Hector strained to hear what was being said, but could not. The intruders paused at the canyon rim as if getting their bearings. They shone green lights on the dirt, tracing the tracks of the men Hector had sent off into the gully to the rendezvous. Hector watched calmly and waited for the small knot of men to head up the gully as well. If he felt anything at that moment, it was chagrin that the people he had led might be caught. But, they knew the risk. He himself didn't sense a threat, and was confident that without the burden of his human cargo he would melt away and leave these pursuers behind. But instead of following the trail leading up the gully, they swung their lights around in measured arcs, looking for additional sign. Hector's eyes narrowed as a faint concern began to flicker in his chest. The lights steadied, focused on a new track.

Hector's.

He realized with a shock of cold certainty that he was wrong about the danger. The pursuers that he had vaguely sensed during the night journey across the border had not been intent on intercepting the men he was delivering. They weren't the Border Patrol. They weren't even interested in the identity or purpose of the men he was smuggling into the US. They had, instead, been following him to learn the secret of the route he had made through the desert. It was a basic foundation of his trade: *control the route and you can control the business,* he thought. He slipped out of the shadow of the rock outcropping he was crouched beneath and began to make his way away from this new source of danger. He moved cautiously, tense with concern that he make no sound. He knew that once a specific trail was known, a guide like himself became merely a liability. And on the border, liabilities were inevitably abandoned to the rocks and sun. Their remains gleamed, bone-white with the passing of years, a reminder to travelers of the danger of the territory through which they passed.

Hector had been a border smuggler for more than five years. He knew all about the dangers. If the desert was harsh, the competing gangs that struggled to control the border's business were even more so. Hector had learned to trust few people, hug the darkness like a friend, and to choose the more difficult and out of the way crossings for his business. A *coyote* had many things to fear.

The Americans were the least of Hector's problems. No matter what their publicity claimed, the Americans could not close the border. The long line between Mexico and the United States was an abstraction on a map. It was an illusion bent by topography and cracked in the desert sun. On the ground, lines on a map had little meaning. The Border Patrol rocked along rutted tracks near the most likely points of access. They scanned the horizon for movement, safe in their trucks, the murmur of the radio a faint under-current in the wash of the air conditioning. Hector the *coyote* had learned the lessons well from his uncles and cousins who had gone before him into this business: go where the *gringo* did not wish to go. Go at night. Move quickly, but don't rush. Plan.

And watch your back. Hector was careful to keep a low profile in the border towns. He maintained respectful relations with the various gang leaders in the area, paid the protection money demanded of him, and relied on a small network of family members to assist in the growing business of smuggling "special" items across the border. They were efficient, discrete, and successful. That was why, when the strangers from the capital had come looking for experienced guides, Hector's people were chosen.

Like most things, there was a hierarchy of services in the *coyote's* world. Anyone could try to cross the border, and any number of eager young men, armed with broken down sneakers and makeshift canteens crafted from old bleach bottles, would offer to serve as guides. The true *coyote* watched them silently through squinted eyes, the skin on their faces taut and etched by the hot breath of the desert. They said nothing and let the young men go. More often than not, their careers were short-lived; the desert, or the gangs, or the Border Patrol people saw to that end. Amateurs were a sad feature of most professions, but not a significant drain on business in this one. In the *coyote's* world, success was survival.

The stakes grew exponentially once the *coyote* moved beyond smuggling *campesinos* desperate to work backbreaking days on American farms and construction sites. There were other things to smuggle, and if the risk was greater, so too was the reward. These were deals that were not cut on a dusty roadside by the rear of an old pickup truck. The men you met were not hungry and weighed down by their past and lumpy bundles of possessions formed into packs with garbage bags and old twine. These deals were made by quietly assured men, whose eyes were as fathomless and glittery as vipers. The parties met in the dim shelter of bars after each side had carefully weighed the competence of their intermediaries, had listened to the rumors on the street, and after each side had scouted out an alternate means of exit.

Hector's people would watch the late model SUV's churn a cloud of dust down the street. When they reached the rendezvous, young men with dark glasses jumped out and scanned the rooflines. They dressed for the city, yet their shiny boots were immediately coated with the powdery dust of the desert. The wind pushed, hot and fitful, at paper trash in the street. You could hear sounds coming from a distant alley, where stringy dogs snarled and fought each other for the gristle and bone remains of something unidentifiable. People scuttled toward doorways, nervously eyeing the men from the SUV—quick, tight sideways glances, before they shut themselves behind the safety of thick doors. The young men didn't seem to react to anything in particular, but took it all in. They watched the pattern of activity, sensitive only to the ripple of the unexpected. At a signal, their principal would emerge from the vehicle and the *coyote*'s people would follow him into the dark room.

In these situations, respectful greetings were always the first item of business. Drinks offered. The conversations were formal, reserved, and terse with an odd combination of respect and tension. The deals themselves were models of simplicity.

Something needed to cross the border. Sometimes it was an object. Other times it was people. The *coyotes* never asked what the packages contained or who the people were. They weren't interested in details beyond the professional assessment of the logistics of transport. A target date for departure was made. Another was established for delivery. The *coyotes* always insisted on some flexibility with the dates for security purposes, but they knew the value of dependability as well. A pickup point was proposed, debated, established. The price for services was negotiated. Payment arrangements were made.

Hector had developed a reputation as the man to come to for particularly sensitive transport jobs. Even the *viejos*, the old timers, admitted that he had a knack for moving through the roughest terrain, of scouting out routes that consistently evaded the American interdiction patrols. He used these routes sparingly, saving them for the most lucrative jobs. The men from the capital paid well for this work, and the high price guaranteed Hector's continuing enthusiasm as well as his silence. But just below the surface of these deals there lurked something more sinister: the potential for violence or betrayal. The chance that it could blow up in your face, or that the price for failure would be higher than you could bear.

Most times, Hector convinced himself that he was too good to fall victim to these undercurrents. He was young and crafty and therefore successful. He was sure that one day he would be a legend on the border. But the old women would watch him silently from a distance and murmur darkly. In life, they knew, there was beauty, and merit, and skill. All these things faded. And the only thing left to you was *suerte*, luck. It was the most fickle of powers, alighting on one man for a time and then deserting him for no apparent reason. They watched Hector, the *coyote*, marveling at his success. But then they crossed themselves and gestured against the evil eye. *The day will come,* their looks said silently. *Even for you, Hector, the day will come when luck will betray you, disappearing like water spilled in the desert sun.*

This latest crossing had been an important one—the arrangements had been meticulous and the deal was cut with great formality between Hector and the men from the capital. They were men of great seriousness, and he treated their need for special arrangements with respect. The three men he was to take across the border were young and fit, dark eyed, but not *Mexicanos*. It was imperative, Hector's clients insisted, that there be no contact with the Border Police. If a crossing were not possible, he was to bring them back rather than risk their arrest. They provided Hector with a cell phone and a number to call once he reached the rendezvous point on the other side of the border. His instructions were to use the cell to make a call once they were across, leave the three men at the location specified, smash the phone and bury the parts, and not look back.

Hector had taken in the instructions without comment, content in the details and the payment. His knowledge of different routes was a valuable commodity. There were various families and gangs vying for control of the most lucrative smuggling routes. Hector went to great pains to avoid observation from rivals, to hoard this knowledge, and to use his most secure routes only for special jobs. His discretion was rewarded with jobs such as this one. His secret trails were as secure as sparing use could make them, and their nature made them practical only for the fittest travelers. His cargo would be up to desert travel, his clients had assured him. And they smiled at each other as if enjoying a particularly good joke.

Hector couldn't remember the precise moment during the

night crossing when he began to suspect that he was being shadowed. He always made a habit of scanning his route ahead whenever the terrain made that possible. He often checked his back trail as well. He paused to listen in the night, having the cargo crouch down in silence at intervals. They did what he said without protest. To Hector, they seemed like men familiar with noise discipline and quiet travel in out of the way places. They waited patiently in the darkness. Their eyes sometimes caught the glitter of starlight, but they said nothing to give away their location, content to let their guide set the pace.

Hector's vigilance had revealed nothing alarming during the night passage. But a nagging feeling, like a faint breath of clammy wind across the nape of his neck, lingered with him. He redoubled his security checks, scanning the night's horizon lines for threats, pausing often to strain to hear the telltale sound of a boot scraping across the hard ground. He typically did not travel armed, but on these special trips he sometimes found a weapon useful. An old long-barreled .38 was tucked into his waistband, covered by his shirt. He had never used the pistol in anger and it gave him little comfort this night. To shoot, you needed a target you could see.

They reached the drop off point two hours before dawn. Hector led the men into a small canyon that opened from a spur of rock that pushed out from the hills rising in a rough jumble of rock in front of them. He walked quickly into the darker confines of the canyon, his hand brushing lightly against the side of the wall. He felt more protected out of the open desert and uttered a faint sigh of relief at completing the journey. He almost laughed at his fears, but some residual sense of foreboding choked off the emotion. He cautiously flicked on a flashlight, the lens covered with a red filter to preserve night vision. The canyon was littered with boulders of various sizes. There was a winding path through them, but it took caution and care. Hector hadn't come this far only to break his leg.

The men he was delivering followed him to the end of the canyon. Here, the narrow defile widened to a roughly circular space perhaps twenty meters wide. Looking up, you could see the night stars shining; remote pinpricks in the remote disk of sky at the top of the canyon. Hector motioned to his travelers to squat down around him. He flicked the light off and could hear their faint panting in the darkness, the sound contained and amplified by the rock walls.

"What now?" one asked him in English. He did not sound like an American. But Hector forced himself not to speculate. These men were packages. Nothing more.

Hector checked the fluorescent hands of his watch. "We wait until four. Then I call." He stood up and stretched his back. He turned back down the trail, straining to see in the darkness of the canyon. Nothing. He faced the men and flicked on his light once more, playing it along the wall of the canyon.

"The Old Ones lived here," he told them. Up the cliff at a ledge some ten meters off the ground, the men saw the jagged opening of a doorway, framed by uneven rock masonry. In the daylight, they would have seen the black stain of ancient campfire smoke that licked out across the dwelling's ceiling and up the doorway's lintel. The *coyote* played the light carefully up the surface of the cliff, showing them the regularly-spaced handholds. "You climb up here to the mesa top. Follow the gully northeast for perhaps two kilometers. It washes out into a sandy bed. The truck will pick you up there."

"And you?" It was the most conversation they had made all night.

"I lead you up," Hector said simply. "Then I go back." It wasn't completely accurate, but it was all they needed to know. When the time came, he made the phone call and then led the way up the canyon wall, playing his light along the surface to show them the handholds. They clambered over the rim at the top and Hector pointed them down the gully to the rendezvous. He squatted in the darkness until the sound of their passing faded, content in a job completed.

And then he heard the clink of a rock kicked loose from the canyon passage below.

Hector felt the adrenalin rush of alarm grip his chest at the same time that he acknowledged that his gut instincts had been right: they were being tracked. Still crouching, he backed slowly away from the edge of the canyon. He touched the pistol in his belt like a talisman, took a deep breath, and thought.

They do not know the trail. Otherwise they would have intercepted us at the end. He squinted off down the gully in the direction he had sent the men he had brought across. *It will take time to discover the way up. By that time, the rendezvous will have been made.* He grunted softly in satisfaction: he had a professional's commitment to completing a job. If whoever was tracking them had hoped to hijack his package, they had failed. All that remained now was for Hector to elude them and make his way back across the border. He hefted his canteen and felt how light it had become. There was water and food stashed in the cliff dwelling below him. He had planned to rest there during the day and return with the coming of another night. Now his pursuers blocked access to his supplies. Hector would have to wait until they realized they had failed to intercept him and left. Then it would be safe to grab the supplies and head home by another route.

The rationality of the plan comforted him, despite the shock of being tracked. He would have to review his security procedures before heading out again. For now, however, he believed that he merely had to hide and wait.

But things hadn't worked out as he anticipated. The approaching day brought with it the awareness that they were coming—for him. Hector began to move away from the canyon rim, throwing glances behind him in the dim grayness of coming dawn, but the shadows and shapes of the rocky desert twilight could have held a hundred pursuers and he would have been none the wiser if they were gaining on him.

Hector worked the pistol out of his waistband. If the men moving up the cliff below him had tracked him across the border and done it carefully, they now knew one of his most closely held secrets. And perhaps this was not the first time he had been followed. He had to admit that this was a possibility.

So why come for me now?

Hector had a sudden mental image of one of the old women of the town, a leather-faced specter with wet, red-rimmed eyes. She had warned him that luck was a passing thing. Now, in the darkness, Hector imagined that she looked at him with the penetrating stare of a *bruja*, a witch. Her mouth moved, and the night around him seemed to mimic her voice.

Perdido the wind whispered. Danger.

Hector exploded across the slope, suddenly breathless with certainty and the need to escape. If the trackers knew his routes, then all they needed to do was eliminate him. *Control the route, control the business.* If they caught him, he would simply disappear in the night, one more *coyote* swallowed up in rock and heat.

The men down below had scaled the cliff. They heard Hector's movement. Their hushed voices sounded strained and urgent, and the sound of their boots on the rock grew louder. Hector stumbled along the slope, hands outstretched for balance. He wanted to use his flashlight, but feared that it would give his position away. His mind was racing reviewing what he knew of the terrain, of the possibility of escape. Of survival.

He skittered along a slope of loose, flat rock fragments. His passage was marked by the clatter of rocks cascading down the hill. He lost his footing and, as his arms windmilled, the pistol went flying from his grasp, clattering into oblivion along with the moving rocks. Hector heard his pursuers closing on him and knew he couldn't waste time searching for the weapon. He reached firmer ground, breathless with effort. But this was no time to rest. He bent double, using his hands to propel himself forward. Hector never sensed the cut in the hillside until he plunged into it. The sudden sense of weightlessness; for a moment he thought he could fly.

Hector went down hard. Although the drop was not more than a few meters, it was studded with rocks that caught him on the tumbling plunge to the bottom of the cut. He lay there, tasting blood, and rock dust, winded. He tried to move, felt the stab of pain in his ribs and almost shrieked out loud when his leg shifted.

Broken.

He gasped, trying to get his breathing under control. Along the crest of the hill, the horizon was lightening. He would be able to see the silhouettes when his pursuers came along the slope, if he waited that long. But Hector knew that to wait was really just to die. He began to drag himself along the bottom of the cut, moving in painful jerks that made him bite his lip with the effort of staying silent. He didn't look back. He didn't see the shadowy shapes of his pursuers, shapes that paused at the arroyo's edge and then fanned out to look for a safe way down.

Hector's world had narrowed down to the dirt and rock of the arroyo floor, to the imperative need to keep moving, and to the jolting stabs of pain that accompanied each lurch forward. His mind raced, seeking an escape. If he could elude them, move toward the rendezvous… He still had the cell phone. He could even call the Border Patrol. They would merely deport him. It was an option to consider.

The fact that Hector could think like this, could plan despite the pain, and could adjust and react to the situation, were the qualities that had made him such a good *coyote* in the first place. That and luck.

He knew now that he would not be able to outdistance his pursuers. His only option was to hide. Another jolt of pain shot through his leg and Hector dragged himself into the meager shadow of a creosote bush. He was panting, he realized, and made a conscious effort to quiet his breathing. *They will hear you,* he reminded himself. Hector strained to listen, to sort out the bird sound and the faint pulse of wind from noises that suggested something more sinister. He was sure that his pursuers were still out there. He closed his mouth, knowing that it would preserve moisture. He would need it. His water bottle had been lost in his shambling, twisting escape from his pursuers. But the need for water discipline was a distant concern. First he had to survive.

The night was fading. The *coyote* could sense the growing power of the sun looming just below the horizon. In the sparse brush along the arroyo, birds had started to chirp, but the only sounds he heard were rougher things: the gasp of his own breath and the scrapes and thuds as he dragged himself painfully over the stony earth. The end of night brought no comfort to him: the heat would kill him if his pursuers did not.

Hector dragged himself deeper into the space between the creosote bush and the rocks near it. He lay there, silent and still, like all animals when they hide from hunters. His heart was hammering in his chest. He closed his eyes and saw the image of the old *bruja*, her eyes red and insistent, boring into him. *Pobrecito. Luck fails us all.*

Exhaustion dragged on him. His body burned, his mind grew fuzzy. His eyelids drooped. Hector jerked his eyes open, unsure whether the sound of a voice was real or something from a dream. In the spreading light of the desert morning, the creature that loomed over him was a thing of shadows and swirls. He had the briefest of moments to react to the terror of discovery, unsure of what he was seeing. A man? Its tattooed visage was more like a devil. Hector's last moments were a jumbled mix of pain and confusion. The clutch in the chest as he realized he was doomed. The sharp throb of shattered bone. The thing above him calling in triumph to the other hunters. Arms that lifted high into the washed out blue of a morning sky, as if pronouncing a benediction.

The jagged rock came down on Hector, again and again, until he lay still, slowly seeping moisture into the hard ground of the borderlands. In time, flies would come to swarm over the sticky pool of fluid until the sun rose, fierce and full, and baked the moisture of Hector's life away, sucking it deep into the desert's heart.

2

LESSONS

The things we remember best tend to come to us in special ways—often linked to extremes of emotion like joy and fear. Or pain. My teacher had been shaped in a tradition where both fear and pain were constant companions because, the old masters believed, an authentic life was one that didn't deny these most inevitable of experiences, it just learned to transcend them.

Yamashita is a *sensei,* or teacher, of the martial arts—the *bugei*—of old Japan. The *bugei* are many things—ways of fighting, of physical training, aesthetic disciplines forged out of the most horrific of practices. My teacher is a master of the form and the essence of these systems, a lethal man whose spirit is as keen and polished as the blade he teaches me to wield. He is simultaneously demanding, exasperating and amazing. I've been banging around the martial arts world for almost thirty years now, and I've never seen anyone like him.

I use the word banging literally. Lots of people today think they know something about the martial arts—black belts and Zen, *ninja* in dark pajamas jumping across a movie screen doing cartwheels that would make an astronaut toss his lunch. The death touch. Wispy masters who never sweat and are never defeated. But Grasshopper, this is all an illusion.

To train in the martial arts is like being apprenticed to frustration, to the burn of effort, and the unattainable criteria of perfection. There's no glamour, no reward beyond the ones you create in your own heart. You struggle along the path and your teacher goads you or challenges you, always three steps ahead and always waiting, his eyes betraying nothing but demanding everything. And you try to give it.

In the process you take some lumps. I've broken my fingers and toes more times than I can count. Some ribs. Until a few years ago, my nose was intact, but that's a thing of the past. It's probably not a huge tragedy—I have a relative in Ireland who once said I have a face like a Dublin pig. When I do my warm up stretches in the morning, I can feel the tug of years of muscle damage all over me and the buzzing reminder of an old dislocated shoulder. There are small white scars on both my hands from a morning when I tore through jagged undergrowth, focused only on the fight to come. I have a long slash of a scar down my back that I got in a sword fight on the night when I began to truly understand what all this training had turned me into. And there are other, less visible marks.

Late in the night images sometimes come unbidden, and I'm pulled back into a whirl of adrenalin and heat and blood. But you cope. You learn to breathe deeply and wait for the sweat to dry. You wait for morning to come and with it the light to remind you of the present. My scars suggest where I've been, not where I am. Most days, I'm in Yamashita's training hall, honing my technique in closer imitation of him and putting his lower ranked students through their paces.

The *dojo*—what Japanese martial artists call their training hall—is a big space, with high ceilings and a polished floor of tightly fitted hardwood strips. There's a mirror on one wall that we use to check ourselves for correct form. Sometimes I catch a glimpse of my features while I prowl the room, and the face is both familiar and strange. For at times it appears to me that my eyes have become as hard and flat as my master's.

That day, I was grinding some swordsmen through a particularly tricky exercise. My teacher has started to hold seminars lately for martial artists who aren't his regular students, but who study related arts and are looking to deepen their skills. We get people who are trained in all sorts of systems. They enter the training hall in uniforms that have been worn into supple functionality. Some are in the karate or judo uniforms known as *gi* and have tattered and faded black belts riding low on their waists. Others wear the more formal pleated skirt known as a *hakama* and tops of white or blue or black. They all stand quietly, people who are centered, balanced, and coiled like steel springs ready for release. They don't impress Yamashita too much, because just to be accepted as one of his regular students you usually need black belts in a few different styles, recommendations from some seriously advanced teachers, and an almost infinite capacity to suffer. But I watch the seminar students carefully and treat them like dangerous, barely domesticated animals.

It's not paranoia on my part. The presence of outsiders at our *dojo* is new, and at first I was puzzled about why Yamashita would allow this. My teacher doesn't advertise anywhere and just to find the converted warehouse where we train, you have to know where you're going and be willing to thread the obscure backstreets of the Red Hook section of Brooklyn. But a small stream of fanatics do make the journey along the hard cement and past the harder eyes of Red Hook's less desirable element. It took a while, but ultimately Yamashita's reasons for sponsoring these seminars became clear: he wasn't interested in letting people in to see him; he was letting them in to see *me.*

I'm his senior student, although when you say it like that it doesn't begin to get at the core of our relationship. He has forged me into something, a version of himself, and we are tied together with filament so fine and so strong that the link is as invisible as it is undeniable. I struggled against it for a time, but I've come to learn to accept it. I move just like him now, and if my footsteps take me along slightly different routes, I know that in essence we travel the same path.

So these seminars were Yamashita's way of letting people know who I was and that I would one day assume leadership of the *dojo*. We have both been scarred by our pasts and now, imperceptible to most, my teacher's movements tell of his wounds. It's something I try not to think about: it's bad for my head and my heart.

But I'm not just being sentimental. My teacher has taught me better than that. I watch the trainees with slightly narrowed eyes, judging them, measuring their skill, and trying to divine their intent. They look back in much the same way. Bringing a bunch of highly skilled fighters together, pointing someone out and implying that he's better than everyone else in the room, is the martial arts equivalent of pouring chum into shark infested waters.

These seminars have the feel of those old Westerns where a bunch of new gunmen stalk into town looking to take on the local prodigy. You can hold up your hands and protest you're not interested in a fight, but people just smirk in disbelief and you know, deep down, that you'd better go get your weapon.

In the martial arts, we meditate and talk about the nature of training as a *Do*, a path, to enlightenment. But there are lots of ways to accomplish this end that don't involve pounding on people in the way we do. Ultimately, no matter how hard we deny it, there's part of us that *likes* that aspect of the *bugei*. The heat. The contact. The fury, trapped and funneled into something truly dangerous. No matter what the particular martial art system is called or what the techniques look like, there's a basic pattern to advanced training: you get pounded and you pound back. The easily bruised should not apply.

I've taken my lumps in the *dojo* and in places far more terrifying as well. I prefer to approach training as a way to fine-tune my technique. I save punching on the afterburners for the real thing. But no matter how calmly I speak to people at these seminars, no matter how much I stress that we're here to learn from each other, I can see that deep down they don't buy it. They wait and watch, hoping for an opportunity to prove to Yamashita that there was a better choice for his top student than the guy leading the exercises. I brace myself to prove them wrong.

And, I've come to realize, this is also part of Yamashita's plan. Everything in my master's world is a means of training. The fact that someone at a seminar may take a run at me is not necessarily a bad thing. From Yamashita's perspective it's more like icing on the cake, or a pickled plum in the middle of a rice ball.

It's not all tension, of course: a few participants at the seminar weren't strangers. Some of the *dojo* regulars were there to help out. A while ago, Yamashita and I had met a woman named Sarah Klein who practiced *kyudo,* the Japanese art of archery. We had both been attracted to her, although for different reasons. Yamashita had been intrigued by her focused energy, and while I had been drawn to that spirit, I was intrigued by so much more. What she saw in me was anyone's guess, but I was glad that she saw something. And I was glad she was at the seminar today.

Sarah's not a big person, but when watching her slight figure move, you got a sense of grace and strength rare in most people. It may have been that suggestion of physical potential that made Yamashita take her on as a student. She was dark-haired with big eyes and a heart shaped face. Just seeing her across a room usually made my stomach flip. Today, as I moved around the seminar participants, she'd occasionally catch my eye for a split second and I'd see a hint of the smile I knew she was suppressing. Sarah has a great smile.

I kept my *sensei* face on, however, and resisted the impulse to wink at her. For now, I had to keep the seminar participants in check. We were executing a series of moves that in the beginning look a lot like the *mae* routine in your basic *iaido kata*. *Iaido* students focus on practicing a series of connected techniques known as *kata* that involve the art of drawing and cutting with the Japanese sword. In the first *kata* that they typically learn, students sit in the formal kneeling position, their swords sheathed. As they sense an attack being launched from the front, they rise on their knees, then draw the sword from its sheath and cut in a wide lateral arc across their front, planting their right foot forward so that only the left knee remains touching the ground.

In the sequence as traditionally practiced, the lateral swipe is followed up with a vertical cut. The idea is that your attacker, kneeling before you, starts to move. You swipe at him, but he jerks back just out of range. You follow up by drawing yourself forward with your right leg and then cutting down in what is meant to be a decisive attack to the head.

As I say, it's pretty standard. Except in Yamashita's *dojo*. He doesn't think it's particularly realistic that someone who has dodged your first strike would remain seated and waiting for your follow up. Much more likely, he says, that the attacker would rear up and then back away, well out of range.

Which means you have to chase him.

It sounds simple enough, but Yamashita is always as interested in finesse as he is in functionality. In many ways, he doesn't even consider them two separate things. So in his *dojo,* after the first cut, the swordsman has to lunge far forward while remaining crouched. Your opponent is standing up by this point and expects you to rise as well. So, my teacher explains, you do the opposite and pursue him from the lower position, driving forward while remaining alert to the possibility of counterattack.

It sounds easy, but is difficult to pull off. The crouching position is awkward, and it takes time to get the knack of using your muscles correctly. If you rely too much on the left foot to propel you, you tend to topple forward, providing a dangerous gap for your opponent to exploit. Too much right leg, and you drag yourself forward and can't move fast enough or far enough to be effective. In years past, when Yamashita demonstrated the technique, it looked as if he was being jerked across the floor by an invisible wire: a feral gnome bent on your destruction. His posture was impeccable, and his hips drove him forward while his legs worked smoothly together to close the gap between him and his opponent, his eyes intent and his sword boring in for the kill.

The visual memory of that attack burns in my brain like the afterimage of a lighting flash. I work every day to replicate it. That day, I had demonstrated the basic idea and a less terrifying version of the move itself to the men and women at the seminar. They watched me coldly, nodding as I shot across the floor. I could see the thought flash across their eyes: *if he can do it, I can.* Then I began what for those people was probably one of the most unpleasant hours of their lives. Because the only way to begin to learn something like this is through repetition.

I had them lurch back and forth across the *dojo* floor. The line of trainees completed the awkward trip. "Good," I commented flatly. "Again." They churned across the floor once more. When they got back, more than a few began to stand to take some of the strain off their legs. I shook my head but didn't say a word, just swept my arm back in the direction that they had come. Off they went.

After thirty minutes or so, their faces were flushed with effort, their palms sweaty on the handle of their wooden training swords. Out of the corner of my eye, I saw Sarah blow a strand of her fine brown hair away from her eyes, draw a focusing breath, and stoically continue. She needed no prodding.

Breath control was second nature to most of these people, but even so I heard some gasps. I knew that their leg muscles felt as if they were on fire. But I kept them at it. It wasn't just that as long as they did this exercise I didn't have to worry about what else they might try to pull on me. It was because my teacher and his teachers before him and now, I suppose, even I, believed that the best learning takes place at the white hot juncture where the body and mind are thoroughly fatigued. And as I looked at the trainees, I sensed that some of them were starting to make the move their own.

That's what training in the martial arts is about.

After a few more tortuous minutes, I called a break. I wanted to burn these people, not break them. They stood up gladly and walked around the room, blotting their foreheads with their sleeves, waiting for the muscle cramps to ebb a bit. I edged over to Sarah.

"How's it going?" I asked quietly.

"I don't know what you had planned for later tonight, Burke, but dancing is definitely out of the question." She smiled.

"The Irish don't dance," I informed her.

"Come on," she protested, "I've seen those girls in those fancy little dresses jumping around. What's it called?" I had recently taken Sarah to a *feis,* a festival that featured Irish step dancing, bagpipes, and other forms of Celtic torture.

"Step dancing," I told her. She nodded silently at my answer, as if her point were made. "But did you ever notice," I continued, "that when they dance, they keep their arms pinned to their sides?"

"So?"

"That's because in the old days, when the English lords would make the peasants dance, the Irish knew that they had to do it, but they decided that they would refuse to enjoy it."

Sarah looked me up and down, quietly pensive. "It explains so much about you, Burke," she concluded. Then I saw the laughter in her eye and knew I was being teased.

The seminar wound its way through the morning. We worked hard with *bokken,* the oak swords that are the basic training weapon here. We also did some empty-hand techniques, stressing joint locks and pressure point techniques that made the nerves jangle. It wasn't totally new stuff to most people in the room—trainees in arts like *iaido* or *aikido* or *kendo* can see some faint hint of their styles in what Yamashita does. But there's a difference: a harder edge, a more concise motion—it's difficult to explain in words. To see it revealed clearly, you have to experience it. Which can be a problem. In the *Yamashita-ha Itto Ryu,* my master's system, a full-bore demonstration usually leaves someone moaning on the ground.

The demo had to come eventually, of course. It was what

they were all really here for. They'd heard about Yamashita; they wanted to see the real deal. But so far, all they got was me. I could tell it was bugging them. Yamashita Sensei was there, of course. He drifted along the edges of the room, silent and contained, but you could feel him and sense his energy. Martial artists at a certain level of training can pick up the psycho-kinetic energy called *ki* . We all emit *ki*, but it viscerally pulses off someone like my teacher. You can suppress it somewhat or, if you're really good (and Yamashita is) you can ramp up the energy projection until even the dimmest pupil can feel it.

He was doing it on purpose.

As the men and women here today trained, they felt the pulse of Yamashita's *ki,* his energy, washing over them. Yet he stayed in the background, content to let me run the class. And what did they sense from me? I'm not sure. Most of them were probably too caught up in trying to master what I was showing them, in trying to look good in front of Yamashita. That kind of thing tends to dim peripheral awareness. In any event, they were glancing occasionally between the two of us as if com-paring. Average looking white guy versus Asian master whose energy field was pinging off them like sonar. Who would you watch?

Eventually, Yamashita looked at me and nodded. It used to be that he gave me a great deal of verbal direction. He said he was compensating for the damage done to me by all that study-ing for my Ph.D. in Asian History. He didn't need to say much to me anymore.

I called the class to order. They sunk attentively to the left knee, which permits everyone to see the instructor and hear his words. "OK," I said. "You're looking good." Many of them looked like they had been soaked with a garden hose, but they were all hanging in there. I liked that. "Relax for a minute." They settled in a rough circle around me and sat with crossed legs on the hard floor.

"We've been working this morning on various things—movement, sword work, some nerve points. In lots of ways, it's a sampling of a continuum of aspects in the system we train in here." I winced inwardly at the word *continuum*. Over the years, I've tried to lose some of my pointy-headedness, but I guess Yamashita is right—I *have* been damaged. I saw one guy smirk slightly at my choice of words. I didn't respond to it, but an idea was forming in the back of my mind.

"Most modern martial arts forms tend to focus their training on a limited range of techniques," I told them. It was nothing new to them. I could see that in their eyes. "At the higher level—where many of you are—you've got to expand your practice to include the integration of other techniques, other perspectives." I held up my hands, fingers splayed, and then joined my hands together. "Meld them." I began to walk around the circle a bit, making some eye contact with individuals.

"The exercise we practiced this morning that was based on *mae,*" I continued, "is a case in point. Depending on how you play it, it's got elements of sword-drawing and weapons use, of *aikido*-like entering techniques, and then the potential for an almost limitless series of applications using strikes or locks or throws." I watched them carefully as I spoke. There's a well-honored dictum in the martial arts world that people who talk about technique can rarely *do* technique. First, I had used an egghead word like continuum. Now I was going on and on, making some points that had to be patently obvious to people with their experience. So I watched their eyes. Some were expressionless, but I saw one guy—the same person who had smirked—looking at me with just the type of aggressive skepticism that I needed.

"Now let's take a look at the application, OK?" I saw a few satisfied nods around the circle and got the message—*it's about time.* When I gestured to my smirking friend, he rose eagerly to his feet in a smooth, powerful motion. His look told me that he had been waiting for something like this all day.

I made the rest of them back up and widen the circle. There was no telling how this would go. My opponent and I sat about one and a half meters apart from each other, just out of attack distance. As we settled down into the formal sitting position known as *seiza,* I held up my hand. "You want to wear *kote?*" I asked my opponent. They're the padded mitts that protect the hands and wrist in arts like *kendo.* They come in handy sometimes.

He looked at me pointedly. "I don't see you wearing any."

I nodded.

He smiled tightly. "I'm fine, then." He was probably in his late twenties. His hair was cut short and you could see powerful cords of muscle anchoring his head to his neck. This guy was built. He was also taller than I was—not a surprise, since most men are. He thought that when I offered the *kote* that I was asking him a question. Maybe he thought I was being overly conscientious. Or perhaps I was trying to needle him. There was probably some aspect of all these things at work. Mostly, however, I was just playing for time, getting a good look at him, registering the length of his arms and legs, and figuring out my options. It wasn't a particularly fair tactic. It's what Yamashita calls *heiho*—strategy.

We took our places and prepared. Usually, the senior person

serves as attacker, but since I was demonstrating the full application of the technique, my partner would start. We sat for a moment, breathing quietly, wooden swords at our left sides. The man sitting across from me on the floor seemed calm. Confident. Contained.

His sword began to move. I had been watching him and the others all morning. They were all pretty good. So I knew that if I lost the initiative here, his sword would have swept across me. At his first twitch, I had already begun to move.

My *bokken* swept in an arc across his face, forcing him to pull back. I scrambled forward in the crouch we had practiced and he shot up and backwards to avoid the pressure I was bringing to bear. This much was standard, almost scripted, and everyone in that room expected it. But now the interesting stuff was going to happen.

Because once my opponent stood up and got slightly out of range of my sword tip, he had a variety of options. His attack could come in many forms. The trick in doing something like this wasn't just in mastering the awkward series of scrambling motions we had practiced, it was in being able to cope with what would happen once your moves brought you into the radius of your opponent's weapon. Like now.

I tried not to give him the option to think too much by continuing to jerk myself forward in that low crouch, my sword seeking a target. He parried and backpedaled, and I could see the awareness in his eyes, his realization that whatever he was going to do would have to be lightning quick, because I was moving in, and if he didn't do something I was going to churn right through him.

He moved slightly to his right as I came forward and he snapped his sword down at my left shoulder in a quick, hard motion. I whirled in toward his blade, simultaneously moving my left shoulder out of range and bringing my own sword around to beat down his weapon. The wood shafts barked on contact. But he was pretty good: he held on and kept trying.

His impulse was to get the sword's blade back up for another try at me. He went with the force of my parry, sweeping his *bokken* down and then up in a counterclockwise sweep that was designed to bring his weapon into the high position, ready for a strike.

As his arms came up, I shot beside him in what the *aikido* people call an *irimi*, or "entering" movement. Now we were both facing in the same direction. I used my left hand to grab his neck from behind. I squeezed hard. It's not that I was going to make much headway against those muscles; it's that people hate to have their head or neck held in any threatening way.

He jerked his head to his left as if trying to look over his shoulder—it's a reflexive action—but he also moved to try to break my hold at the same time. As movements go, it was OK, and perfectly understandable. But for that one split second he had lost focus on his sword. I was still beside him and his right arm was stretched out, gripping the haft of the wooden sword.

I lifted my *bokken*, the point straight toward heaven, and then brought it down vertically, slamming the butt into the cluster of nerves on the inner edge of his right forearm.

It's a funny feeling. Sort of. I heard him gasp and then the *bokken* fell out of his hands. I dumped him on the ground and put the tip of my own sword about an inch from his nose. He wasn't stunned by the fall and his eyes crossed slightly as he focused on the tip of my weapon.

I moved away carefully, taking three steps backward to bring me out of range, and bowed formally to him.

Yamashita strode forward. He picked up my opponent's sword and looked around the room. "So…" he commented to the watchful trainees. "Application is always more interesting than rehearsal, *neh?*" I saw some heads nod ruefully. In more than one face, I saw a dawning gratitude that someone else had been selected to serve as a training partner. Yamashita moved toward the man I had put on the floor. He got up, but I knew that he wasn't going to be able to use his right arm for a while. His eyes bore into mine. For the first time that day, I let my own eyes bore back into a trainee's eyes. *Shoulda used the kote, bud.*

Yamashita watched the silent exchange. "What we have seen here is a lesson with two aspects. Like a sword blade, there are two sides, *omote* and *ura,* the front and the back, the obvious and the hidden." He canted the wooden sword in his hand to show one side of the blade, now the other. I saw some frowns from the group as they failed to follow his logic.

Yamashita saw it, too. He sighed. "*Omote.* Burke Sensei has clearly demonstrated how the technique you began to train this morning can be finished in a match. It is not the only application, perhaps," he said and paused to give me a subtly arch look, "perhaps not even the most elegant. But certainly effective."

Heads nodded, and Yamashita stood there for a minute, saying nothing. The lights of the *dojo* made the wooden floor gleam and, if they seemed to make his eyes deeper and darker, they also made his shaven head shine in imitation of the hard surfaces of his world.

Finally, someone raised a hand. "Yamashita Sensei," the question came. "What was the second lesson?"

My teacher looked up and regarded the expectant circle of trainees. He smiled slightly. "Ah. The hidden lesson?" He looked around. "You spent all your time waiting for me. Doing what Burke Sensei said, but waiting for me. The wise warrior keeps himself hidden, in the shadows. *Kage.* You know the word?" Heads nodded.

"Just so," my master finished. "My pupil keeps himself in shadow. Like most people, there is more to him than meets the eye."

The lesson was over.

3
TALES

I was talking to a bunch of mystery writers about the realities of fighting: how it works and the toll it takes. And how long it takes to recover. The overfed guy was incredulous.

"A week!" he protested, his eyes blinking in outrage. The conference room was a soothing beige and the hotel's mammoth air conditioning units kept the desert heat from seeping into the building, but I felt a bit warm anyway. The fluorescent ceiling lights played on the lenses of the man's round steel-rimmed glasses. He had a big mustache that helped balance out his jowls and he held a hardcover book to his breast, front cover out, so everyone could see. *Look. This is mine. I wrote it.*

I nodded and held my hands up to calm him. "A week to ten days," I repeated. The rest of the audience murmured in displeasure as well.

"But I can't have my main character laid up for that long," the writer continued. "It would destroy the pacing of the novel!"

I nodded in sympathy. "Sure." But it seemed that they wanted something more from me. I looked around the conference room at the fifty or so people whose eyes were sharpened in concern. I began again. "I'm not telling you how to write your books," I pointed out. "But the fact is, when you a take a good beating, you can figure that you're going to be like the walking wounded for at least a week. Trust me, in the real world, people don't take punishment like that and bounce back right away."

They were all deeply disturbed. They had been raised on Hollywood's version of combat. Most had never been in a real fight. You could probably stun three quarters of the people in the room into immobility with nothing more lethal than a good hard slap to the face. These folks were mystery writers. Their fictional activity dragged them over just a little into my world but its rules didn't mesh well with theirs.

I could see that the other panelists for this little talk were eyeing me uncomfortably. When the conference organizers invited me to come to Arizona's premier mystery and thriller writers' conference to speak about the reality of unarmed fighting, I think they had something else in mind. Tales of derring do. Nifty tricks. Lethal uses of toothpaste.

Actually, they had someone else in mind as well, but my brother refused to go.

Micky had snickered when he showed me the invitation. "Hey, check this out. You know that guy from the *News* who wrote the book about that Ronin guy?" I nodded. A columnist from the *Daily News* had churned out a breathless true-crime paperback about a case we had been involved in. It had all the elements of a best seller: a tale of revenge featuring serial murders and the exotic world of the martial arts. And, as far as I was concerned, the ending was great because Micky, Yamashita, and I got to walk away from the scene of the crime. Actually, they took me away in an ambulance, but that's beside the point. The guy from the *News* did a halfway decent job, but for some reason the book never did catch on—that season the reading public was interested in other things. But the author did his best to plug the book whenever possible, and was asking my brother to join him on a panel in an upcoming mystery writer's conference.

I had handed the letter back to my brother. "Why not?" I asked. "You were the cop who was featured in his book. You could tell those people stories that would curl their hair."

Micky had been a policeman for twenty years. He and his partner Art had just retired and started their own security consulting firm. They had spent the last decade as homicide detectives in New York City. That and a recent brush with Philippine terrorists had provided them with a wealth of contacts and tremendous street cred. As a result, business was booming. But although my brother no longer carried his gold detective's shield, not much else had changed. Growing up, Micky was always a handful. As he's aged (I'm not sure whether matured is the right term) he's gotten quieter. But it's not a comforting type of quiet.

We've got a big family and we get together often: a dense crowd of Burkes washing across various rooms and backyards. My brothers and sisters follow the old ways. As a result, there is a small army of Burke children that regularly alights on my mother's house like a swarm of Mayo locust. The adults settle on chairs and sofas or cluster in the kitchen to rib each other with the ease of long familiarity. The kids pound up and down stairs, on fire to eavesdrop on the adults, yet torn by the equally powerful desire to consume the salty snacks strategically placed like lures in the family room and basement, far away from their parents.

It's a benevolent type of chaos, a restless celebration of connection. But in the midst of it all, you'll often spot Micky sidling off to a window or the backyard and staring into the distance.

They say that cops either care too much and burn out, or grow callous out of self-preservation. Micky's opted for a third way. My brother seems to have mastered the art of keeping his inner filament intact, of stoking a fire that burns but doesn't consume him. It makes him a great cop, but it also creates an outlook that's pretty cut and dried: just the facts, ma'am.

"Connor," my brother had told me, as I emerged from my reverie, "the world is full of bullshit. Why should I contribute to it?" I nodded in silent agreement. Micky eyed me slyly and pointed at the invitation. "You, however, would be natural for this sort of thing."

Which is how I ended up in Arizona, in a room full of writers, annoying the Walrus Man. The conference people had offered to pay my expenses, and Sarah had a consulting job lined up in Phoenix that she'd been putting off, so we flew in together. I dropped her off in Scottsdale and headed south toward Tucson. We planned to meet up in a few days and drive north. The Grand Canyon. Cliff dwellings. The wide-open spaces. It was going to be great if I could just avoid being assaulted by the people at this writer's conference.

The audience was still waiting for something from me. A retraction? I wasn't sure. During my brief speech, I had gotten up to talk and had moved away from the table where three other speakers sat. Now I looked over to my fellow panelists in a mute appeal for help. They were silent for an awkward moment. I got the feeling they were happy just to be out of the blast zone. Then one cleared his throat and stood up.

He was a lean, youngish guy with a full head of dark hair, wearing jeans, a dark turtleneck shirt, and a sport jacket. He looked every inch the best selling writer that he was. He had a self-confident, easy manner that probably came with being on the "A" list. All day people had been nodding and smiling at him, pointing him out surreptitiously and gazing in rapt admiration. So far no one had fallen to their knees and tried to touch the hem of his garment, but the day was young.

"What Dr. Burke has done for us," he said smoothly, "is to remind us of the real challenge of the writer's craft." He smiled at me and I smiled back. I couldn't help it. The guy was good. And besides, the crowd seemed to buy it. I slipped into my chair and listened while he distracted the mob.

"What we do as writers," he continued, "is combine the world in our imagination with just enough reality to engage people's attention; to gain their trust. And then we spin a web with language that makes them suspend something of their critical faculties." He paused and the crowd seemed to hold its breath. "Then," he concluded, "we pull them into *our* world." His fellow panelists nodded in agreement and there was a general bobbing of heads all over the room.

No one asked me questions after that. I had, I suppose, been officially noted as someone who would never enter *their* world. Fair enough. The session broke up and people milled around chatting and hoping for a private audience with the other luminaries on the panel. I was left pretty much to my own devices. I cut across the room and started to move down a side aisle, putting the rows of metal banquet chairs between me and the writers lingering for a last word. Some of them still looked annoyed with me. A vigilant defense is a successful defense.

I escaped without incident into the foyer, which was located at the center of a series of conference rooms. People milled about display tables with colorful flyers and paperback books on racks, or sat along the walls at small café tables, chatting and drinking coffee. Everyone in this section of the hotel had to have little plastic ID cards around their necks to show that they were bona fide conference participants. Presenters like me had a little red star on their card. After my performance I was wondering whether they'd yank the star off.

I glanced at my watch. It was too early to call Sarah. I figured I'd get changed and visit the health center at the hotel. Traveling always makes my leg and back muscles tight and, after all this time, you get addicted to the regularity of some sort of training.

I noticed some people moving down the hallway. They didn't look like conference members. For one thing, they were missing their little plastic ID cards. And they were better dressed. The man was young and professional looking and was wearing a blue blazer with the hotel crest on it.

The woman with him was a little older, but still on the young side of middle age. Frosted blonde hair. Blue eyes. She wore some sort of linen suit that fell around her in a way that made you think it was expensive. The guy with the blazer was gesturing toward me. *Uh-oh. There goes my star.*

The woman walked right up to me and extended a hand. She moved with a smooth, controlled quality that betrayed toned muscle. She was good-looking, and you got the impression that she knew it and had practiced moving so that you would know it, too. It was a little too studied for my taste, but it didn't make her any less attractive.

"Dr. Burke?" It was a rhetorical question and she didn't even wait for a reply. "I'm Lori Westmann, the general manager."

I shook her hand and smiled. She didn't even bother to introduce the guy in the hotel blazer. His nametag identified him as "Roy." As far as Westmann was concerned, Roy was invisible. Being in charge means you get to pretty much treat people any way you want. Or at least that's what I hear. Roy didn't seem offended by the omission and just stood respectfully at a slight distance from us, ready to serve.

Lori Westmann smiled back at me with even white teeth. It was a practiced smile that didn't really communicate much—just a standard visual cue in the conversational sequence.

"What can I do for you?" I said.

She glanced about her at the guests. "I have a business proposition for you. Perhaps you'd care to join me for an early lunch?" She leaned in slightly toward me, cocking her head as if listening for my silent agreement. Then she moved off without waiting to see whether I was following or not.

We were seated with a bit of understated hysteria by the restaurant staff. It was clear that they were all pretty intimidated by their hotel manager. It suggested to me that her looks were probably deceiving. The blue-eyed blond with the long legs who was sitting across from me was easy on the eye in the same way a statue was: hard and cold.

The restaurant was hacienda themed; fake adobe partitions with rounded timbers jutting from little tile roof sections that were meant to create a pattern of cozy little nooks for customers. The focus of the place was inward, to the table and the meal, but you could look out through the tinted windows that ran across one end of the restaurant. Inside it was cool and dim, but out there you could see the hard light pounding down on the sere landscape in the distance.

The restaurant manager materialized to take our drink orders. He was almost quivering with attention. Lori Westmann ordered a chardonnay. I quickly perused the beer list and ordered a Sierra Nevada Pale Ale. I'm on a personal mission to try every beer ever made. Some varieties merit multiple tastings.

The drinks arrived. "Are you enjoying the conference?' she asked. "The accommodations appropriate?" She was running down a mental checklist. Ms. Westmann didn't look like someone deeply concerned about other people's enjoyment. She did seem focused on efficiency, however.

"It's fine," I assured her.

She smiled. A flash of white teeth and a tight motion of the lips. Then back to business.

"I was surprised to see someone like you at this type of conference, Dr. Burke."

I wondered whether this woman would ever get to the point and why she was so obviously engaging in small talk. She didn't seem the type. But I was in no rush. I shrugged at her statement and took a sip of the Sierra Nevada. Looked out the window into the shimmering hills and wondered idly how hot it was out there. "The accommodations are nice. The beer is even better," I said.

She frowned slightly at that—a small crease at the bridge of her nose. Lori Westmann probably was not exposed to a great deal of levity from underlings. She gave her head a little shake as if dislodging a troublesome fly. "I would expect someone like you at a conference of academics, not mystery writers."

She was overestimating my place in the scholarly community, but I let it go, and explained how I got here.

"And how are you enjoying this group?" she asked when I had finished.

"Not a question of how I'm enjoying them," I replied. "Mostly, I don't think I'm what they expected."

She eyed me over the rim of her wine glass. "How so?"

I thought for a minute. "I'm too… reality based."

She sat up a little straighter. "Excellent. So am I." The

waiter came and we contemplated lunch. Westmann didn't even look at the menu when she ordered. I had a chicken sandwich. Burke, culinary adventurer. When the help had gone, Westmann got back to business.

"I'm looking for someone with your research expertise to assist me," she began. I raised my eyebrows questioningly to encourage her to continue. Lori Westmann took a deep breath as if preparing herself for something unpleasant. "A month ago, my father was found dead at home."

"I'm sorry."

She waved the sympathy away as irrelevant. "The cause of death was listed as an accidental fall. I disagree."

I thought I saw where this was going. "Ms. Westmann, I'm sorry for your loss," I started, "but this is probably something you need to take to the police. I'm not a trained investigator." This point was, in fact, a huge understatement. I've blundered around a few crime scenes to help my brother Micky, but, as he reminds me, my major talent is that I know obscure things that most people don't care about. I also have a knack for getting in way over my head and clawing my way back out again.

"I'm well aware of your background and qualifications," Westmann commented. "I have a number of people working on this from the forensic angle."

"And?"

"You know as well as I do that if a murder isn't solved within forty-eight hours it's probably not going to happen." She waved a hand. "The police are overworked. They feel the evidence for a crime is shaky at best and that I'm a typical grieving child incapable of accepting the sudden death of a parent."

She didn't look all that broken up to me, but she did seem like someone who didn't take no for an answer. Our lunches came and I ordered another beer. Lori Westmann had been sipping at her wine since it arrived, but the glass seemed as full as ever.

"And are the cops right?" I asked. "About you, I mean."

She looked at me directly. I didn't think the cops were right. Her eyes had a hard glint to them. "I have very good reasons to think that my father's death was not accidental, Dr. Burke."

"Such as?"

I had picked up my glass to take a drink. Lori Westmann leaned across the table toward me. "Dr Burke," she said intensely, "my father was Eliot Westmann."

I put down my beer.

Eliot Westmann was a lunatic of the first order. He was notorious in Asian Studies circles for writing a series of books about his alleged adventures studying with a mysterious sect in Hokkaido, far to the north in Japan. Westmann and his publisher maintained that the books were true accounts; most scholars considered them a blend of personal fantasy and faulty scholarship.

Westmann had been awarded a doctoral degree by an obscure little Midwestern university. As an undergraduate he had a double major in marketing and theater. Everyone should have seen it coming. His book, *Inari-sama: Tales of a Warrior Mystic*, hit the stands in the late sixties and made him a cult favorite. I had looked at it years ago. It seemed a weird first-person journey through a confusing mix of Tantric Buddhism, recycled Asian stereotypes, and fragments of martial arts stories about *ninja* and *samurai* masters. He eventually published another five or so books on the same subject. Specialists scoffed and the public devoured them.

Westmann had always maintained that by writing about the secret community of *Inari-sama*, the Fox Lord, he had put his life at risk. He claimed that the members of the sect vowed a horrible revenge on anyone who revealed their secrets. Special assassins, marked with a mystic diamond tattoo at the base of the neck, would be dispatched from the cold mountains of Japan's remote north country to hunt him down.

The only people who hunted him down, it turned out, were fans. Nothing annoys scholars like popularity, but, Westmann, true to his theatrical penchant, reveled in the spotlight. He eventually dropped any pretense of connection to the academic establishment. He and his considerable royalty payments simply moved on. The last I had heard, he was dabbling in Native American mysticism, ostensibly still vigilant against assassins, still reclusive and as controversial as ever.

Westmann's daughter Lori watched me as I reacted to the mention of her father.

"So," I finally said trying to tone down my disbelief, "you think Inari-sama's people got him?"

Her mouth tightened with displeasure. "It's not a joke, Dr. Burke. We're talking about a man's life here."

I took a breath. She had a point. "OK. What do you want from me?"

"I never knew my father as a child. My late mother was his first wife. In the last five years we had reconnected and he told me about his experiences in Japan." She saw my skeptical look. "Never at any time did I get the sense that he was being anything but truthful." She tapped the table for emphasis. Her nails were short but manicured, professional. "I'm in a business where I have to read people constantly, Dr. Burke. My father was not lying."

"OK," I said. I wasn't going to argue. "How do I fit in?"

"My father was killed. I'm sure of it. I've got investigators looking into the crime. What I need is someone to do an objective assessment of his works." Her words came more quickly, fueled by an unexpected emotion. "Someone," she continued, "with a background as a scholar who can vouch for his integrity and rehabilitate his reputation after all these years…"

Oh boy. "And," I concluded, "someone to provide a motive for his killing."

Lori Westmann sat back in her chair, eyes bright. "Exactly."

I took a sip of beer. "Ms. Westmann, I've got to be honest with you. I read some of your father's stuff years ago. I thought it was entertaining, but I never took it seriously. All I could provide you would be an honest assessment of your father's work from a scholarly perspective…"

"That's exactly what I want."

"You'll want it unless it comes back with an unfavorable conclusion," I pointed out.

"I'm convinced an objective evaluation will clear his reputation and lead the authorities to his killer. And you're just the type of well-credentialed skeptic I need," she concluded briskly. She looked at me with a firm, almost clenched-jaw expression: woman of action brooking no resistance. Then she looked around into the dim recesses of the restaurant and made a motion with her hand. Roy appeared almost magically and placed a leather portfolio on the table. She opened it and pulled out a slim golden Montblanc. "I'm proposing that you spend approximately a month going through my father's notes and manuscripts, evaluating his work, and providing me with a confidential written report. Shall we talk about compensation?"

I have an obscure research specialty and a genius for alienating potential academic employers. I spend most of my time and energy training with Yamashita. As a result, I cobble a living together in the most unlikely of ways. I looked at the lady across the table and gave a mental shrug. *I've had worse jobs.*

Lori Westmann was waiting, tapping her elegant executive pen on an open page of checks. I thought about what I would make in a month in a typical year. Then I doubled it. I told her that was my fee and she didn't bat an eye. She started to write in the checkbook.

You idiot. You should have tripled it. "Plus expenses," I added hopefully.

She looked at me shrewdly. "Of course." She carefully completed writing and pulled the check free. "This is a retainer for the first two week's work." She stood up and extended a hand, smiling her pleasant and mechanical business smile. "Roy will provide you with the information you'll need to get started."

"I'll be able to get going next week," I told her.

Her smile disappeared. "I would prefer that you start immediately."

If I were thinking straight I would have wondered why she was in such a rush. Eliot Westmannn had been an academic laughing stock for decades and he'd been dead for over a month. It would take weeks for me to research this stuff. I thought she was merely being imperious.

I shook my head and smiled to soften the disagreement. "I'm sorry, but I've got other commitments over the next few days..."

"If it's a matter of money," she started and began to re-open her checkbook.

I held up a hand. "No. The retainer's fine. I'm just

unavailable until next week."

"I see. Do you mind telling me why?"

"Yes, I do." She blinked at that, and seemed at a momentary loss for words. "I'll be back early next week. If you can accept that, we've got a deal. Otherwise, it's been nice chatting." I handed back the check.

She looked at me with hardened eyes. "I made calls about you, Dr. Burke. They told me that you can be… difficult." But, she left the check on the table.

Ms. Westmann, I thought to myself, *you have no idea.*

4
WANDERERS

Sarah and I drove north, marveling at the arid expanse of land along the highway and equally amazed at the familiar-looking strip malls and fast food joints that dotted the desert landscape. It was a juxtaposition of the strange with the familiar. There were McDonald's and Burger Kings, K-Marts and pizza joints, odd samplings of American popular culture jettisoned out onto territory that looked as foreign to me as the surface of the moon.

An early spring snowfall dumped eighteen inches around Flagstaff, and we spent two days there, enjoying mountain air redolent of pine and biting with frost. As we drove toward the city in a thickening cloud of white, I saw huge forms moving slowly way back in the trees, like ghosts. Elk. It made me think of mountain men and times almost forgotten.

We slept at a place called the Pony Soldier Motel. I picked the name out of a list because it sounded like something from a John Ford movie. It was, in fact, just like any other mid-priced chain motel, except it had a full-size statue of a horse out front.

The next morning dawned sunny and the snow began to melt under a sharp blue sky. We ventured out. A few miles east on I-40 was Walnut Creek Canyon. Sarah and I scrambled down the cliff trail maintained by the Park Service, peering into dwellings that were centuries old before Europeans ever glimpsed the "new" world. You could stoop and enter the chambers of the old cliff dwellings, noting the dry-stone construction, the lick of soot along the door lintel from ancient fires, and try to imagine life in a vanished world. The north slope of the canyon was protected from the full blast of the desert sun and was greener than the south slope—differing ecological zones a stone's throw from one another, separated by a trickle of silver water some six hundred feet down at the foot of the canyon.

We shopped for souvenirs back in town. I couldn't resist buying a cowboy hat; every little boy wants to be a cowboy. And, the next day, the road north was clear. After driving through another stretch of high desert, we hit the tourist mecca of the Southwest. People were scurrying around like ants. Buses and cars lined up at the park gate. Ultimately, however, you got through, and all that hassle faded away into the expanse. Sarah and I walked along the rim of the Grand Canyon, silent so as not to disturb the immensity of the vista, of the colored striations in the canyon's walls, and the line between earth and sky that seemed to melt in the distant haze.

As the day faded, we headed back across the Sin Agua Mountains toward Williams. It sprang up from a flat landscape: a small, erect, compact place. Its buildings had the facades of the Old West, and there was nothing around it but the flat empty land, the interstate, and mountains that reared up like a dark barrier wall to the west. It looked like something from the movie *Shane*.

The next day we drove south and saw Tuzigoot National Monument and Montezuma's Castle. We ate in small restaurants, snapped roadside pictures on cheap disposable cameras, and laughed a lot. In the evening, Sarah and I would make love and hold each other, creating a sense of familiarity and connection and comfort, a secure space in a strange and transient landscape.

We'd talk quietly in the darkness.

"She's using you, you know," she told me as our trip was drawing to a close. Her head was resting on my chest and I stroked her back. The words she spoke were a soft murmur, but I heard the warning.

"It's not a big deal," I said.

"You don't think it will hurt your academic reputation?" Sarah asked.

She's sweet. I didn't want to disillusion her by stating I had no reputation to protect, so I reassured her. "Don't worry. I'll do the analysis and it will show—guess what?—that Eliot Westmann was a fraud. When his daughter gets the report, it'll never see the light of day."

"Do you think she really believes that he was telling the truth? It'll be sad for her to have him exposed as a liar."

I thought about that for a minute. "I don't know," I finally said. "She seems pretty hard-nosed. She's got her reasons for wanting this deal, but I don't see her getting all broken up about it. Mostly she'll be sad she shelled out all that money for me to do the research."

"Hmpph," Sarah murmured and snuggled a little closer. I pulled the sheet up over her back and held her. In the distance, cars whined down the highway. I listened to the rhythm of her breathing slow, felt the gradual loosening of her grasp as she drifted off into sleep. My eyes began to droop as well, and my arm slip off her. I shifted slowly. I made sure my arm was still around her. *Never let go.*

The next day, we said our goodbyes at the airport, a quick embrace and whispered assurances in the exposure of a public place. Sarah made her way through the security check and turned once to wave. There was the quick glint of her smile, eyes flashing, and then she was on her way back to New York. I sighed and headed back toward Tucson, into the harsher light of southern Arizona.

I showed up back at the hotel a little before lunchtime. Roy, efficient, alert, and as crisp as ever in his little hotel blazer, saw me coming and offered a solemn greeting and a limp handshake. He leaned over the high front desk, retrieved a manila envelope and ushered me through the main reception hall and back outside. Roy glanced at the gear slung over my shoulder clearly disdainful that that was all my luggage. He was used to people with matched luggage sets the size of piano cases. I had a duffle bag and the ratty little canvas satchel I call my briefcase. Security people at airports eye it warily and it's routinely searched for explosives.

"Will you require a porter, Dr. Burke?"

I hefted my gear and said I was fine. Roy looked doubtful, but carried on, gesturing as we came through the doors. Sprightly, tanned young people in pink polo shirts and khaki shorts bounced around the walkway, piling luggage onto carts and ushering people to various locations in little electric carts. One of them glided up in front of us and we got in.

"Ms. Westmann has given me explicit instructions that I'm to facilitate any requirements you may have, Dr. Burke," he began. Roy opened the envelope and began pointing things out to me. The hotel was a sprawling complex of stucco buildings, pools, and pathways. "You'll be staying in one of our detached suites for the duration of your assignment. As a guest of the house, your food and entertainment expenses are complimentary." He handed me a gold plastic card. "Simply use this card when you sign for things. It's also your room key."

We drove sedately and silently along a palm-lined path. The cart's motor whined faintly, but the sound of the rubber tires was louder than the engine. Roy traced our progress on a little map of the grounds. "The health club is close to your suite, and there are six pools at different locations around the facility. Restaurants and shops here," he touched the map lightly, "and here, and here."

"I'll need high speed Internet access and computer gear for research," I indicated.

He nodded. "Arrangements have been made with our Executive Support Center. A laptop should also be waiting for you in the room."

We tooled by a pool, the water's deep blue set off by the almost blinding white of the surrounding cement. The sun was hot and most people stayed in the shade or under the awning of the outdoor bar. Machines in the bar's eaves sprayed a fine mist that kept the patrons cool. It would be bad for business to have the guests collapse from heat stroke.

Our driver pulled neatly up a path and we got out. A small flowering tree shaded the entrance to the bungalow. A dark wooden door set in the stucco wall opened onto a spacious living room. The furniture was finished to make it look like it had been bleached in the sun. The color scheme was muted pastels, and understated Southwest art was on the walls. The AC had been on for some time and the place was about the temperature of a meat locker. Roy ushered me around the different rooms in the suite, pointing out the wet bar and fridge, the flat screen TV, the directory of services bound in something that was probably plastic but was meant to look like rich Corinthian leather. Both the living room and the bedroom had sliding glass doors that opened onto a small, walled-in patio. I slid the glass doors open and the heat hit me like a hammer. Small birds chirped in the greenery along the tops of the patio wall. I could smell flowers and something very like dry herbs. It was elegant, private, and restful. If Sarah were here, I would have liked it a great deal.

Roy must have seen the expression on my face. "I hope everything is acceptable?" he said anxiously.

I smiled. "First-class, Roy."

He smiled back. His was very professional. Hospitality is a serious business. "I'm so relieved," he told me. I looked carefully, but could detect no sarcasm.

I tossed my bags on the bed and he handed me the envelope filled with stuff. "Your research will mostly take place at the Westmann estate," he told me. "No autos are permitted on these grounds, but a hotel car will be yours to use when traveling. The bell staff at the main entrance are aware of this and will provide you with the keys."

"Where is the Westmann estate?" I asked.

Roy had a tight smile that was more like a grimace. "Ms. Westmann has arranged for you to be briefed by our chief of security on a number of items." He looked at his watch. "Would you care to freshen up or have a bite to eat before the meeting?"

"No, I'm good," I said. I took a last look around the room, pocketed my magic gold pass and went with him, back out into the harsh light.

The hotel's chief of security was a relief: you could see laugh lines etched in the tanned skin around his eyes.

"Charlie Fiorella," he said, shaking my hands. His white shirt was pressed and immaculate, the cuffs carefully folded back. Fiorella had freshly cut silver hair brushed back from a pleasant face that looked like it had seen a great deal. *Cop,* I thought.

He sat down behind a desk that had a gold nameplate, a black phone with lots of buttons, and a carefully placed pen set that had some sort of engraving in the base. The desktop was polished and totally devoid of paper.

"So you're the researcher," he smiled. It wasn't a crack; Fiorella seemed relaxed and open to my presence. "Lori told me you'd be coming by."

"I guess you're supposed to bring me up to speed so I can figure out what to do next. That's what Roy tells me."

Fiorella made a face. "Roy. What a troll. They get you set up okay, with a room and everything?"

"Yeah," I nodded. "A bit more elegant than the Motel 6."

Fiorella grinned. "Just a bit. I gotta warn ya, though. Lori will want her pound of flesh…"

"She seems like someone who's used to getting what she wants."

Fiorella's eyes went slightly out of focus as if he were mentally reviewing data for a second. "That's probably a pretty accurate observation, Dr. Burke."

"Connor," I told him.

Fiorella looked at me and squinted. "I got the background on you. I ran across your brother once at a conference in New York." He seemed like he wanted to say more. It's not an unusual occurrence when I meet people who've met Micky.

"You're not from around here, are you?" I was trying to place his faint accent.

Fiorella smiled. "Not many people are. The Southwest is filling up with people from all over. Nah," he said, getting to my question. "I retired as chief of homicide in Buffalo and decided that fifty-five years of snow was enough."

"How was the transition?"

"You know, Connor, every time there was a homicide in the city of Buffalo, the chief had to be called in. Day or night. Holidays. Weekends. I spent so much time at crime scenes talking to the TV people, that my friends started to call me Captain Video. Here? I get to sleep nights. I can get a full round of golf in before work. I got a good staff of young, ambitious types and a bunch of rich people staying for a few days, maybe drinking too much or screwing too much, but that's it. I keep a lid on the over exuberant and keep the troops from stepping over the line. It's like a paid vacation."

"You've got a homicide on your hands now," I reminded him. "Or at least that's what your boss thinks."

Charlie Fiorella grimaced. "There's some differing opinions on that…"

"But she's got you working it, doesn't she?"

He smiled. "You too."

I held my hands up. "I'm just supposed to read her father's books and render an opinion."

Fiorella stood up: a pretty good size, but trim and fit. He was wearing creased gray trousers and shiny oxblood loafers with little tassels on them. He swung a navy blazer off a chair, straightened his tie. "Let's take a walk, Connor."

"What? The walls have ears?"

Fiorella shrugged. "Who knows? Probably. Mostly, it's time for me to make the rounds. Show my face to the troops."

We wandered around the hotel grounds. Fiorella moved with an easy economy, like someone who'd done it for a long time. He'd stop occasionally and have brief, low-voiced conversations with various people. They all smiled and seemed both respectful and genuinely glad to see him. If Lori Westmann's presence made everyone stiffen up, Charlie Fiorella seemed to have the knack for making people feel comfortable. Probably not a bad skill for an investigator.

"You know what Lori wants you to find don't you?" he asked me as we ambled along a shaded colonnade by a pool. Attendants were busy collecting wet towels and taking drink orders from vacationers in various stages of sunburn. Dressed to be part of the shadows, fully clothed people flitted silently in the background, sweeping walks and working the various pieces of invisible machinery that spins below the surface of any resort. Fiorella greeted them by name. They looked up to respond with brief smiles, then saw me and quickly returned their eyes to their work.

"Sure, I know what she wants," I answered him. "She wants me to prove that her father's books weren't fiction and that he was murdered for revealing the secrets of some ancient sect of mystics."

Fiorella nodded as I explained. We stepped to one side as another electric cart whizzed by. "Anything about this strike you as odd?" He pressed.

"Well, yeah," I admitted. "Like why wait thirty years to send a hit squad. The damage was long done."

Fiorella smiled. His teeth were bright against the tanned skin. "Good start. Anything else?"

"Why bother killing someone for revealing secrets when most of the world thinks they're not true anyway?"

Charlie Fiorella led me up to a bar. We sat and turned to watch the action in a pool with a huge slide and dozens of screaming kids. The bartender greeted him and slid two cocktail napkins into place. He snapped the tops off two Coronas. The bottles made a happy little fizzing sound. The bartender slipped some lime into them. "I like the way your mind works, Connor," Fiorella said. He reached for a bottle. "Cheers."

We sipped the beers for a while. The kids shrieked and bobbed and splashed around. Their parents sipped fruity drinks under awnings. Fiorella watched it all with a benign watchfulness. I'm pretty sure I detected a pistol in an ankle holster.

"So," he continued. "I've got some friends on the local force. I get copies of the crime scene report. I talk to the investigator of record."

"And?"

He shrugged. "Eliot Westmann was a flake. His personal life was a mess. He'd been through three marriages and would shack up with almost anything in a skirt. Big with the New Age crowd. Spent most of his time at his retreat up in the hills. Nice place."

"Is that where he died?"

"Yeah. They found him at the bottom of a staircase. Stone steps. Hard landing, ya know? He bled a bit, but basically he broke his neck falling down the stairs."

"No sign of…"

"Foul play?" he asked playfully. "Far as I can tell, the people from Stolichnaya did him in. The guy was a drinker, and the blood work confirms that he was severely intoxicated at the time of the incident."

"So I don't get it," I told him. "The locals think it's an accident. So do you. Why is Lori Westmann so hot to pursue this?"

Fiorella thoughtfully finished the last of his Corona. Mine was done as well, the slice of lime sitting sadly at the bottom of the bottle. The bartender approached and looked at me. I shook my head no. Out of the corner of my eye, I could see Fiorella watching the exchange with approval.

"There are any number of explanations, I suppose," he began. "People have a hard time accepting accidents of this type."

"Were they close?"

Fiorella pushed off the bar and we headed off in another direction, away from the crowds. "That type of closeness is not something I tend to associate with Lori," he said judiciously. "Her father had been mostly in and out of her life at best until a few years ago."

"What happened? Late life crisis of conscience?"

He shrugged. "Maybe. Drunks get that way. I'm not discounting it."

Something in his voice told me that he was skeptical. "But what?" I pressed.

He grinned, and the lines at the side of his eyes creased in pleasure. "It's my own little theory that he had bought that big place out in the hills with the idea of turning it into some New Age retreat center. And maybe, because he was a flake and drinker, he realized that he needed a little help with the project. You know, math and contracts and managing the help…"

"Lucky he had a daughter with some real world skills."

Fiorella snorted. "You could say that. She's a tough cookie. Anyways, I'd be surprised if some of their newfound affection wasn't fueled by a profit motive."

"How nice," I commented.

"The world's a complex place, Connor. You see it for what it is."

I'd heard that before from my brother. "So they had some mutual business interests. But why her insistence on pursuing the murder theory? It's not an insurance issue is it?"

He shook his head. "Investigation would slow down a settlement."

"She the sole heir?"

"Yep. All the ex-wives are dead. No other kids."

"So," I pursued, "then I don't get it. Is it just that she's got this fixation and isn't used to being told no?"

"There may be some of that," he admitted. "But she's someone who's got her emotional side pretty well caged up. I'm like you—I can't quite figure the angle." We wandered along a twisting path, the blank walls of private patios and carefully manicured bushes offering a sense of privacy to the conversation. "And I don't know whether I really have to."

"She's got the money to pay for any investigation she wants, I guess."

"And she usually gets what she wants," Fiorella concluded.

"It's a bit cynical," I commented. We emerged into a more open area, turned left and found ourselves at my suite.

"I read about you, Connor. All the Asian martial arts stuff." He paused. "What's the definition of the word *samurai*?"

I was monetarily puzzled at the change in topic. "Well, they were the hereditary warrior class of feudal Japan…"

He waived the explanation away. "What does the *word* mean?"

"Oh," I said, getting his point even as I spoke. "It means 'those who serve.'"

Fiorella stopped and smiled at me. "The lady's father dies and she's got money to spend to make sure nobody's overlooked anything. Who's it gonna hurt? The guy's already dead. In the meantime, you get to spend some time out here in the sunshine." He smiled pleasantly. "Get yourself settled in. I'll have the crime scene report sent over for background. I've also got some biographical stuff on Westmann. Have a nice dinner, maybe a swim. Tomorrow, I'll take you out to his place. All the books and notes are in his library there."

It seemed fair enough. I shook his hand and headed toward the door. Then a thought occurred to me and I turned to ask a question.

"Charlie?" He stood smiling, squinting in the sun.

"Anybody who might have a grudge or motive, however farfetched? Anybody in the mix here look like they were hard enough to do Westmann in?"

"Connor," he laughed. "You mean outside of you, me, a coupla dozen members of the Tucson underworld, and your fabled Asian assassins?"

"Yeah."

"The only other person I can think of is the nice lady who employs us."

Now there was a comforting thought.

5

JIZO

In Japan, small stone statues of Jizo stand silently in deserted places and graveyards. In Buddhism, Jizo is, among other things, the patron of travelers and pilgrims. I stood in the dust of the high desert, watching the eyes of the men surrounding me. Jizo often carries a six-foot staff. I wished I had one with me now.

I'd picked up a hotel car that morning and followed Charlie Fiorella out into the hills toward Westmann's desert retreat. We wound our way up along roads that were increasingly devoid of signs of human presence, with only power lines strung along the wayside to serve as a connector to town.

Westmann had used some of his abundant royalty money to invest in a failed resort property that he had attempted to transform into a personal refuge and a mystic conference center. He gathered transient groups of like-minded "seekers": kids pushing the envelope of life, rejects from interdisciplinary graduate programs, and old hippies nearing retirement who were saddled with money to burn and a backlog of unanswered questions. He called it The Kiva, after the ritual centers of the old pueblos. I read the report that Fiorella had provided about the place. I wasn't impressed: it seemed both self-indulgent and unfocused. The Kiva consisted of a few hundred acres with several unattached buildings clustered around a central courtyard. You came into the property through stone pillars artfully crafted to look ancient. The road dust helped as well. We got out of our cars. The sunlight was white with intensity. In the quiet, you could hear a faint musical tinkling coming from a wind chime that moved fitfully under the eaves of a deep front porch. Our car engines pinged faintly, throwing off heat into a world that was already far too hot for my taste. There were a few pickups with a contractor's logo on the doors parked in a steadily diminishing pool of shade. Other than that, there was no sign of life.

The main building was a big two-story adobe affair. The door was unlocked, and we moved gratefully into the dark coolness of the interior. It took a moment for my eyes to adjust after the glare of the courtyard. The first floor featured a great room with a cathedral ceiling and a stone fireplace big enough to cook a bison . There were clerestory windows high up along the walls, and shafts of indirect lighting cut through the space. There were smaller rooms for conference groups and a kitchen and dining area to the rear. The second floor was entirely occupied by Eliot Westmann's personal quarters, including his library. It was where I'd spend most of my time.

We walked up the wide flight of stone steps that led to the second level. I tried not to look down for stains.

Charlie read my mind. "This is where the old man took the fall," he confirmed. The staircase grew wider as it led downward, a dramatic architectural sweep that must have been designed to permit truly memorable entrances from above. Unless, of course, you got totally smashed, lost your footing, and tumbled down. The stairs had small risers and the steps were made from gray flagstones, dense and hard-edged. I imagine that falling down them would not be an esthetic experience—the only thing they offered was a series of punishing blows on your bounce to the bottom.

Westmann's library had a wall of tinted windows that provided a vista of the dusty hills as they tumbled down into the rough and broken desert terrain that stretched out to Mexico and beyond. His desk was set at an angle to the wall of glass, and I could imagine him sitting there, rubbing tired eyes and turning to face the wide world, to escape for a time into the expanse of tan and brown and faded ochre that waited out there under a wide and uncaring sky.

The other walls were windowless and packed from floor to ceiling with books and unbound papers stuffed in dark brown file folders. There was a worktable in the center of the room with a few hardback chairs around it. The desk itself was devoid of clutter. A flat computer screen stood in isolation on the polished expanse of cherry wood. I looked around the room expectantly, as if something there would help give me a sense of Eliot Westmann. I looked in vain. There were no posters or paintings. No decorations of any type. None of the other typical junk you find in people's offices, either: plaques, odd statues, paperweights, souvenirs. And no photographs. There was nothing in the room to give me a sense of the former owner's personality, that he had been connected to places and things other than those in his own mind. Eliot Westmann's sparse legacy was a steely-eyed daughter and the books and papers in the sagging shelves all around me.

I looked at Charlie. Wiped my hand along a bookshelf. "This place has been cleaned since he died, hasn't it?" It looked too tidy. Most writers I know have working spaces that look like a tornado has recently blown through them.

He nodded. "Sure. The Criminal Investigations people from the State DPS took a look, dusted for prints in various rooms."

"Anything unusual?" I knew I wasn't supposed to be involved in this end of things, but hanging around with my brother has had an effect on me.

Charlie smiled knowingly. "No identifiable prints other than Westmann's and the staff. Some smudges of indeterminate origin. Mostly, the state guys were just going through the motions to make Lori happy. Short of a message written in blood on the wall that said 'I did it,' it was pretty clear that Westmann got loaded and took a header down the stairs. End of story."

"And yet…" I started.

"… here we are," Charlie finished.

"I hate spinning my wheels," I told him.

"Easier to take when you're on an expense account," he reminded me. *Cop wisdom.*

We agreed that I had better get started, not that I was entirely sure what that meant. Contrary to appearances, Charlie said there were staff members around and they'd take care of me. I walked him downstairs and out onto the porch. A big van with the hotel logo on its side curved into the courtyard, kicking up some dust. A bunch of people swathed in sunscreen, large floppy hats, and sensible shoes emerged. The driver popped out and began unloading daypacks and camelback water units out of the rear of the van. He was dressed in hi-tech outerwear— what looked like climbing pants, a white sleeveless shirt, and well-worn hiking boots. His long jet-black hair was pulled back into a ponytail. His skin was burnished a deep reddish brown and his eyes were hidden behind wraparound sunglasses with lenses that shimmered in a rainbow effect. The man with the ponytail glanced at us, but gave no sign that our presence had registered at all.

I looked at Charlie and nodded at the van. "What's this?"

"Desert hike. Part of the service from the hotel. This place has lots of trails and Lori's been encouraging their use."

"Who's the driver?"

Charlie snorted. "The Chief? His name is Rosario Contreras. Outdoor freak. Hiking. Rock climbing. He works at the hotel setting up desert excursions."

"Chief?" I asked incredulously.

He grinned. "Nah, I just call him that to needle him. He's big into Native heritage on both sides of the border. Calls himself Xochi."

"Showchee?" I asked, and Charlie spelled it for me.

"That's not Spanish," I observed.

"No. It's something different. Aztec or something." He jutted his jaw out in mock seriousness. "Reflects pride in heritage."

We watched the group get organized and head off down a path that led out into the surrounding hills. I peered out at the sky from the cover of the porch. "Call me crazy, but if I were taking a walk around here, I'd do it really early or really late."

Charlie nodded. "So you would think. But you're a practical guy. Not an entrepreneur." I looked at him quizzically. "He takes them out for a hike," he explained to me. "They stumble around for twenty minutes, worried about rattlers. He tells them about rocks and stuff. By this time, they're swimming in sweat. They take a break for a while and drink most of their water. They gasp their way back to the van. Then back to the hotel and into the bar for something cold and frosty. They pay for the hotel room. They pay for the guided trip. And they pay for their drinks."

"Ecotourism," I commented. "It's a beautiful thing."

"Lori says it's a form of recreational synergy," Charlie commented.

"What's that mean?"

"That she's found another way to squeeze money out of her guests, I guess."

"She's an evil genius," I laughed.

Charlie Fiorella made his way to the car and looked at me over the open door. "Hey. That's my employer you're talking about. I prefer to think of her as a fearsome yet creative presence." He gave me a grin and drove away.

I spent most of that day getting organized and dreaming up a strategy. I had some biographical stuff on Westmann and a list of all his book publications. I'd also searched the Internet for any related sites that could flesh out his profile. I got into some on-line archives that had old reviews of each of his works. I did a lot of cutting and pasting and saving stuff to disk.

But I knew that I was simply dodging the inevitable. Eventually, I was actually going to have to *read* all the stuff he wrote. I had a vague recollection of looking at his books years ago when I was young and impressionable. Even then, as naïve as I was, I had put Westmann's work down, convinced that the guy was a fraud. And I had seen nothing in the literature from the academic community that suggested anything different. Yet it was a type of opinion that was widely held even though the reasons were not particularly well documented. People had suggested that Westmann had recycled excerpts from various obscure tomes, fit them together into an outlandish fantasy of his own making, and then tried to pass it off as scholarship.

In some ways it was a beautiful scheme. The world of academia is like most other worlds—filled with fine people, but also with its share of freaks and phonies. Mainstream scholars dismissed Westmann, but somewhere in the few thousand obscure little colleges around the country you could always find some charlatan with a shaky Ph.D. who'd defend what one book dust jacket described as "a groundbreaking exploration of a secret world of mystic warriors, penned by a courageous scholar."

In the post-modern academic world, truth is often alleged to be relative. Westmann's stuff didn't seem plausible? Who are we to denigrate an individual's unique perspective? Nobody seemed to be able to substantiate his claims? Nobody could locate the leader of the secret society who was his main informant? Easily explained. It's a *secret* society.

It all made me roll my eyes. Serious readers with any familiarity with the topic would simply dismiss Westmann's stuff. And few people would have the need or the time to do a very thorough research job to prove or disprove his veracity. Only a nut would devote any time to this.

Or someone in the pay of Westmann's daughter.

I sighed and pulled his books off the shelf, lining up copies of reviews for each of them. Then I went back to the Web, tried to track the book reviewers down, and e-mailed a message outlining my purpose to the ones who were still alive, asking whether they could point me in any direction. No sense reinventing the wheel.

The task was uninspiring and I grew antsy. I looked out through the wall of glass at the shifting patterns on the desert floor below me. I thought about the group from the hotel. Maybe a little hike to end the day?

The van with the tourists was long gone. I headed over to the gravel path that led out into the rough terrain around the property. A finely-crafted wooden sign with a vaguely Indian stick figure pointed the way onward. Who was I to argue?

The sun was dropping down and the wind, while hot,

offered the illusion of relief. I wandered down the track, thinking of nothing in particular, just glad to be moving. I could see boot prints from the tourist group in the dust on the path. It wound up and down slight inclines. In a few places, it paralleled the edge of the ridge to permit panoramic views of the desert floor. The rocks around me were awash in the rose-orange glow of a setting sun, silent watchers, stolid sentinels who would never voice an alarm.

After a time, the path ended in a small, boulder-studded cul-de-sac. This was obviously the limit of hotel adventure. I, however, am made of sterner stuff. I noticed a very narrow trail leading up through the boulder field and over a ridge. I followed it up.

Here, the view was even better. I could look back and see the buildings of the Kiva, lit up by the sunset, and an even wider expanse of desert terrain, studded with lengthening shadows. The pathway arced away around the hillside and out of sight. In another ten minutes or so of walking, the ridgeline began to soften and the incline leading to the lower elevation became more gradual. I came across what looked like a four wheeler track. It crossed the path I was on and sloped down the hill. I looked at the setting sun, aware that I didn't want to get stuck out here after dark. But I figured that I still had time. Roads always lead to something. Way out here, I wondered what that was, so I took a left and began to follow it down.

In retrospect, I should have been more alert, more sensitive to the subtle vibrations that could have warned me that this was not a good idea. I could argue that I was in a strange place, a very different environment and that the sensations, while present, were not familiar enough yet for me to interpret. But there's no real excuse. My *sensei* admonishes us that there are two important things in a warrior's life: intention and result. And results matter more. Excuses are both meaningless and potentially distracting. Which means they're dangerous.

I was bounding along the track as it switch-backed down the slope, loose limbed, and just enjoying the hike. So I pretty much blundered into their midst before I or they knew what was happening. The old battered Jeep Cherokee was covered in dust and old baked-on mud splatters. So were the men standing around it, smoking. They were in work clothes, wearing construction boots and frayed, sweat stained hats. Their skin had been burned by desert labor and their brown eyes were bloodshot from heat and sweat and work. These guys saw a great deal of the outdoors. They probably preferred dark, cool places. So if they were here, it was for a reason. And it wasn't to admire the sunset or take in the scenery. I also noticed that one of them held a pair of binoculars and a small radio.

They were not happy to see me.

One pushed himself off the car, stuck his cigarette in his mouth and regarded me through menacing eyes. He gave a curt order to one of the others, the youngest in the bunch, who circled me warily and then trotted up the trail to see who else was coming.

The men silently spaced themselves in arc in front of me. Three of them. Four counting the kid at my back. I didn't see any weapons, but I figured knives were probably a certainty. I, on the other hand, was only armed with my trusty gold laminated hotel card.

Trained guy that I am, I got that visceral jolt that was the body's deep knowledge: *you're in deep trouble Burke.*

When I first started training, I didn't know how to interpret the feeling. The clench in the gut, the elevated heart rate, and the cool tingling along the outer arms and neck. I thought it was fear. But it's merely the body's quick read of the situation: you're going to need to do something violent soon, and you better get ready because the outcome will be important.

"*Habla Ingles?*" I asked, exhausting the remains of four years of high school Spanish. They smirked a little at that but didn't say a word. I watched the shift of their eyes. They were waiting for word from their scout up the trail. No need to waste words at this point.

One of the men in front of me reached into the jeep and pulled out a roofer's hammer. It had a longish handle and a really nasty looking spike on one end. It was a weapon, but not a gun, so part of me was relieved. Blunt trauma is part of my world. Plus, now I knew who was probably going to take the lead when things heated up.

The goal with multiple attackers is to keep them from getting to you all at once: you shift around a bit in the hopes that they'll get in each other's way. But it's tricky. Above all, you don't want people getting behind you. Particularly when they're carrying a hammer.

I heard the scuffle of feet as the young guy came back.

"*No hay nadie,*" he said, puffing a little bit from running.

That was all they needed. The guy with the hammer came in at me without any kind of indicator, no need for a windup or a command from his pals. He wasn't big, but he was stocky, arms and chest thick with years of hard toil. His bones would be dense, his muscles hard sheaths of fiber, his hands blunt and strong.

He swung the hammer around, seeking to smash my head with a powerful blow to the temple. His mouth was slightly open with excitement and I caught a glimpse of big, stained teeth. I moved in toward him, bringing myself into the safer zone that lay inside the arc of his attack. I could smell the tobacco on his breath. Most people with weapons expect you to back off when they attack. But Yamashita's basic rule is to never do what people expect, never be where they anticipate you'll be. He's pounded it into my head over the years and it's a great strategy, providing you can read people correctly. Read them right, and you've gained an advantage. Read them wrong and you hope for another chance to get it right.

It's not like the movies. You don't meet an attacker and push him away and then go on to the next guy in the circle. Because if you do, the person you pushed away is going to come back again. And, eventually, they'll wear you down. It's the basic strategy of all pack hunters.

So I got my left sword-hand up to block the blow, redirected his arm out and down and back up again. I spun him around in a classic *shiho-nage* technique, controlling his arm and bending it so his palm faced his rear and I was locking the arm up at wrist, elbow, and shoulder. The body positioning is designed to take someone right off their feet, and I could feel him start to shift. In the practice hall, you line up the joints so as not to hurt your partner. But now I swirled around that dusty place and purposefully brought the arm out of alignment. I could smell his body odor, and the dry dirt smell of the hillside. When you're really focused in the middle of a technique, sensations get imprinted in the strangest ways. So you don't remember all the details of the things you do. But I remember how he smelled.

And the sensation of tearing joints that vibrated up his bones to where I held him. That and the sound of his shriek.

I dumped him down as hard as I could, although I didn't

have time to look for a really big rock for him to land on, because I was spinning around to deal with the next guy. Fortunately, it was the kid. The young have energy, but not much wisdom.

I drove up from a crouch, pivoted toward this new threat, and rammed a left into his solar plexus. I heard the wind go out of him. I slapped him on the side of the head for further distraction, and spun him around to get him between me and the other two guys. The kid was barely standing, but the spin made him fight against the loss of balance and his head came up a bit. I formed a tense arc with the web portion of my hand between the thumb and forefinger and popped him in the throat. Not too hard. But he fell backward onto his rear, sitting down hard enough to make his teeth snap together audibly. He started to gag a bit.

I backed away, trying to get up the trail while watching the last two men. We were all crouched with arms slightly extended, animals waiting for the next snarling lunge of an attack. I could hear the sound of my breath sawing in and out. My mouth was dry and I could taste the alkaline dust that swirled around us.

From the rim of rocks toward the southwest, near the drop off to the jumbled stretch of land that led to Mexico, I saw a shape loom up out of the corner of my eye. The figure was black against the red sky, and I was afraid to look too closely, afraid to take my eyes off the men from the Jeep.

"*Paratelos!*" a voice commanded. The two men still standing looked at the man on the rocks. They paused momentarily. On the ground, the man with the hammer was moaning, cradling his arm, and trying to sit up. The kid had vomited all over himself.

There was a flurry of excited discussion in Spanish. A lot

of pointing at me and at the two men on the ground. I edged slightly away and got a good look at the man on the rocks. It was the desert guide who called himself Xochi. His stylish shades were nowhere in evidence and his face was flushed with anger. The horizon was brightly lit, but in the little dip on the trail where we stood the light was beginning to fade.

Xochi hopped down from the rocks, light-footed and confident, while the argument continued. He moved to my side.

"Thanks," I murmured.

He looked at me, his eyes flat and disapproving. "You should not be here," Xochi said flatly.

I looked at him, surprised at his attitude. But he seemed to be getting the boys with the hammer calmed down. *Drop it, Burke. Leave it. Walk away.*

"Consider me gone," I told him.

"That would be wise," he said. "Hurry. You are losing the light. The desert at night is a dangerous place." His tone of voice was flat.

I backed my way up the slope, taking a last look. The bodies sprawled in the dirt—the blood red sky. Shadows like wraiths, growing and twisting as evening approached. And five men watching me as I made my way out of the wasteland.

6
CENTERING

"I miss you," I told her. I was tucked away in my hotel room, safe from men with hammers. I stared up at the textured ceiling, dismissing the minor bruises from the fight, and conjured up an image of Sarah, all those miles away in New York.

"I miss you, too," she said, and I imagined that I could hear the slight smile over the phone line. "But I'm getting some really focused training in with Yamashita now that you're not around to distract him."

I snorted. "Yamashita doesn't get distracted."

"Oh yeah?" she countered. "Something was bothering him tonight in the *dojo*."

"Bad technique?" I teased.

"Be serious, Burke. It didn't seem to be anything we did, that I could see, but he'd occasionally stop and well, if it wasn't Yamashita, I'd say daydream."

"A disturbance in the force…" I suggested, using my patented James Earl Jones voice. But I could hear her exasperation even through the filtering of the electronics, and so quickly followed with, "I know what you mean. I've seen the same thing. Sometimes… I don't know. I've come to accept that he's some sort of receptor and picks up on things we don't even know are around. It could have been almost anything."

"Well whatever was happening," she said, "By the end of the night, he was really agitated."

I did the mental arithmetic of the difference in time zones

and got a cool tingly feeling, thinking about where I was around that time and what was happening. The Western part of me dismissed it as coincidence. But I'd been with my teacher for too many years not to consider that, on some non-rational level, he perceived the world in ways that none of us could imagine. But all I said to Sarah was "Huh."

We talked some more, saying the kinds of things people say when they're apart and wish they weren't. I gave Sarah a highly-edited description of my day. I didn't mention the fight.

I once asked my brother Micky how much detail he shared with his wife Deirdre about his adventures as a cop. He squinted at me. "Connor," he said. "Life with me is not a laugh riot in the first place, ya know? I try not to clutter our life up with every bad thing that happens on the job. Ya put it in a box and you don't let the family peek inside unless it's absolutely neces-sary." It seemed to me like good advice.

But, Sarah saw through my edits, much, I suspected, as Deirdre sees through Micky's. In their case I think it's for Micky's peace of mind, not her's, that Deirdre allows Micky his silences. Sarah chose instead to softly edge into my deletions.

"What's really happening Connor?"

"It's nothing," I said, still trying to protect her.

The silence on the other end of the line crackled with tension.

"You don't see it, do you?" she finally said.

"What?" I protested.

Sarah took a breath. "It's like you're being sucked in… into this black hole of Yamashita's life."

"It's my life too."

"Do you think? I wonder." Her words were cutting. "Some-times I think you're just following out of blind loyalty."

"What's wrong with that?"

"Burke, loyalty doesn't have to be blind. But if you can't see that, then your decisions will always be, oh I don't know—tainted. It's dangerous to live blindly in his life. I respect Yamashita and I don't think he means to bring you into harm's way, but, there's something about him—his life is shrouded in violence."

I felt defensive. "You don't know what you're talking about. Yamashita's not even here and he had nothing to do with my coming out here."

"Okay, Burke, have it your way. By the way," she added, her voice tight and raspy with irony, "Yamashita says he needs you to do something." She had me write down a name and a telephone number.

"Hasegawa Sensei," I noted. "Here in Tucson. I got it. What's the deal?" Trying for normalcy in my tone and not really pulling it off.

"I'm just the messenger," she said. Her voice was curt and resentful. "Tell Burke he must call," she said in her best Yamashita style. "*Ima wa*," Now.

"*Hai*," *Yes*, I conceded with resignation to the presence of my teacher, invisible but nonetheless real.

I rose at dawn and went out for a run. The sun had edged up over the jagged hills that studded the horizon, but it was still cool outdoors. Sprinklers hissed everywhere on the manicured grounds of the hotel property, lush grass a deep green sparkling in the sunlight. Birds chirped and uniformed service workers moved quietly around in the half-light, cleaning walks, tending the pools, and stocking up on towels in the cabanas.

The hotel had a measured running trail that wound around

the edge of the resort and up a little ways into the seared hills. You'd think after yesterday, I'd know better, but I had to run and that was where the path led. It was an old pattern in my life. I got to the trailhead and started some stretches. A fit-looking, deeply tanned woman arrived right after I did. She was wearing a stylish pastel ensemble, including a pink baseball cap. Her streaked blonde hair was pulled through the back of the cap, a high ponytail. It bounced along with the rest of her, as if her good health couldn't be contained. She smiled tightly to acknowledge my presence, a tight flash of white teeth in a lean face. Then she turned away and, with a show of great focus, began her own warm-ups. Exercise is serious business.

Or maybe she didn't approve of my outfit. I was wearing a pair of ratty shorts that were questionable even by my standards and a faded T-shirt that proclaimed "I've Seen Elvis!" It had a few rows of pictures of the big E variously disguised as a nun, Marilyn Monroe, and a Russian soldier to name just a few. Maybe the lady in the hat was a fan of his. Or maybe she'd actually seen Elvis and knew he wasn't living in a convent.

I shook off the vision of too many Elvises and hit the road.

The trail wound past the hotel golf course, behind the corral where the electric carts were penned up, and then out into the hills. The transformation from manicured lawn to brown earth was dramatic, as if a line had been drawn across the terrain. Without the constant irrigation of sprinklers, the wild land beyond the hotel's property appeared as sterile as the surface of the moon. But the light was soft and the desert landscape was soothing. I settled into the rhythm of the run, happy that the path was long, the terrain open and I didn't see any suspicious characters in a Jeep. After twenty minutes or so, I headed back. I could feel the growing force of the sun as it climbed higher into the sky. As I approached the hotel grounds, I looked up and caught sight of a still form standing deep in the shade of a tree near the pro club, watching me. *Xochi*

He was motionless, and I doubt I would have noticed him at all if I weren't still a little on edge from yesterday. People who spend a great deal of time outdoors have a knack for silence and stillness. Good naturalists have it. So do hunters. So, I noted, did Xochi. I looked back down to the trail, as if concerned with my footing. I didn't want him to know that I had spotted him.

He faded back around the corner of the building as I came closer. I headed off toward my room, taking a winding route in the hopes of catching another glimpse of him. But Xochi was gone.

Charlie Fiorella was at his desk, though, reading a report of some sort. His blue pastel golf shirt was pressed and his forearms were brown and thick. He looked up and peered at me over his reading glasses.

"I got jumped last night," I started as I sat down and filled him in on the details.

Charlie pursed his lips as if tasting something unpleasant. He took the report he was reading and carefully filed it away in a desk drawer. Then he got up from the desk and quietly closed the door to his office. His gray pants had a crease as sharp as a blade; his tasseled loafers gleamed.

"You OK?" He asked softly as the door clicked closed behind him. I nodded and he continued. "You want to file a report with the locals? I've got some contacts."

"Would it do any good?"

"Honestly? No. A big waste of time."

I'd come to the same conclusion. I could imagine myself telling the story to the cops: out-of-towner takes a wrong turn down an unmarked trail, comes across a few locals, gets in a scrape, and gets away. I didn't know who they were. I didn't get the license plate number on the Jeep. They could follow up with Xochi the guide, but he would probably stonewall and claim he had just wandered by. Nothing against the law about being a Good Samaritan. Cop work is an exercise in triage: you identify the crimes you've got a good chance of solving and pretty quickly get a feel for what you can't. The cops would take my report, make mooing noises at me, then file it and forget it.

But I had some questions I wanted to pursue. "What's the deal with this Xochi guy?" I asked.

Charlie stared off at a wall. "Ah, our friend Rosario. He's been kicking around the university here for a while. Picked up master's degrees in Native American Studies and Cultural Ecology."

I shook my head. I never understood why anyone in their right mind would get two master's degrees, when in academic circles a doctorate is the only really acceptable degree. "How long's he been on unemployment?" I asked sarcastically.

"Oh, he seems to do pretty well. He's big with promoting Native rights and moaning about the Anglos destroying indigenous culture. Works as a counselor at the university part time. And he's developed a pretty good business taking tourists for desert hikes."

"So he doesn't like Anglos, just their money," I commented. Charlie grinned but said nothing. "He spend a lot of time out there in the desert?" I continued

"A bit," he said cagily.

"So what's that suggest to you?"

Now he had his poker face on. "What do you mean?"

I leaned forward. "Come on, Charlie. Those guys I met

yesterday weren't out for a nature hike. They had binoculars and a radio and were waiting for something. What do you wait for out there?"

He shrugged. "Lots of things. People. Drugs. Whatever's coming over the border."

"That's right," I said. "And what does it tell you that this Xochi fella got those guys all calmed down long enough for me to get away? Seems to me that it suggests he may have some involvement."

"You could be right, Burke," he said quietly. "You hear things. The Homeland Security people have tightened the net in a lot of spots. We're seeing more activity in some of the rougher border areas around here."

"And Xochi?"

He held up his hands. "The guy's plugged into a lot of different groups with ties on both sides of the border. He's an expert on the desert. "

"Did you run a check on him?" I asked.

"Didn't get as far as I'd like," he admitted, and sighed quietly.

"Why not?" I demanded.

He bridled a bit at my tone. "Hey Burke, don't you think I know my job?"

"Seems to me that your job is to do a thorough check on your employees, Charlie."

His eyes got a little hard at that. He started to say something, then moved his mouth silently as if he were chewing on his words.

"Look," he finally said, "I started making some inquiries, but got pulled off it."

"Pulled off it? By whom?"

He didn't answer me directly. He didn't have to. There was

only one person at the hotel that could do that to him: the general manager, Lori Westmann. Charlie looked me in the eyes and said quietly, "Leave it Burke. They're close." He paused for emphasis. "*Very* close."

I wiggled my eyebrows suggestively.

"Look," Charlie said, "when the old man took the tumble, Lori had a lot on her plate: major restorations at the resort, some big contract negotiations. She needed someone out at the Kiva to be her eyes and ears... so she settled on Xochi. He's out there practically every day anyway. He cleaned things up, got the old man's papers organized. Nothing sinister."

But it was just another strange wrinkle in the story. I headed off to Eliot Westmann's place and spent hours rummaging through his library. Something bothered me. I couldn't put my finger on it, but it was there in the back of my mind. I pressed on. There were files and files of manuscript notes that were dated, and so could be correlated to his publications. They were all Xerox copies, however. I wondered why, and also wondered where the originals were. I got some e-mail responses to my inquiries, most of which indicated that the people I had tried to contact were either no longer around, or really not interested in assisting me in my goofy little project. So I was essentially on my own, faced once again with an unpleasant task.

I was really going to have to read Eliot Westmann's collected works. I suppose that it's an essential part of literary forensics, but from what I knew about his death, I suspected that the cops were right and that all of my work was going to be pointless. And besides, it didn't interest me all that much.

So I procrastinated. I poked around the library some more. Westmann was a prolific, even a compulsive writer. He hadn't had much published, however, in the decade prior to his fatal tumble. The sterile little office didn't give me much insight into what he was doing.

I decided to poke around a bit more. The entire second floor of the main building had been Westmann's living quarters. I wandered through them, feeling a bit self-conscious at invading a dead guy's space. There was a living room, decorated Southwest style. It had tasteful pottery on shelves and a fine-looking Navaho rug hanging on the wall. The furniture was square, darkly stained mission-style stuff. The room also had a big leather sofa, a matching recliner, and a big screen TV. Aha! Finally, something that looked like a person actually lived in this place. It was still tremendously sterile, however.

I slipped into his bedroom. More mission furniture. I poked around in the drawers of night tables and a small desk. They contained the usual junk you discover in small drawers: tissues, an old battery, a few paperclips, assorted plastic pens without their caps. I would have thought the meticulous Ms. Westmann would have had the house cleaned out by now.

There was a walk-in closet. Westmann's wardrobe was casual: denim and chinos. A canvas barn coat. A dusty daypack was dumped in a corner on top of a pair of well-worn hiking boots. There was a battered straw cowboy hat on a peg. The closet smelled faintly of old cologne, wood smoke, and tobacco. Finally, a place that didn't appear to have been totally sanitized. The clothes on hangers and shelves were neatly arranged, but there was stuff in here that hadn't been cleaned, as if someone had been reluctant to scrub away the last private vestiges of Westmann's presence on the earth. Maybe she was more sentimental than I gave her credit.

As I looked around the closet, I noticed that there was a nail high up on the inside of the door's lip with a braided leather lanyard hanging from it. I took it down, the leather felt soft and worn. A single key hung from it, shiny with use.

It took some skulking, but I eventually found the lock that the key opened. Actually, even with the skulking, I wouldn't have found it, except that I tripped on a rock in front of the door, and to save my graceful self from bashing my head on the wall, I put my hand on the door and it gave just enough for me to notice the entrance. The key slipped into lock easily, and when I swung the door open, I knew I had found the mother lode.

The room was small and seemed dark and cramped when compared to the library in the main house. A heavy old wooden table was piled high with papers. I closed the door and switched on the reading lamp that waited there. It threw an intimate, yellow light across the table, and made the shadows in the corners seem to swell and draw nearer. I sunk down into a cane-bottomed chair that creaked with old age. I looked around open-mouthed.

I shouldn't have been surprised, I suppose. Eliot Westmann was a bit of a recluse, someone who hid himself purposefully from others. Even in the security of his own retreat, old habits must have been hard to shake. Nestled here in this aromatic cell, protected by wood and stone, were the pieces of his life that he hid from view. Here were the pictures, newspaper clippings, and other scraps that marked his passage through life. A ceramic ashtray held a well-worn pipe, its bowl grown cold.

A thick, crude shelf rested on rounded pegs driven into the wall. It held an oil lamp, its glass globe partially blackened with use, and a book of matches. Two good-sized rocks served as bookends, encompassing a series of leather-bound journals. I brought them down and carefully made a space on the battered old table.

Westmann had a spidery, although legible hand. The volumes appeared to go back a few years. I surveyed the pages quickly, intending to go back in more detail later. Westmann's journal was a combination of personal diary and a record of ongoing work. There were details of parties and people he met. His love life. There were a few snapshots shoved in among some particularly lurid pages. Young women in a hot tub smiled at the camera. The desert sky was dark behind them, with only a faint orange line across the horizon. The camera flash highlighted the contrast between the tan lines on their naked torsos and the pale skin of their breasts. There was another picture of Westmann in the water with them, his face flushed with alcohol and his eyes slightly crossed. He had an expression on his face that suggested that the lights were on but no one was home.

"Ick," I said out loud to no one in particular.

Westmann's party life wasn't what I was interested in. I was looking for clues about how he thought and how he worked.

Eventually, I grew adept at filtering out the more personal stuff and focusing on the entries dealing with writing. At first glance, there wasn't much here that related to his old books. His recent journal notes suggested that he had developed a fascination with the indigenous peoples of the American Southwest, their relation to the land and their expressions of spirituality. The notes were a jumble of reflections on sand paintings, the Kachina, vision quests, and anything else he could grab at. There were copies of maps folded in the latest volumes.

By evening, I'd come away with the impression of a man

who had long put aside his early interests and was in the throes of a new intellectual passion. He didn't seem worried about a visit from Asian assassins bent on revenging a decades-old betrayal of secret lore. He was interested in sweat lodges and mystic chants and figuring out a way to tap into the American fascination with the generically exotic.

In other words, he was still a shyster. A talented guy with a keen eye and an ear well tuned to the pitch of popular culture, but a shyster nonetheless. This was not a revelation to me. There was little in the journals to pique my interest. Until the entries that began to mention the help Westmann received from a guide in the ways of the desert: Xochi.

Was reading this stuff technically connected to what I was getting paid to do? No. I hadn't finished my research, but I was coming to some conclusions. Westmann mostly seemed pretty sad to me: a person always trying to work the angles, in search of things not for the joy of discovery, but because the process led him to other things: notoriety, women, a good buzz. But that wasn't what was holding my attention. I couldn't let go of the question about the attack in the desert, or why Lori Westmann's desert guide Xochi was taking an interest in me.

Xochi. Did he hide the existence of Westmann's retreat from Lori to protect her mental image of her father? Or was he playing some other angle? Perhaps there was a value to the journals that I didn't understand.

Looking back, maybe I shouldn't have read the journals. But I had a sense that somewhere in these pages, there were answers for me. And besides, part of me really hated the type of shyster-scholar that Westmann had become. If I was going to research him, I wanted to uncover the truth and not whatever Lori Westmann was trying to peddle. Finally, I remembered

Yamashita's admonition: in the warrior's life there are two things: intention and results.

I spent some hours working the copy machine in the library, placed the original journals back where I had found them, then closed up and headed back to town. I had an order from Yamashita to obey.

Hasegawa Sensei was probably in his early forties. He had a bristly salt and pepper mustache and short dark hair with some silver on the sides. His torso was thick and his handshake was powerful.

"Hey, Dr. Burke," he said. "Pleased to meet you. I'm Steve Hasegawa. We got a call that you might drop by." *Sansei*, I thought: at least a third generation Japanese American.

I smiled at him. He had good presence; the body relaxed yet fit looking, his face open and friendly. "My *sensei* doesn't want me getting rusty while I'm out here for a while on a consulting job," I explained. "He obviously thinks highly of your *dojo*. I was wondering whether you might be willing to let me train…"

It was a decent looking training hall. The ceilings were high enough for weapons use. The space was big and empty and unadorned—always a positive sign in my experience. You go into a place and see a Bruce Lee poster or a velvet painting of the Buddha, it's probably best to walk right out again. Hasegawa's work space consisted of a battered metal desk. Behind him on the wall were framed certificates of rank, a posted practice schedule, and some black and white photos. A few showed a much older Asian man in action, a still center amidst the blurring motion of falling bodies. Another was of Steve Hasegawa conducting a class. Another photo captured him as a younger, cockier man wearing camouflage BDU's with a Ranger tab on the shoulder and cradling a scoped sniper rifle.

"Interesting," I said.

He waved a hand. "Ancient history. Let me show you around."

The room was dominated by the broad expanse of hard-looking mats. The walls were white with worn wainscoting, and fluorescent lights pulsed down without remorse. It was a serious training hall. The only concession to fashion was a small shrine along one wall with a scroll hanging there. The calligraphy was bold and fluid. It translated as "Relentless as Fire." My kind of place.

But it's always dicey to show up and ask to be let in on practice. It's not unusual in the martial arts world for complete strangers to wander in off the street, imply they're advanced students, and ask to train for a while. They've got the gear in a battered bag and know the lingo, but they're almost always a royal pain. Inevitably, they're either not as trained as they think, which puts them at risk, or they've got something to prove, which puts others at risk

Hasegawa's smile didn't fade when I made the request to train, although his eyes shifted a bit. "Well," he said, "we're always interested in new students, but I don't know what benefit there would be in a short-term membership."

"Did my teacher speak with you?" I asked. "Sort of describe what I'm looking for?"

"Uh, no," he replied. "Actually the contact was through my father. It's his school, but I've been sort of running it lately…" He trailed off as if there was explanation there but he was unwilling to supply it. Then Hasegawa moved over to a desk and pulled out a form. He looked up at me, still skeptical, but obviously thinking about whatever his father had told him.

"Maybe you could fill this membership form out, give me some indication of your training background…"

They gave me a rental *gi* to wear. It was soft with repeated washings and had the number "4" written on the collar in magic marker. The standard uniform you see in judo and other grappling arts, the *gi* was an off-white color. I had worn something very similar years ago when I first started studying the martial arts. In Yamashita's *dojo*, we wear the deep indigo training tops of the traditional sword arts with a matching *hakama*. They're links to an older, formal age in Japan. In some training halls, appearing in just a *gi* without a *hakama* over it is considered the equivalent of appearing in your underwear. But in other styles, like Hasegawa's, *hakama* are only worn by people with black belt rank.

They gave me a white belt to tie around my uniform. When the class was called to order, I made sure I sat at the end with the beginners. Everything in a traditional Japanese training hall is related to issues of rank: it conditions whom you bow to and how, the roles of people in paired exercises, and how you're supposed to behave in general. Even the room is divided into spheres of higher and lower status. Higher ranks line up closest to the place of honor where the scroll hung. As *sensei*, Hasegawa would sit at that end. The line would stretch away from him, across the room, and as individual rank decreased, so your place in the line grew farther and farther away from the teacher.

I sat near the door, with the kids. As the class sat down in the formal position for the ritual bow, the front door opened and an elderly woman pushed a man in a wheelchair into the room. All activity stopped. Steve Hasegawa leapt up from his position, kissed the woman, and gently took control of the wheelchair. He moved the old man onto the mats, placed him with care in the spot of honor, and then knelt down in front of him, facing the wheelchair-bound man with the rest of the class.

His voice was strong as he called "*Sensei ni... Rei!*" and we bowed in silent unison toward the figure in the chair. He sat immobile, slightly slumped over, but his eyes glittered in acknowledgment of the salutation.

This was probably the Hasegawa Sensei that Yamashita was thinking about when he sent me here. As I watched Steve care for the old man, placing him with care in a spot where he could watch the training, I realized that my first impressions were right: this would be a good place to learn things.

It didn't mean that it would be an easy place, however. The Hasegawa school was rooted in the traditions of judo and aikido. The advanced students worked with wooden swords and the short staff known as a *jo*. They handed me one of the staffs, which were made from white oak.

We moved through some basics, practicing movement and strikes in isolation. Then we progressed to paired techniques. The old man watched me, his body almost totally motionless, but his head and eyes moving slightly to track me, to measure me, to weigh my skill. His son was doing the same, moving around the room, correcting and encouraging, but always coming back to evaluate me.

At one point we took a rest and at some signal I couldn't decipher, the old man called his son over. Steve bent over the chair and his father whispered something to him. The younger man nodded and straightened up.

"*Kata*," he called. *Kata* are the formal practice routines of the old arts, choreographed actions developed from traditions where the slightest error with a weapon could maim your opponent. Some martial artists disdain *kata*. When done right, true *kata* practice can make the sweat stream off you and your hair stand on end.

In the paired exercises focusing on *jo,* the attacker uses a wooden sword and the defender wields a *jo.* There are twelve *kata* for *jo,* and they grow subtly more complex as you progress through them. As a junior ranked person in this school, I got to defend with the *jo.* I was looking about for a partner, when Steve Hasegawa slipped into place in front of me carrying a wooden sword. He grinned slightly as we bowed.

But when we came together, he was all business—focused, smooth, and lethal. We started with the *kata* called *tsukizue.* Hasegawa was holding back a bit, getting a feel for my skill level. As we advanced through each form, his movements grew crisper, harder, and faster. His eyes tightened in concentration as my response kept pace with the increasing intensity of his actions.

By the time we had finished the final *kata* called *Ranai,* we were both sweaty. We brought our weapons down and bowed formally to each other. The smile was back on his face. I glanced around me and noticed that the rest of the class had sat down to watch. Thinking back, I remember the fleeting impression that most other activity had stopped some time ago.

"Thank you, Sensei," I said. "That was the sort of thing I needed."

"My pleasure, Dr. Burke," he said, and sounded like he meant it. He called the class to order and we began to line up for the formal bow that would end the session. I started to move down to the end of the line, but Hasegawa laid a gentle hand upon my arm.

"Oh, no." He gestured beside him in the special spot reserved for teachers. "You sit beside me here."

When the students were seated, Hasegawa Sensei addressed them. "I hope you were watching carefully this evening," he began. "It's not often we get to see this sort of thing. Dr. Burke will be with us for a short time. I hope that you use that time to learn what you can from him."

He called the group to attention, we bowed to the old man in the wheelchair, then to each other. As the class broke up, Hasegawa called to one of his senior students. "Keith, please see whether we can rustle up a *hakama* to loan to Dr. Burke." I glanced over at the old man in the wheelchair. His eyes closed slowly and he painfully, ever so slightly, inclined himself in my direction.

As the week passed, I settled into a rhythm, sifting through the papers at Westmann's estate, working more eagerly with his journals, and training with the Hasegawas in the evening. It helped me feel a bit less adrift, more myself as I pursued what I was coming to believe was a fruitless search for clues to a non-existent crime related to Westmann's death.

That night, after almost a week at the *dojo* I'd come out at the end of a training session, still damp from the shower. The street was a busy one, and if I expected a wash of stars across the desert sky, I was disappointed—the city lights bled upward, obscuring the heavens.

I was heading toward the car. Down the road an engine roared into life. Cars whizzed past. I was loose and calm, with the almost narcotic sense of well-being you get from a solid workout. As I headed toward the car, a voice called my name.

I turned to see one of Hasegawa's students, a burly guy with a military style haircut. He came up to me, casting a glance up the street.

"Dr. Burke," he repeated. I looked at him pleasantly, figuring maybe he had a technical question. The expression on his face was serious.

"Tony Villardi," he said. "I'm with the Tucson P.D."

"What can I do for you, Tony?"

He looked around again. "You know anyone in this town, Dr. Burke?"

"No, not really. Why?"

"We tend to get out of the training hall at about the same time every night. When I come out, I always look around, you know?"

I nodded encouragingly.

"At first I thought it was just a coincidence, but I've been watching all week."

"Watching what, Tony?"

"Every night, there's a car parked across the road. A couple of guys are always in it. When you come out, they start up the motor, wait for you to pull out, and follow you."

So much for my powers of observation. "Did you run the tags?" I asked him.

He shrugged. "It's a different car every night. Different guys for all I know. But it's the same pattern. And I didn't get a good look, but it seems to me that these guys are sporting gang colors."

"Gangs?" I asked.

He nodded. "We got 'em all over the area. They're involved in everything from dope to guns to border trafficking. You got any reason to think you've run afoul of these people?"

"No," I lied.

He shrugged. "Maybe I'm imagining it, but I don't think so. You want to keep your eyes open, Dr. Burke. These guys are not real smart, but they're mean."

I thanked him for the warning and drove back to the hotel. My steering was a little wobbly because I kept trying to spot gang members in my rearview mirror. My vigilance earned me nothing except a few rude gestures from other drivers.

7

TRACKERS

In the mesquite and dirt of the Tohono O'Odham reservation, Oliver Jackson squatted, reading sign. The five other members of his team waited patiently. They, too, could read the significance in the boot prints they had discovered, but he was the senior man and had been doing this for almost twenty years. They waited out of respect, and because their trade demanded it.

It was a time when infrared sensors and pilotless drones were just a few of the hi-tech tools that Homeland Security used along the Mexican border. But HSA was willing to use almost any technique if it worked. And sometimes, the most effective tools were the timeless use of men on the ground; men who had been raised to read the subtle signs left in the desert, and to track prey with a silent, dogged intensity.

All of Jackson's men were Native Americans. They had grown up in the outdoors hunting, tracking, and coming to know the land in a way few people could. A Dineh, what most people knew as Navaho, Jackson was stocky and compact, his skin like leather from years in the desert sun. His short cropped hair was just showing some silver in the tips. His dusty desert camo uniform was rumpled, but his gear was meticulously cared for and the CAR-15 slung across his back was well-oiled.

The Tohono O'Odham land stretches across southern Arizona into Mexico, a vast area larger than the state of Connecticut. Seventy-six miles of the border with Mexico are contained with the Tohono O'Odham territory. In the seventies, the Tohono had agreed to let federal agents onto their land, but only if they were Native Americans. It was the genesis of the unit Jackson had served in for all these years.

Although the border was long and easily crossed, the best routes combined terrain features that made crossings harder to detect and also provided possible resting spots and water sources. It narrowed down, somewhat, the choices for Jackson and his men. They tracked smugglers through this remote landscape intercepting groups of men lugging sixty pound bales of marijuana through the blasting heat of summer or the frigid desert winter. And lately, the activity had been picking up.

Jackson's team had been tracking a group of about ten smugglers since before dawn. In places where they left tracks, the team could see that their boot prints were deep and widely spaced—a sure sign they were carrying heavy loads. The latest imprints that Jackson looked at were clean ones, devoid of the tracks of nocturnal animals or insects. He knew that the men he was tracking were probably only a few hours ahead.

The smugglers were headed north, away from the border. Jackson took out a map and laid it across his thighs. A thick finger traced their route so far. He showed his team.

"Here," he said. "They're heading here." The team nodded in silent agreement. Smugglers would typically come across the border and trundle their bales some forty miles north to little used roads where they would be transferred to trucks. Today was no exception.

The sun was high overhead, pounding down on the group as they squatted amid the thorny scrub. One of the team noticed a small piece of fabric clinging to a bush. He plucked it, bringing it to his face and sniffed. He smiled and passed it on to

Jackson, who cupped it in his hand and held it to his nose. The scent of burlap. A smuggler had snagged his load on this bush, leaving this thread in the passing.

"OK," he said. "Huddle up." The team clustered around him. "Another hour or so and we should overtake these guys." He eyed his men: they squatted comfortably in the sun, eyes invisible behind sunglasses. They drank quietly at camel-back canteens; the small sips veterans take who know water discipline. Nobody seemed tired. Everyone was eager for the hunt. "When we start to get close, I want to hold up and get ourselves set. The briefing last night said that the natives are restless."

His men grinned at that: brief flashes of white teeth in dark faces. They *were* the natives.

"Border Patrol units have been fired on recently. The number of incidents is increasing. And the armaments being used are not your typical border guns." Jackson scanned the jumbled terrain that stretched before them. "Something's changing out here. I can feel it. I don't know what it is, but I don't like it…" He looked out into the far hills, straining to sense a clue embedded in the gusting heat of the desert.

Jackson was a quiet man in the field. His team was used to silence and comfortable with his quiet competence as a tracker. But he was also a *hitaali,* a singer, among his people. He practiced the old ways of healing and the chantways of the Dineh. There were times when his team members swore that his success as a tracker was due to more than just skill.

Jackson was a legend, a man at home in the desert who had an almost mystical link to the land. He could see minute traces of a smuggler's passing that nobody else noticed. He could intuit a prey's intention with almost no clues. It was said he saw things on the wind.

The team members looked at one another quizzically, but made no sound. Their people knew of the power of the men who could read signs in the air and see far distances. When Jackson gazed off into the invisible world, it was best not to rouse him. After a moment, Jackson stirred, returning to the imminent. What was the lanky form he had seen, trotting among the shimmering rocks? *A coyote. A bad sign.* He looked down, taking a deep breath to shake off the sense of dread. "When we get close, keep alert. Stay down and behind cover, till I give the signal. I've got a feeling…"

He looked from one of his men to the other. They nodded solemnly. "OK," Jackson said, "let's go."

A sandy patch of open desert bore clear evidence of the smugglers, a churned trail of boot prints leading to a dirt road that was sketched in on Jackson's map. The afternoon sun began to take its toll, and even Jackson's men began to tire.

Almost there, he thought, checking his map. The others sensed it too: Jackson could see the renewed eagerness of their movement. *They love the hunt. But we're tired. And eager. This is when mistakes get made.*

He held a hand up and waved it in a circle. The team collected around him in the shadow of a sandstone rock that was angled into the sand like a listing vessel. Jackson spread out the map, pointing out terrain features and what seemed to him like the likely route to the smugglers' transfer point. He directed individual members of the team to take up positions on high ground overlooking the rendezvous site.

When he was sure that everyone knew their role, Jackson unslung his rifle and pulled the charging handle back to load it. His men did the same. Jackson paused and sniffed the wind. He moved slowly up a rise, ears straining for sounds out of place. The land was too rough for clear line of sight and its gnarled terrain created acoustic shadows that swallowed sound. He knew that somewhere around this slope and downhill, the road would come into view. But he was moving blind. And the feeling of unease was growing stronger. He listened intently. Wind. Birds calling in the distance. He sniffed the air: sometimes you could smell tobacco or the pungent aroma of the marijuana bales. There was instead a faint oily scent, something mechanical and deeply out of place.

He brought his weapon up and crept around the slope, motioning his team into position with hand gestures. When the road came into view, Jackson's gut lurched.

The smugglers had reached the drop off point. But they would never return. A late model Ford F-150 sagged, riddled with bullet holes. He could see a body slumped over the wheel. The smugglers' bodies were scattered across the churned-up sand of the rendezvous. The blood that had not seeped into the dirt had thickened and grown black. Flies congregated and birds were wheeling in anticipation.

Jackson and his men lurched warily down the slope and checked for survivors. There were none: all the smugglers had had their throats cut for good measure. *We were too* late, he thought. The tire treads of multiple vehicles crisscrossed the area. The marijuana bales were long gone. *Ambush.*

"Bad medicine, Boss," one of his men commented.

Jackson thought of his vision of the coyote loping ahead in the shimmering distance, tongue wagging as if in mockery. He sighed and radioed for help.

8
LAIR

I was summoned to the dragon's lair a few days later. I'd been working steadily, putting together a picture of Eliot West-mann and the process he used to write his books. In the evenings after I came back from Hasegawa's *dojo*, I worked my way through the hidden journals as well. They weren't directly relevant to the issue of authenticity in his books, but they gave me an insight into the man and, as an aside, also fleshed out what he had been up to just before he joined the Martini Diving Team.

I got a call from Roy just before 10 PM to let me know that Ms. Westmann would expect me in her office tomorrow morning to present a status report. In my mind's eye, I could picture Roy, poised with quivering pen over a checklist of tasks he had to complete for his mistress.

"A status report?" I said, and my tone must have betrayed something of my amusement. It was not an emotion that Roy associated with his employer, however.

"Ms. Westmann is very eager to hear the details of your work to date, Dr. Burke," he told me earnestly. "A brief written synopsis should do—Ms. Westmann is extremely busy—along with an oral report. Please let me know whether you'll require anything from our business center—a projector for a presentation, copying services. We're at your disposal."

"How nice," I answered but I could sense that I was going to be a real disappointment to Roy. There wasn't going to be a

PowerPoint presentation in my briefing. No handouts. I toyed with the idea of multicolored pie charts, but dismissed that as well. I could pretty much deliver a report on my progress without audiovisual aids. The only thing I had to work on was to find a nicer word than "shyster" to describe Eliot Westmann.

I did show up as requested—time has mellowed me somewhat. The Burkes have a lifelong issue with authority. It may come from the unique cultural experience of being raised as Irish Catholics. It was composed, in part, of a dramatic emotional oscillation between struggling to stand on your own two feet and being forced to sink to your knees. Either way, someone was always pushing you around.

I had made some quick notes for the meeting, but I left my laptop in the room. Bad enough that I had to show up when ordered. There was no sense in appearing eager or overly efficient—an attitude that is responsible for my notable lack of career advancement.

Charlie Fiorella was waiting for me outside Lori Westmann's executive suite. He was as dapper as ever; looking relaxed and fit in a lightweight tan suit. He seemed at ease in the corridors of power. The office suites of the powerful smell faintly of good cologne and furniture polish. There's a subdued, efficient-sounding hum pulsing out from secretarial cubicles. The air is heavy with importance.

I'm always suspicious that the people in these sorts of places have invited me there to help move furniture. It's delusional, of course. The people there are just people, but they're working frantically to prove that they are smarter and better than everyone else. Some of them may be smarter than I am, I don't know—I've ceased evaluating people in that way. What I do know is that in places like this, generating a collective sense of importance is vital. The alternative is often too painful for these folks to contemplate.

Lori Westmann was as smooth and well coiffed and hard as ever. She was wearing a dark blue business suit with a pink collarless shirt of what looked like silk. Her large office was finely appointed, but the curtains were drawn and muted lights set in the ceiling created pools of brightness amidst a general gloom. She sat strategically in a cone of light that made her appear to glow. We were relegated to a less brilliant zone. Westmann gave me a cursory smile from the other side of her large desk. Roy pointed me to a seat. Charlie followed me in and sat down, crossing his leg casually but being careful to hike up the trouser leg to preserve the line of the crease. His socks matched his suit color perfectly. I wasn't sure what color my socks were. I couldn't even remember whether I was wearing any. It seemed to me that our chairs were slightly lower than Lori Westmann's.

We exchanged ritual pleasantries. Roy brought us all coffee, but once the fidgeting with cups was over, his boss simply turned an inquiring look my way. I launched into an overview of my activities. When Westmann concentrated, a small crease appeared at the top of her nose, pulling her well-plucked eyebrows closer together.

"So," she interrupted at one point, "your work to date has been in large part a re-reading of my father's works as well as commentary from various reviewers?" Her tone was not pleased. She was a woman in a hurry and the sooner I could complete my analysis, the better.

"In part, yes," I answered. "The structure and themes and images your father employed in his work are central to any analysis of his ..." I hesitated for a moment trying to find the correct word, "... authenticity."

"And?" I thought she seemed a little testy so early in the morning, but I suppose that a chief executive's work is never-ending. Then again, I did notice that her nails appeared freshly manicured.

"His writing is highly creative, certainly," I offered. "But any evaluation of his claims to have used primary sources is going to be built on a comparison of his writing to published sources available at the time." She looked at me skeptically. Her eyes were very blue, like the slick underbelly of an iceberg. "I'm not disputing the fact that your father was a talented writer, Ms. Westmann. That's not what you hired me to do. I'm looking for elements in his books that could or could not have been lifted from other sources. It's the only way to begin to prove any original scholarship."

"Your opinion, Dr. Burke," she put a sarcastic emphasis on the doctor part. "After reading the material, what is your opinion?" She began to tick points off one by one, tapping a forefinger on the desk for emphasis. The pink of the nail polish matched her blouse. "The whole description of the mountain temple, the prevalence of deep red color symbolism, fox statues. Even the name for the trainees there…"

"*Kitsume*," I supplied. "Shape shifters." I began to suspect she knew more about her father's work than she had let on.

"Precisely," she said. "I've done my homework, Dr. Burke," she said scornfully. "I expected something more from you."

I probably let a little too much energy seep into my answer, but she was beginning to annoy me. "They're the type of details I can dig up in about thirty seconds using the Internet. When your father wrote his books, it probably took a bit more digging, but I'll bet there were sources available that he could have drawn from. Not his own experience."

"Prove it!" she demanded.

"I will. But there are other things that don't fit with my knowledge of the literature. Sure, the Shinto deity Inari was sometimes thought of as the patron god of sword smiths. But there's no record that I know of that speaks of a secret cult of nature worshipping ascetics training in warrior systems up in Hokkaido." I now had a full head of steam up. "And I'm a little disappointed at the resources in your father's library. Most of the stuff there seems to be copies of manuscript pages…"

"My father was very protective of his life's work. He routinely made copies and sent the originals off to an archive," she noted dryly.

I waived it away. "I can live with the copies. That doesn't matter. But the types of notes a scholar would make before getting to the point of a completed manuscript aren't present. Some marginal notes relating to sources appear occasionally, but not enough to permit a reconstruction. And there are frequent notations that simply say 'PO'. What's that all about?"

"My father told me that meant 'personal observation.'"

"It's not enough for scholars. Without field notes or journals from the time to back it up, it's going to look like it means 'permanently obscure.'" I couldn't be positive, but out of the corner of my eye, I thought I saw Charlie's lips twitch in a suppressed smile. Roy looked appalled. I had leaned forward in my chair as my temper got the better of me, so I sat back and waited.

Lori Westmann took a little sipping breath, swung her chair around so she could look out at window of her office, perhaps expecting her laser-like executive glare to pierce the curtains. She swung back to me, her face flat, but her eyes piercing.

"What else do you need to make the complete assessment?"

"I need access to whatever field notes or journals he kept at the time. I know your father kept a personal journal pretty faithfully…"

"He seems to have stopped that in recent years," she told me.

I shook my head. "No, he never stopped," I corrected her. "I've seen them."

"What!" she demanded. The discovery seemed to shake her. At the time, I thought it was that she simply disliked being surprised. She was, after all, a woman who prided herself on being informed and in control. Not much happened in her little universe that she didn't know about.

I described finding the journals, careful to point out that they shed light on Eliot Westmann, the way he thought, and his approach to life, but really had not contributed much toward my analysis of his contested works. Lori made careful notes about the journals and their location. She looked at Charlie for the first time that morning. "I'll want those journals secured," she ordered. He nodded in silent agreement.

She turned back to me. "Do you have a report for me?"

I was puzzled for a moment, and then I realized that she was expecting some sort of formal document. "You just got it," I answered.

She was seething, but kept it pretty tightly under control. "I'd like a written summary of your activities to date and your observations on my desk by this evening." The words were pronounced carefully and flew out like bullets from a gun. "Plus a concrete list of what other resources you'll need to access and a timeline for completion. A *short* timeline."

"I'll need to see his journals from back then," I countered. "The ones you say are in the archives…"

"His agent maintains them," she snapped.

"Fine, I'll go see him," I said cheerily. It was fun needling her. Dangerous, but fun.

"He's in New York City." She glanced at Roy. He made some notes.

"Even better," I said, my voice bright. *Home.* "The library at Columbia should give me the other resources I need."

Lori gave Roy a string of orders. I was dismissed with a curt nod and Charlie and I sauntered back out into the daylight.

We strolled along the pathways, bordered in the deep emerald of well-manicured lawns.

"You are some piece of work," he said with a slight smile.

I shrugged. "She hired me to do a job. I know my work. She ought to let me run with it."

"She's used to getting her way," he noted. "Not many people don't fold when she pushes hard at them."

"And another thing," I said, not even bothering to comment on Charlie's observation, "she's skewing the data I've got, trying to steer me to certain conclusions—she's holding back sources that I need to make an objective assessment. As if I wouldn't notice."

"She's paying you," he said simply. "She figures she owns you."

"She figured wrong," I told him.

Charlie smiled again. "I think she realizes that now."

As we walked up the path toward my suite, I looked at him. "How do you stand it? Working for her?"

He shrugged. "She needs me and she knows it. She tends to stay out of my way and I let her pretend she's in charge. She's unpleasant to be around, but the salary is good and every morning I can almost count on…"

"…getting in a full round of golf," I finished for him.

He patted me on the shoulder. "You got it."

I stopped and faced him. "I'm assuming I should probably start packing?"

"That would be a safe assumption. Old Roy will make sure you turn in your little book report tonight and probably have you on the first plane out of here."

I nodded in acknowledgment and headed toward the door. It was slightly ajar.

"That's funny," I said, "I would have sworn I locked it."

Charlie pushed me gently aside. "These doors are self-closing," he commented quietly. He reached down and took a small handgun from an ankle holster and pushed the door back into the room. A small piece of wood had been wedged in the bottom of the jam.

I looked at him questioningly, but he shook his head and did a quick sweep of the room. I looked around, but everything seemed fine. Charlie moved quietly into the other rooms, checking closets and corners. He called to me from the bedroom.

He was standing there, looking at the wall above the bed. Some characters had been spray painted there. And driven into the wood of the headboard was a small throwing star, the archaic weapon of the *ninja*. The points that weren't embedded in the wood gleamed as if they had been recently sharpened. My laptop lay on the bed, the screen up as if it had just recently been used. When I had left for the meeting, the computer had been on the desk.

"Don't touch anything," he said, but it was unnecessary—I'd been at crime scenes before. I just stood there looking at things, picking up details, and trying to make sense out of it.

He nodded at the wall. "Can you make that out?"

"Sure," I nodded. "It's crude, but it's legible."

"And…" he prompted.

Two characters, one below the other. "*Okuden*," I read.

"And?" he said again, with a trace of impatience.

"It refers to hidden teachings," I told him. "In the martial arts world there are layers to what students get taught. The *okuden* are the special secrets of your teacher and not to be revealed to outsiders…"

Even as I said it, I began making the connections.

"I've seen these things before," Charlie commented, pointing to the throwing star. "Kung fu, right?"

I smiled. "It's a *shuriken*. A throwing star. Pretty common in various arts."

"They all have the little design in the center?"

"No," I sighed. Etched in the center of the star was a small diamond. A diamond, the *kongo* symbol that Eliot Westmann claimed was the mark of the followers of Inari-sama's secret sect in Hokkaido.

"You still think Lori's jerking your chain?" Charlie asked me quietly.

In fact, I didn't know what to think. After the cops arrived and checked things out, I was left to puzzle over recent events. Roy moved me to another room, this one small and on the third floor of the main building, and also informed me that I was scheduled for a mid-day flight out of Arizona the next day. He appeared deeply concerned by the strange chain of events. I imagined that he wasn't so much worried about what happened to me, since I was on his boss's black list, as he was upset about the fact that someone had defaced hotel property in one of their more elegant suites.

I sat down in my little room for a while, staring at the walls. After a time, I moved out to the postage-stamp sized balcony. There was a white plastic chair and wobbly table, tangible evidence of how far I had fallen in Lori Westmann's estimation. I gazed out over the resort property, the winding paths and rooftops, the lush deep green of grass and the bright blossoms of flowering plants. I lifted my eyes higher and into the rougher, less forgiving ground of the distant desert. We try so hard to make our worlds pleasant and tidy.

I sighed, turned around, and brought my laptop out to begin the chore of writing a report. But it wouldn't boot up. I tried a few different things, but got the same result. *Great. Now I'll have to do it from memory.*

I made a call to the business center and the folks there were more than happy to take a look at the computer. The word of my fall from grace had obviously not percolated down to the troops. I wandered down to the main reception center, taking care to make sure my door was securely locked. I was alert to the possible presence of danger. The most alarming thing I saw was an obese woman in a bright, expansively flowered bathing suit. She was alone in the deep blue of the pool, paddling slowly with the odd, languid grace that heavy people display in the water.

They ran a check on my computer. All the components were working.

"So what's the deal?" I asked the tech.

"It's been wiped," he told me matter of factly. He was probably still in college, reed thin, with a spiky hairdo.

"Wiped?" I said.

"Sure," he shrugged. "The hard drive's been wiped out."

"And the data?" I pressed him.

"Gone." He saw my expression. "I can reformat the drive for you. It'll take a while, but you'll be able to use it again."

"How's something like this happen?"

"Pretty easy," he explained. "All you need is a fairly good magnet. You wave it across the drive and it scrambles everything."

I had wondered why the laptop was left on my bed. If the point of the break in was to warn me about discovering old secrets from Westmann's work, then someone had to worry that there might be information on the computer I was using. I thought about the odd juxtaposition of things: a crude, scrawled warning in Japanese characters on the wall, the more sinister message of the *shuriken*'s point driven deep into a wood frame above the place where I lay, and now the destruction of my notes. As if to say that the revelation of secrets begun by Westmann so many years ago should finally be put to an end.

It was creepy. But something about it bothered me: The lore of Japanese assassins is replete with various types of exotic equipment: blowguns, blades, smoke bombs. Westmann's books had described a sect of warrior monks armed with the typical set of Japanese weapons. As far as I could remember, I don't think his *ninja*-like assassins were equipped with computer-destroying magnets.

I spent a few hours in the business center, hogging the use of one of their computers. I wrote down what I could, padding my text with information and sources I could pull from the Internet. The advanced education I had received while earning a Ph.D. has almost no useful application in the real world. But after years of graduate school, one thing I can do is write a book report.

I printed the report out and delivered it to the Dragon Lady. Then I took a ride out to Hasegawa's *dojo* to say goodbye. Steve

Hasegawa was puttering around the empty space, sweeping the mats in preparation for the evening's class, and he seemed genuinely sad to learn that I wasn't going to be around any more.

"It was good training with you, Burke," he said and shook my hand. "The students will miss you."

I shrugged the compliment off. "All good things come to an end," I said.

Steve nodded sadly. "Sure." He looked down at his feet, but I don't think that was what he was seeing. I wondered for a moment whether he was thinking of his father, once a martial artist of accomplishment and now a prisoner in his own body. Then he looked up, back in the moment, and summoned up a smile. He tapped the side of his head with the heel of his palm in mock surprise. "But hey, I'm forgetting my *reigi.*"

Etiquette. It's part and parcel of training. He rummaged around in his desk drawer and drew out a small folded piece of cloth wrapped in cellophane. It was a *tenegui,* a small cotton towel used in the martial arts for a variety of things. It's customary when visiting other *dojo* for people to exchange them, since each school has *tenegui* made in different colors embodying different slogans representative of their unique character.

I accepted it with two hands in a gesture of respect. "I have nothing for you in return," I admitted, "except my thanks." The *tenegui* was yellow, with crimson calligraphy. The color scheme echoed the state flag of Arizona, but the sentiment written upon it was the same slogan that guided the students in the *dojo* of the Hasegawas.

Steve shrugged and smiled. "I know you like the motto," he commented.

"Relentless as fire," I recited.

He nodded. "Real old-time hard core, Burke." But his tone

led me to believe he had more to say.

"And?"

"You know what's really relentless as fire, Burke?" I shook my head no. "Life," he said simply, and turned back to cleaning the mats.

When I returned to the hotel, Charlie Fiorella was waiting for me. I barely got the car parked before he emerged from the shade of the front portico of the hotel reception area.

"Hi Charlie," I said brightly enough, but then I registered his serious mood.

"I've been waiting for you," he said grimly. He looked slightly disheveled, and I noticed a smudge or two on his sport coat.

What's up?"

He didn't answer me directly. "Where have you been for the last few hours?" he asked.

"Here, for the most part," I said, puzzled.

"Witnesses?"

"Sure, I was in the business center." I didn't like the direction of his line of questions, but I liked Charlie and was willing to give him the benefit of the doubt.

He nodded at the car. "And now?"

"I took a drive out to the martial arts school I was training at to say good bye."

"Can it be confirmed?"

I nodded in the affirmative. The brisk, focused series of questions was familiar: it was something I had seen my brother Micky do any number of times as he interrogated people who might or might not be suspects in a criminal investigation.

My responses seemed to reassure Charlie; his face relaxed

somewhat, and he took me by the arm and guided me along the shaded walk so we'd be out of earshot of the staff.

"Look," he said quietly. "After the meeting I went out to the old man's place to get that journal you found. I had a couple of issues pending in the office, so I didn't get out there until after lunch."

"And?"

"When I got out there, the place had been torched. The main building was pretty much gutted. And the room you described had been ransacked."

"No journal?" I guessed.

"No journal," he replied. "No nothing. Every single scrap of paper in Westmann's library is gone."

I wasn't sure that this was a major literary disaster. And I was pretty sure that Charlie didn't care much about the loss of Westmann's notes either. He wasn't focusing so much on what was done; he was more concerned at the fact that it had taken place at all. It was a turf issue, a pride issue. But mostly, it was a cop thing. These guys work hard at keeping a messy world in some semblance of order. Their self-image is intertwined with the abilities they display on the job. Someone like Charlie could deal with any number of disasters and take them in stride. But this event was personal in an odd sort of way: an insult to his competence as head of security in the tiny efficient empire of Lori Westmann.

"Do you have any suspects?" I said.

He squinted at me. "We usually look to disgruntled employees." I nodded. "People with an axe to grind." He saw that I wasn't getting it. "Someone," he said with emphasis, "who might have recently been called to a meeting and argued with his employer and whose work was judged to be unsatisfactory."

"Oh," I replied, finally getting it. "Ah."

Charlie started to laugh. "Burke, get a grip. I don't seriously think you're a suspect. And, fortunately," he told me, "you've got an alibi."

"True, but imagine that my tab at the poolside bar is not going to be honored anymore."

"If you're not packed yet," he told me in confidence, "I'd make that a priority."

The staff didn't line up to bid me farewell. Charlie had hosed down Lori Westmann enough to ensure that I wasn't arrested on suspicion of arson. I signed the bill with a sense of relief and prepared to escape. As I settled up, I asked them to retrieve the package I had deposited in the hotel safe a few days ago. It was fairly bulky, and when the clerk passed it over the high counter to me, some of the papers spilled out. The sheets swirled to the floor. I scrambled to pick them up and get them out of sight. Anyone who knew his handwriting would recognize the copy I had made of Eliot Westmann's journal. I was focused on getting the pages back into the package and yet simultaneously trying to see whether anyone was taking an undue interest.

It wasn't until I was almost out the door that I caught a glimpse of Xochi watching me with a still, shocking intensity.

I clambered into the limo that was taking me to the airport. If I had been driving, I would have hit the gas so hard that the wheels would have been smoking. As it was, the chauffeur moved us smoothly and sedately away from the hotel. I half expected Xochi to throw himself across the hood of the car. But he stayed in the shadows and the limo headed, unmolested, out into the hard light of the highway.

Home, James.

9

KIME

I tried not to think too much about the Westmanns for a while. And, truth be told, it wasn't difficult. I had spent a great deal of my early life thinking too much and I was making up for lost time.

CRACK! I parried Yamashita's cut at my wrist with my own wooden sword. The *bokken* is dense, white oak, and the vibration of the blow hummed deep in the bones of my arm. I could feel the sweat seeping out on my forehead. I moved warily to one side, watching my teacher. My partner. My opponent. Yamashita flowed over the surface of the wooden floor, his face a flat mask and his eyes dark and narrowed with merciless concentration. When I first began studying with him, the sheer psychic force of his presence when we crossed swords was enough to take my breath away. But I had learned to control my breath. It was just as well. Today, I was going to need it.

We were engaged in a demonstration *kata* for the students who sat, mute on the floor around us. Some would be entranced by the flow of action. The really good students would acknowledge the contained ferocity. Each knew the implications of the scripted moves and the toll they could take on the trainee. Symbols and rituals and hints of an exotic culture surround the traditional Japanese martial arts. It's easy not to see them for what they really are. Despite the skill and grace, the elegance of the techniques and philosophies associated with them, these are systems that take as their subject the destruction of other human beings. Unlike more modern martial arts forms, these are not sports. They're physical and sometimes beautiful, but never nice.

My countering thrust was as hard and focused as I could make it. The point of my sword was driven by explosive movement generated from the hips. It was a technique of full commitment; its goal was to have the opponent choking on a blade that skewered the neck. The thrust known as *tsuki* has been known to make the strongest swordsman flinch. I gave it everything I had.

In the final instant before my sword tip could make contact, Yamashita's body shot to one side as if it were being yanked along a wire. My momentum carried me forward and he prepared for the final, killing blow.

I spun around to face him, dropping to one knee. My sword was held horizontally out above my head, my left hand supporting the blade in anticipation of the final blow that would end the *kata*.

CRACK! It came, as focused and powerful as I expected. I steeled myself into immobility as was required. Some people think that martial artists only study movement. They are wrong. We study control, and it takes a variety of forms.

The two of us remained frozen for an instant, our eyes locked. Finally, my teacher relented. His blade came away and he stepped back.

"So..." he said in the musing, sibilant way the Japanese have. Then he bowed and I bowed back. I noticed that his shaven head was dappled with oily perspiration.

We had reversed roles for the demonstration, a slight and

imperceptible concession to our changing condition. Age and wounds pulled at my teacher, and sometimes when the *dojo* was empty but for the two of us, you could see him struggle against the bonds that time had wrapped around him. But in a demonstration like this, he could, for a time, summon the old fire, and he moved with all the crisp force of a blade singing through the air.

I gave a command, and the circle of students kneeling in a watchful circle paired off to emulate the form we had just demonstrated. Then we walked the room's perimeter, my teacher and I, watching a new generation struggle along the path toward mastery that we had pointed out for them.

Yamashita's voice was low, a murmur as we made our rounds and the walls rang out with the clack and stamp of the *kata*.

"It is good that you are back, Professor," he told me.

"Nice to be missed," I said. We glided along the hardwood floor, our eyes baleful, alert. I saw Sarah working hard with another woman to get the timing of the attack just right.

Yamashita saw the direction of my gaze. "Some, I think, missed you more than others," he said with a faint smile. Then his face grew stern. "The consulting work you are doing… it is a distraction."

"It is a minor thing…"

But he waved me to silence with a chop of his hand. "The *dojo* needs you, Burke. All this other activity…" Yamashita was silent for moment, and I could tell that it was not merely annoyance that was giving him pause. His next words were slow and halting, as if they were difficult to say. "I can still work with them, Burke, but you supply…" He paused once more to find the right word.

I knew then what he was getting at. And how hard it was to

admit, even to me, that the years and damage were slowly dragging him down. I swallowed and made my voice light. "What? A little dash?" I suggested teasingly. "A hint of roguish danger?"

Yamashita has gotten use to my sarcasm over the years, as I have come to finally note and appreciate his own odd, dry humor. But we both knew what I was doing now. He looked at me and shook his head. He opened his mouth to say something else, but his eyes suddenly narrowed, and all that came from him was a soft hiss.

"I see it," I told him, and headed over to correct a student's technique. Each person in the room except for Yamashita dropped to one knee as I explained what needed to be changed. When I was done, the students bowed and sprang back up for more training. It's part of the old style of etiquette. Like most things in the martial arts, it's got more than one purpose. It reinforces good manners and lets the entire group see what's going on, of course. But all that bobbing up and down also builds strong leg muscles. The old masters were nothing if not wily.

Yamashita and I resumed our walk, our heads swiveling watchfully while we spoke without looking at each other, relieved that the pull of the moment had distracted us from more troubling things.

"Do you know when I first sensed that you would make a good pupil, Burke?" he asked me. I shook my head and my *sensei* continued. "It was during the first months of training. You were working with Komura-san."

Komura. He was a fairly high-level executive with Sumitomo, a thick, stolid swordsman who spent his days at the office repressing rage and the evenings venting it in *dojo* all across Manhattan. He was notorious among the junior students: a guy who never said much, carefully folded his pin stripe suits in the dressing room, and emerged onto the training floor with a curt bow and a murderous gleam in his eye. Some of us thought he was a psychopath. For his part, Yamashita seemed to enjoy having Komura around and used him to test the mettle of students.

Yamashita described for me the match he had observed so many years ago. I had a vague recollection of sparring any number of times with Komura, but who cherishes unpleasant memories?

"You had been here long enough to know what you did not know," Yamashita reminded me with an approving tone. I could remember those days: the sense of something akin to despair when, after almost a decade of training in judo and karate, I had entered the blast furnace of training in Yamashita's *dojo*. The black belts I had achieved were revealed as virtually useless: they merely served to get me in the door of his school. Where I was left completely unprepared and virtually defenseless.

I nodded slowly as I thought back. "I remember one time when Komura hammered me pretty good," I said.

"Indeed. I told him to," my teacher said with satisfaction. "You had been working diligently to master the basic forms, but there is nothing like working with an opponent."

"The guy was a lunatic," I reminded Yamashita.

He pursed his lips as if suppressing a smile. "Komura's faults were also his strengths," Yamashita mused. "His technique was good, very good... and more to my purpose on that night, it was not tempered with mercy."

It was coming back to me. Yamashita had paired me with Komura, and we went through a seemingly endless series of parrying drills designed to teach me proper blocking and the consequences of improper technique. I squinted into the past and remembered the sweat and frustration as, seriously over-matched, I furiously attempted to avoid the slashing blows of Komura's wooden sword. He came at me like a machine, flat eyed and pitiless. By the end of the session, I had welts all over my forearms and sides.

I sensed Yamashita looking at me. "You remember now, I think," he commented.

"Oh yeah," I acknowledged.

"And do you know why that event made an impression on me, Professor?"

"Because I would take a beating and still come back for more?" I asked.

Yamashita cocked his head. "Endurance is a good thing for a warrior to have, certainly. But no. At one point, just at the end of the night, Komura had pushed you to your limit. And I saw you set yourself and try, one last time. In fact, you went on the offensive."

"I was pretty steamed," I told him.

"Indeed. You were supposed to be 'steamed' as you put it. But when you attacked, it was not a wild thing. It was very contained. Focused. There was something… dangerous in it."

"I did *tsuki*," I remembered. The thrust to the throat we had just performed in the *kata* tonight.

"Just so. And it was a good, even a very good *tsuki*. A killing technique."

"I seem to remember that he dumped me on the floor."

Yamashita waved it away. "Burke. Of course. He was your senior and much more experienced. But Komura later confided in me that, for a brief moment, his spirit quailed under the force of your *kime*, your focus. And that is when I knew that you would be a good student."

"Because I got angry and attacked him?"

"No. Because you grew angry but contained the energy and channeled it. It wasn't your endurance or even your aggression that impressed me. It was the brief glimpse of *kime*."

Yamashita moved his head slightly to indicate the students we were watching now. "It is what they strive to learn. Your Sarah Klein, for instance. She has the potential to use the sword well. There is an elegance there." It was true. I felt that way whenever I caught a glimpse of her. Something of that quality carried over into her work in the *dojo*.

"I sense a 'but' coming," I prompted him.

He nodded, his eyes down on the floor, watching the slow process of his own feet as they slid across the hard, polished wood. "She lacks as yet the focus needed for a killing blow."

"It will come in time," I said.

"Perhaps," Yamashita mused. "Perhaps it is not something that she truly wishes to acquire." Then he looked up from the floor and changed gears. "We will see. But I am glad that you are back, Burke. You will finish this study for the woman in Arizona soon?" I nodded in assent. "Good. Then your focus can return fully here. Now go and tell that young man to hold the sword properly or I will demonstrate how to take it away."

That would be bad. As I said, sometimes he can still stoke up the old fires.

Eliot Westmann's literary agent was a man named Jonathan Roberts. He had a head of snow-white hair pulled back into a tight ponytail. His face was pink, glowing with good grooming and incipient hypertension probably brought on by too many business lunches. He greeted me with the false enthusiasm of a truly professional schmoozer.

"Dr. Burke, yes," he purred. "Lori Westmann mentioned you might be by."

He leaned back in a high-backed desk chair. The leather groaned in luxurious understatement. Roberts regarded me pleasantly, silently, his bright blue eyes amused either at me or at life in general.

"Good," I said. "I'm finishing up some consulting work for Ms. Westmann and she indicated that you are the custodian of Eliot Westmann's archives."

"Ahh, Eliot," Roberts sighed. "What a gift the man had! I say it not only as someone who became his good friend over the years, Dr. Burke, but as an individual with some considerable experience with the range of literary talent out there in the world." He looked at me knowingly.

"Do you have any insight on the authenticity of some of his work?" I said. It couldn't hurt to ask, and at this point anything would be better than what I had.

He looked at me with a sly expression. "Dr. Burke. Really! One doesn't question talent. One celebrates it." He licked his lips as if savoring the remembered taste of a delicacy. "It was my privilege to represent Eliot Westmann and transform his amazing talent and vision into a considerable writing career."

It was your privilege to get fifteen percent of whatever deals you could cut. It was pretty obvious he wasn't interested in telling me anything.

"OK," I said slowly, drawing the sound out as I thought. "Perhaps you could arrange for me to get into the archives so I can do some cross-checking on things for my report?"

"Dr. Burke," he beamed, "nothing would give me more personal pleasure..." He paused significantly. "Unfortunately, I'm under rather emphatic instructions that the Westmann literary archives are not to be opened for anyone at this time."

"Are you sure?" I said. "Ms. Westmann was supposed to make arrangements. There must be some mistake."

"Oh, no mistake," he said, his voice suggesting sympathy, certainty, and a total lack of real engagement. "I met in person with Ms. Westmann just this morning and she was very definite as only she can be." He smiled brightly.

"She's here in New York?" I asked, confused.

"Oh, indeed." He smoothly passed me an envelope. "She instructed that you be provided with this final… gratuity and that you be informed that your services are no longer needed." He stood up, carefully buttoned his jacket and made sure that the line of his expensive suit fell with appropriate elegance around his figure.

"She's here in New York?" I repeated. My mouth often continues to function when the brain stops.

"Oh, yes. We're lunching today with our publisher to celebrate the re-issue of Eliot's seminal works." He pushed a button on his phone console and ushered me toward the door. "Really, a pleasure meeting with you, Dr. Burke. My charming assistant will see you out…" He gave a jovial wave and, as I left, disappeared back behind his office door, which snicked closed with a definite, firm, yet elegant sound.

"So she cut ya loose," my brother Micky said. "What did you expect?"

"I dunno," I shrugged. "I figured she'd at least insist that I finish the report."

He and Art were sitting across from me in a restaurant booth, eyeing me like I was an exhibit at the freak show.

Art is burlier and seems more easy going than my brother,

but differences in size and coloring and temperament are irrel-evant: they've been partners a long time and share a certain unique perspective.

"So what's the problem?" Art began. "My poor wayward child. Always so down." He took an appreciative sip from a pint of beer. Since they had transformed themselves from homicide cops to security consultants, Art and Mick's hours were a bit more normal. They had gotten a plum contract working as trainers with the NYPD's new counter-terrorism unit. The pay was excellent, there was no overtime, and they were determined to enjoy the experience.

"Let's see what's good about this." Art held up a thick hand and began ticking things off on his fingers. "You got an extended, all-expenses paid trip to Tucson, golden resort capital of the sunny Southwest…"

"You also got paid," Micky added.

Art frowned at the intrusion. "You were asked to put the fine yet obscure skills you have honed through years of higher education to use," he continued.

"And the fact that anyone would pay you to do that is a minor miracle," Micky cackled.

Art held up a third finger. "Although there appeared to be certain… uh, let's say bumpy spots, there was none of the carnage typically associated with your unescorted forays into investigations…"

"And you got paid," Micky reminded me.

I nodded and took a first, appreciative sip from my glass. It was a black and tan, a smooth, creamy mix of ale and stout. I think of it as the chocolate milk of beer—so good and so good for you. I looked from one man to the other. Art smiled and nodded at me encouragingly.

"But something about this doesn't make sense, though," I fumed.

Micky snorted. He and Art had spent years in homicide, where logic was typically not a major factor in the commission of crime. But he held his tongue and let me continue.

"I mean, think about this. Lori Westmann hires me to investigate whether her father was murdered..."

"Ah, the Asian Assassins Theory," Art said appreciatively.

"The Yellow Peril," my brother added.

"Ninja with knives," Art countered.

"Guys, please," I started, but I knew it as too late. Micky and Art are vintage movie buffs. For two people so well grounded in reality, they possess a tremendous knack for relating almost anything to old cinema.

"Reminds me of Warner Oland," Art said. "*The Jade Mask...*"

"*The Shanghai Cobra,*" my brother suggested. "That Charlie Chan. A model for us all." He shook his head appreciatively. Then he saw the look on my face and stopped. "Look," he said in a more serious tone of voice, "I made some calls. Fiorella checks out. He was a good, solid cop. If he didn't smell anything out of the ordinary, the death was probably what it seemed."

"Death by vodka," Art concluded. "No need for assassins. The guy essentially killed himself."

"Then why waste money on an investigation?" I asked. "Why me?"

They looked at each other, a silent flash of communication where shared knowledge was acknowledged and some sort of decision was made. Art reached into the bowl of peanuts on the table and methodically broke open the shell, shook out the nuts, and ate them. He had big, thick hands and the tops were covered with pale freckles. Micky drank his beer and watched me.

Art had a few more nuts, the dark wooden table before him growing littered with the paper-thin husks from the peanuts, and then began. "Well, let's see. In the first place, what this Westmann woman has you do is not a reconstruction of the alleged crime. Instead she sends you off on a trip through this dead guy's writing: mystery and martial arts mumbo-jumbo, right?"

"Far as I can tell, he was making it up," I explained. "He did a lot of research, then concocted a story and cut and pasted a variety of facts culled from the sources to make it sound plausible."

"So you can see why she'd choose you," Micky commented. "You've got the background…" but the tone in his voice suggested something more.

Art supplied it. "But you're not exactly mainstream, are you, Connor?" I started to protest, but he held up a calming hand. "I'm not saying this is a bad thing. But look at it from her perspective. You're academically qualified but not part of the academic establishment."

I had to admit that this was true. I had been run out of academia on a rail for some of my extra-curricular activities. And most of my energies these days were focused on running the *dojo* with Yamashita.

"So from Lori Westmann's perspective," Micky added, "you were perfect. I mean, most specialists thought the guy was a fraud, right?"

"Sure. I did, too."

Micky waved that fact away. "She was looking at it from a

different angle. Your credentials would stand up to scrutiny. Most importantly, you seemed available for hire…"

"And when people like her hire you," Art told me significantly, "what they're really thinking is that they've bought you."

"You mean that she expected me to cook my findings to support her murder theory?"

"Uh, gee, ya think?" Micky said sarcastically.

"Put it all together, Connor," Art said. "This lady thinks her father was murdered. Does she pester the cops? No. She asks some Asian specialist to write a report that would substantiate her wacky Asian assassin theory."

"She never asked me to do that," I started.

"Not in so many words," Art agreed. "But again. People like this have expectations. They pay. You play."

"What happened when your research started to poke holes in things?" Micky asked.

"She was pretty steamed," I said.

"And she got rid of you pretty quickly, too," Art reminded me.

"So what was the point?" I pressed.

Micky signaled the waitress for another round. Art mutely held up the empty peanut basket for her to see that he needed a refill there as well.

"I wondered that, too," my brother said. "But the visit with the agent pretty much clears everything up."

"How so?"

Art reached out and touched my arm. "It wasn't about her father, Connor. It was about his books…" They both looked at me expectantly, waiting for the light to go on over my head.

I saw it then. I was a minor player in Lori Westmann's gambit to revitalize interest in her father's writing. If she could create some controversy, the chances were greater that she could sell the idea of reissuing his works. For Lori Westmann, her father was a literary property, not a person. My research was supposed to contribute toward the PR machine.

"So when it didn't work out with my research, she decided to cut her losses?" I commented. "Pursue other avenues?"

"In today's fast-moving world, the successful manager is nothing if not flexible," Art intoned.

"And I guess it worked out for her, based on what the agent said to you," Micky said.

I shrugged in acceptance. "Man. People are such a disappointment."

"Tremendously predictable and yet always a surprise," Micky told me in a tone that hinted at vast experience.

We sat and drank for a while, talking about nothing in particular. Art cracked his way through the basket of peanuts and was finally reduced to poking through the broken shells for any fugitive nuts that might have been overlooked.

"OK," I finally said, "but there's still something that bugs me…"

"I knew this was coming," my brother said.

I ignored him. "From what I could see from Eliot Westmann's most recent journals, he was fascinated with Native American mysticism. The lure of the desert and all that stuff. He was working with that guy Xochi."

"The guy who called the banditos off you?" Art commented.

"Yeah. The journal is filled with descriptions of ancient settlements and obscure desert trails that crisscross the border down there. I wonder whether he hadn't stumbled onto something…"

"We see lots of stuff from the Homeland Security guys,"

Micky said. "There's a lot of activity going on down there. Knowledge of multiple smuggling routes that are not heavily used would be valuable to any number of people. Maybe that guy Xochi was up to something. Maybe he just bailed you out of a bad situation because he knew you were working for Lori Westmann and didn't want the attention your demise would attract."

"Sometimes things are not what they appear," Art explained. "But sometimes they are. You may have just wandered into something. An accident. Like a tourist inadvertently walking into the wrong part of town."

"Stuff happens," Micky shrugged. "It had an exotic locale…"

"*Treasure of the Sierra Madre*," Art interjected.

"… and so it sticks in your mind. But just be happy you got out in one piece, and now you're back here where you belong."

I knew what they were trying to tell me, but something nagged at me about the whole situation. It was like the feeling you get just before a fight is joined—you're not positive about what will happen, but sense the invisible jangling of energy that telegraphs danger.

"*Si, senor*," Art said in his best Mexican accent. "Better for you here, where you are safe, I *theenk*."

He meant well, but was more wrong than any of us could have known.

10

TARGETS

I live in Brooklyn. Immigrants from Europe spawned here after making the scary trip across the gray expanse of the Atlantic. Later waves of newcomers journeyed across different seas, mixing with the Irish, Scandinavians, Italians, and Jews. Today, there are places in Brooklyn where you can still get canned reindeer meat and markets where shopkeepers speak only in Mandarin.

It's no real surprise that Yamashita ended up here. His *dojo* is in Red Hook, inside an old warehouse. The building is made of worn orange-red brick baked before the turn of the century, and it sits on an ugly street in a neighborhood that was grumpily becoming gentrified. Just finding it is an adventure. In the old days, getting home safe was not a given. In retrospect, I think my *sensei* originally chose the location on purpose—it tended to winnow out the faint of heart.

I live in Brooklyn partly to be near the *dojo*. But there are other reasons as well. The Burkes have deep roots in the borough. Rheumy-eyed women, bent with age, still wander these streets and remember my father when he was a child. The Irish American diaspora didn't end with a flight from the city to the suburbs; some of us have found our way back.

The house I live in on 61st street is part of the transitional zone between Sunset Park and the more upscale section known as Fort Hamilton. Many of the families in my neighborhood go back for three generations and the area still has the feeling of a community. The block is made up of narrow, attached houses, their brick faces seasoned with time and peppered with urban grit. They are all essentially the same and only the front porches offer any variety or clue to the owners' personalities. Some porches have been enclosed, as if to shut out the streets. Others embrace it and sport bizarrely green outdoor carpeting and lawn chairs. A few flower boxes are in evidence here and there, and in season bright geraniums and pansies sprout and seek the yellow light of a Brooklyn summer.

Inside, each building has a classic railroad flat configuration. You enter through an outer and inner door into a small foyer. Three short stairs to your left lead to a landing, then turn right and climb up to the second floor. A hall directly in front of you stretches to the rear—a long, dim tube that ends at the kitchen. In years past, my landlady, Mrs. O'Toole, would invariably be there. You'd walk in and smell the odd perfume of her home: old plaster, the faint hint of steam, the smell of onions and meat cooking. The kitchen was a bright, distant rectangle, the room where she held sway, murmuring to herself like a harmless witch and tending a stove that seemed to be perpetually in use.

A pocket door to your right opens on the living room, with a broad window facing the street. This half of the house parallels the hallway and is divided by heavy mahogany pocket doors into two small bedrooms and the larger dining room at the rear, next to the kitchen.

It's all mine now. Mrs. O'Toole had outlived all her relatives and, when she died, she left me the place because, as the note in the will said, "he's an odd sort of fellow and his family must worry he'll never amount to anything." I was grateful for the gift. Kindness is rare enough, no matter the motive.

Sarah had her own place in Manhattan, but after our time apart we were eager to be together. She stayed the night and we decided to spend the next day just knocking around. At dawn, I slipped out of bed, leaving her nestled in the sheets. I padded quietly to the room at the rear of the second story of the house that I had turned into a makeshift *dojo*. I gazed groggily out the window, across the elevated section of the expressway in the distance, toward Staten Island. The sky was still dark over there, and the lights on the top of the Verrazano Bridge twinkled.

I sank to the floor and stretched, my body slowly warming but my mind still sluggish with the last vestiges of sleep. Eventually, I picked up a *bokken* and went through some basic routines. Later in the session, I'd use the *katana* that waited in lethal repose on the rack on a small table nearby. But I have a basic rule of thumb: never use a live blade when you're still half asleep.

I've come to like the dawn, its quiet and the hushed sense of possibility. Part of that potential is increasingly revealed for me in the act of training. It's become a constant companion in my life. I used to think that following the martial path was a journey that had specific destinations in view: achieving a black belt, gaining admission to a prestigious school like Yamashita's, or perhaps mastering a weapon and its techniques. But I was confusing the road markers for the journey. Now, I have come to realize that an essential element of what I do is not lineal, but cyclical. You strive and endure and train, and, at the end of it, the curtain parts. You see more clearly into new territory and understand what will be asked of you anew: effort, endurance. And more training.

I sensed something behind me in the quiet of the room.

It was Sarah, wrapped in a robe, watching me silently with an expression that seemed somehow sad. I put down my sword and went to her, but she moved away.

"Finish," she said, shaking her head. Then she shuffled away.

Later, after lingering over coffee and the morning newspaper, we went out, heading toward 8th Avenue and the supermarket. Sarah still seemed subdued, but outside the day was coming alive. At any given moment, there's a lot of movement on my street. Buicks rock through the neighborhood, their speakers pulsing like the heartbeat of an animal. Kids shout. The gates in the wrought-iron fences that front each home creak and clang as people emerge for the day. I was happy to be back home—happy to be with Sarah. All those things together are probably why I didn't notice anything out of the ordinary.

"Did you ever wonder what's the point of all that training, Burke?" She asked as we wandered through the store. Sarah looked at me pointedly. I shrugged and put some cans of tomato paste into the cart.

"I dunno. What do you mean?" I said. She didn't answer right away, just wheeled the cart slowly down the aisle. Sarah reached stiffly for a box of lasagna noodles. I followed, wondering what was behind her question. I thought about the look on her face this morning.

She continued, "Well, here you are working so hard at something. All these years… And it's sort of, I don't know…"

"Abstract?" I offered. "Archaic? That's probably half the attraction for me." I smiled at her, but she didn't smile back.

"No." She shook her head emphatically. "Maybe in some places you could say that. But not in Yamashita's *dojo*. It's much too serious." We wandered over to the cheese section. She picked up a packet of mozzarella and looked at it, but I don't think that was what she was seeing.

"Well," I countered. "You know something about this from your own experience—The coordination of mind and body—The Way—All that stuff."

"The Way…" she said reflectively. "The Way to—what?"

It was a good question and a hard one to answer in some ways. You hope that the training gives you a better insight into yourself, that the archaic discipline of the martial art makes you more able to deal with the world in the here and now. But the reality is that martial artists are like everyone else: some are good people; some are idiots. The process is supposed to make you a better person through the alchemy of training, but in many *dojo* there are individuals who have walked the path for years and are still idiots. They're just highly-skilled idiots.

"For me," I finally told her, "it's complicated. I enjoy the physical action and the way I can lose myself in it." I shrugged again. "And there's Yamashita…"

She tossed the cheese in the basket and I pushed it down the aisle. One of the wheels turned sideways and the cart shuddered a bit before I got it lined up just right.

Sarah sighed. "I know. But sometimes, Burke, I see you in the *dojo* and the look in your eyes—I've seen it before. There are times when you are—not there. I was afraid that you wouldn't come back in time to stop yourself from hurting a student."

I almost replied that that was a good thing, but I wisely held my tongue.

"I don't know," she concluded as we paid the cashier. "I wonder whether training like that doesn't bring something bad out in a person."

"Oh, come on, Sarah," I protested.

"Come on, yourself. Think about it. I mean, I respect

Yamashita and his training. It's a big part of your life. It's a good part of your life…"

"There's a 'but' coming," I said warily.

She cocked her head and looked at me. Her gaze was remote and objective. "There's a terrible sadness in him, Burke. I mean, a master of his caliber, out in the US, buried in Red Hook?"

I shrugged. "He's got his reasons, I suppose." Privately I wondered whether someday he'd ever share them with me.

"You're travelling blind, Burke." She reached out to touch me, her eyes glistening with emotion. "He's swallowing you up."

I felt a jet of anger. Was she jealous? A faint voice way in the back of my head wondered whether she was intuiting something that I couldn't see. But I ignored it and shrugged off her touch.

"You used to have your university job—awful as it was—it kept you aware of the rest of the world. Now your whole life is Yamashita. And violence." She swallowed. "I worry about you and I worry about me."

I didn't know what to say. In retrospect, perhaps she was more sensitive to a whole range of forces that flitted around us, waiting to pounce. We wandered back to the house in silence.

The lookout probably picked us up when we went to the store. They certainly had enough time to set up. Once again, I was too focused on internal things and not alert to the growing threat around me.

It's not an excuse mind you, just an explanation.

Sarah, still deeply annoyed, pushed into the house clutching her grocery bags, and moved away from me down the hall toward the kitchen. I fumbled with my own bags at the door, watching her recede from me.

Somehow I must have registered the sounds behind me—the clank of the gate, the scuffle of footsteps—but I reacted too late. They pushed in behind me with the force and efficiency of long practice, sweeping me into the foyer. I spun around to face them.

There were three men, all Hispanic looking. They formed an arc in front of me. Two shooters stood expectantly, pistols hanging at their sides. They were thick and experienced looking, calm presences on either side of a man wearing a black raincoat and knit cap. He was younger, leaner, and appeared unarmed. I could see the dark vinelike curl of a tattoo climbing his neck and thought he also had tattoos on his temples that looked like a devil's horns, but the cap partially obscured the ink.

We could all hear Sarah in the rear of the house. The man in black looked to the shooter on my left. "*La mujer,*" he said softly, and the man began to move past me toward the kitchen.

I started for him and shouted out a warning to Sarah. The man in black came at me, a knife appearing in his hand like a sorcerer's trick. It wasn't some cheap brittle street blade. This was a combat weapon, double-edged with the flat sheen of quality steel.

The ones with knives always come at you first—it's why they choose knives in the first place. They like the action, the intimacy of attack. Above all, they like the smooth purr and wet sensation of cutting.

The guy heading for Sarah eluded me. I had to let him go. In that enclosed space of the hallway, my world had narrowed down to the two other men as they launched their attack. I knew in an elemental way that this wasn't about robbery. It wasn't a typical break in or a mugging. They were here to kill us.

You can scoff, but there's a tangible difference between types of violence. And I've learned to sense it. The air around me was thick with intent, as if violence gave off a mist that you could almost see in the air and taste on your lips. Time seemed to both compress and stretch out.

You can't wait on a knife attack. You can't dodge it—a good knife man will keep flicking at you like a viper until you make a mistake and he slices you open or punches into you with his blade. If Yamashita has beaten one thing into my head it was to move toward the attacking blade, not away from it. So my response was instinctual. I rushed inside the strike and clamped my left hand around his wrist. At the same time I slammed at his chin, upward and to one side, using a palm heel strike. If you can make the head move, you can unbalance people. His head moved all right, but he had strong neck muscles and the effect didn't have the stunning sort of snap I was looking for. I left my hand there and gripped his jaw, yanking us around in a tight arc. I could feel the intimate play of bone and muscle in his jaw as I squeezed his chin like a vise.

But also I had to worry about the other guy. The one with the gun. I didn't think he'd risk a shot—in the tight confines of the foyer, there was as much likelihood that he'd hit his friend as he would me. But he'd probably have a few other tricks up his sleeve.

We crashed up against the wall. The gunman was trying to pistol whip me from behind, but I was moving too much for him to be able to strike the spot behind the ear that he was trying for. He rained down blows on my skull anyway, and I could feel the hot burning sensation as my scalp ripped open. In the kitchen, I could hear thuds and muffled cries as well. I knew I had to move fast. A fight is a race to see who can inflict the most pain in the shortest period of time. The longer you take, the less effective you are, the more exhausted you become, and the greater the likelihood that you'll make a mistake.

There was no margin for error here. I gripped the knife fighter's throat and repeatedly slammed his arm against the corner of the entranceway leading into the living room. I kneed him with fast, vicious moves; groin, thigh—anything I could hit. The man behind me hit me in the kidneys and my knees almost buckled. I gasped, but kept at it. I felt the bones in the knife fighter's arm crackle. Then the blade fell from his hand and he rolled away from me into the living room.

I swung down for the knife and spun to face the gunman. He had a clear shot now. I don't know what the pistol was— some automatic, maybe a 9mm, or a .40. What do I know about guns? They tell me that technically a firearm of that caliber is not considered large, but that's the sort of comment made by people who aren't worried about being shot by one.

The gunman was backing away, looking to put a little bit of distance between us so he could choose his target. He didn't have much space to work with in the hallway, but that wasn't critical: most shootings take place at targets closer than fifteen feet. I knew that in about a split second, that black thing in his hand was going to go boom and it was going to be all over.

I couldn't hesitate, so I just followed the momentum of my spin and lunged at him. I slammed the pistol to one side as it flashed into life, a ringing explosion that bounced sound off the walls around us. I felt the burn of a round as it grazed my side, but I was focused on my target. My body would have carried through with the attack even if the bullet had killed me.

I had the knife up high and drove it with all the force I could muster deep into his eye socket. The blade was a long one. It sliced through the eyeball and buried itself deep in his brain. I could feel the edge of the weapon grind against the bone of the orbit. He gave one involuntary gasp and went down like he was pole-axed. We fell together, locked tight.

He dropped the pistol and it bounced away from us. I pushed up off him, looking for the gun. The shooter's legs were jerking slightly, his heels drumming on the floor, but he was dead. It was a grisly sight, but there's no nice way to kill someone with a knife.

I glanced toward the kitchen and started to move that way, toward Sarah. Then I heard the sound behind me and knew that I was doomed.

The man in the black raincoat had gotten his hands on the gun.

He looked shaky and his knife hand hung uselessly at his side. The gun was in his left fist and it looked awkward there. But at this range neither precision nor elegance would be needed.

His nostrils flared with rage. "*Puta!*" he spat and began squeezing rounds off. One gouged out a splinter in the floor. Another shot by me and buried itself into the dense plaster of the old walls. The third one slammed into my arm, knocking me back onto the staircase. It was like having someone clip your arm with a baseball bat—hard and powerful, even if it was glancing.

It was a freak shot—his aim was off because he was firing left-handed, he was in pain, and he was angry—but it was enough.

The slug had torn its way across the inside bend of my arm and the artery was spurting blood all over the hall.

I could see the gleam of satisfaction grow in his eyes. I was clasping my arm, trying to get some pressure on the wound, to slow the thick pulse of blood that was soaking my side and everything around me. If I didn't get a tourniquet on it soon, I was going to bleed out right there on the stairs. And he knew it, too. It's what animated the cruel smile that broke out on his face.

The man with the tattoos came closer to me, a look of deep satisfaction in his eyes.

"*Y ahora,*" he said. "*No hay mas preguntas.*" *Now there are no more questions.*

There was a ringing in my ears and it was growing hard to hear him. I was feeling dizzy, slightly sick. My vision began to blur. The hall seemed a dimmer place, and I could focus only with difficulty. His cruel face was still there as I began to slip under. I saw him raise the pistol for one, last, finishing shot. His lips opened to say something.

The double impact rocked him and his mouth opened wider to belch forth a deep crimson bubble. The sounds of the gunshots hardly registered on me at all. I was slipping away, vaguely aware of Sarah standing there with a gun in her hand, wide-eyed.

"Burke!" she screamed and came toward me, looking panicky, overwhelmed at sight of the bodies. There was blood everywhere.

"Burke!" she screamed again, but it seemed far away, a distant call that blended with the approaching wail of a siren, the two merging to make something that sounded to me like a small despairing wail.

11
TWINS

I drifted, for a time, in a place between worlds. I have a vague recollection of voices, movement, and distant sensation, but nothing pierced through to wake me.

After a while, I imagined myself in a dark, low-ceilinged room that stretched away from me on either side. I was confused, and kept spinning around, frantic with an unfocused sense of having lost something important. At one distant end of the room, a figure crouched in a pool of warm light. I moved toward it, eager to go and yet hindered by a nagging sense that what I really needed lay somewhere behind me. When I turned to look there, I was confronted only by blackness. And the room seemed to stretch and lengthen even as I fought toward the lighted figure. No matter how I struggled, I had the despairing sense that I would never find what I had lost somewhere in the gloom, nor would I ever reach the light. I squinted into the brightness at the remote figure that sat there, solid, dense, and immovable. Suddenly, his eyes opened. "Burke!" Yamashita called.

"Mr. Burke," another voice said. It was gentle, yet insistent. I felt a hand on my arm and I opened my eyes. The doctor, chart in hand, gave me a quick smile when my eyes opened. "Welcome back," he told me.

I licked my lips and blinked. Took a look around. The hospital room was dimly lit and I was on the only bed in it. I had a big bandage on my left arm. There were wires attached to my right hand and one of those machines that displays your vital signs was playing the Burke's Awake Show through the spiky medium of a heartbeat monitor. I shifted my body to check the muscular connections, felt a slight tug of pain in my side and some soreness on my head. But, since the last thing I remembered was being bathed in blood that was mostly my own, things were looking up.

"Nice to be back," I answered him thickly, and then cleared my throat. The doctor had a pocket protector full of pens and bags under his eyes. He pulled a chair close to me and flashed a small light in my eyes. He grunted.

"I'm Doctor Weiss. You were pretty banged up when they brought you in this morning," he began thoughtfully. He consulted the sheaf of clipped papers in his hand, "But I can see that you've been in this sort of situation before." Weiss looked at me expectantly.

"Yeah," I had to admit.

"Well, you were lucky that your friend got a tourniquet on you as soon as she did. You were down pretty low."

I was slowly gaining focus, recalling the last images I had of Sarah standing over me. "How is she?" I asked Weiss.

"Hmm?" he said, distracted by the notations on my chart. "Oh, she was fine. A little shook up, obviously…" A nurse came in and whispered in his ear. Dr. Weiss nodded. "Give us a minute," he instructed her.

"OK," he concluded as she left. "We got some units of blood into you and repaired the gunshot wound. The bullet nicked the brachial artery, and I'll want you to take it easy and stay with us for a few days. You've got a fractured rib and a surface contusion on your side—you're lucky the bullet there just grazed you—and I put some stitches into your scalp. How do you feel?"

"A little tired, but OK," I said.

"You're able to focus all right?" he queried. I nodded gently. "Good. There are some people outside from the police department who want to get a statement now that you're awake." He made some notes on the chart and hung it back on the foot of the bed. "Nurses will be in frequently to check your pressure…"

"In case I spring a leak?" I teased.

"Precisely," Weiss told me in all seriousness. "We'll see later today whether you can get up and move around. I don't want you bedridden for too long. Pneumonia's a common complication in cases like this…"

"Hey, I want to get out of here as soon as I can," I assured him.

Weiss looked skeptical. He jerked his head toward the door. "I wouldn't be in a rush. They've got a guard on your room, Mr. Burke. The police seem to think someone's trying to kill you."

"Somebody was," I corrected him.

"Well, they almost succeeded," he shot back grumpily. "Get some rest." And he was gone in a swirl of lab coat.

A pair of detectives from the 68th precinct came in to talk. I'd had some contact with the people in the 68th a few times in the last few years, but I didn't recognize these two, which was probably a good thing. Cops live in an untidy world and accommodate themselves to that fact, but they still get upset when you keep kicking buckets over on their turf.

These two had the standard moves down. One asked questions, the other hung back and watched. I'd seen my brother and his partner Art do it often enough. The questions come at you in no discernible order. The logic is subtler than that. They push and prod, listen to the timbre of your voice, watch the movement of your hands, and note the flicker in your eyes.

"So you never saw these guys before?" the lead cop asked after a while. His name was Berger. His face was big, and middle age had wrapped him in a thick, even blanket of fat that made him seem larger and more powerful than he probably was. Berger's eyes were sharp, though. Ice blue and alive.

"No," I told them, shaking my head. "At first I thought it was just a push-in robbery." You hear about them all the time: a thief hangs around and times his approach to catch someone as they open their door. Then he simply pushes the victim inside. It's got a certain simple elegance to it from the criminal's perspective. No need to fiddle with locks.

"At first?" Berger's partner asked. He was leaning quietly against the wall and his body language didn't make it seem like he was particularly interested in my answer.

"Yeah. Two things were wrong about it," I replied. Berger just raised his eyebrows to encourage me to go on. "In the first place, this kind of crime usually targets someone who's easy to overpower. The elderly. Women."

"They got in at your place," Berger reminded me.

"It took three of them," I said. "How inconspicuous did that look? Three Hispanic guys piling through my front door?"

Berger shrugged. "They're crooks," he told me. "Nobody ever said they were geniuses."

His partner smirked. "Lucky for you. The old guy across the street saw them force the door and called it in to 911. Probably the only reason the EMT's got to you before you pumped out."

I said nothing while that thought sunk in. "What else?" Berger finally prompted.

"Huh?" I was still thinking about how close I came this time to not waking up.

"You said there were two things that weren't right about this," he reminded me.

I closed my eyes for a minute. "Yeah. The second thing was that these guys were armed to the teeth. And it wasn't street junk. The knife was a pro's weapon… "

"How do you know that?" Berger asked suspiciously.

I shrugged and the action tugged a bit on the leads to my hand. I saw the lines on the monitor near the bed jump a little.

"You can feel it in the balance, the heft of a weapon," I explained. "Particularly something like a knife." The cops looked significantly at each other.

"You know a lot about things like this," Berger said. It sounded like an indictment.

I got a quick flash of a knife jutting from an eye socket. The ring of gunshots. Blood. "Hey," I told them, "they broke into my house. They weren't there looking for my social security check or to steal the stereo."

"What do you think they were there for then?" Berger pressed.

I paused. I fidgeted a bit and the monitor spiked again. "They were there to get… me." I concluded.

"They came close," Berger's partner observed. He was watching me half the time and eyeing the heart rate monitor the other half.

But Berger was focused on me. He sat down in the chair next to the bed, as if he had finally heard something worth his time.

"And why were they after you, Mr. Burke?" he said quietly. Berger's blue eyes glittered. His partner didn't move a muscle.

I shifted in the bed. "I don't know," I replied, shaking my head wearily. And it was partially true.

"You never saw these men before?" Berger pressed. He sounded incredulous. I signaled no. He sighed and slipped a folded piece of paper out of his jacket. It was a printout of mug shots. He flattened the paper out and laid it gently in my lap. I looked at the two pictures there. The photographs captured the stolid features well enough, but didn't convey the air of menace these men had in person. I recognized them anyway.

"These two gentlemen are Geronimo Martín and Xavier Soledad. They've got a rep on the street that's pretty fierce," Berger told me. "They're shooters. They don't come cheap. And they always work together."

"They call them *Los Gemenos*," his partner chimed in. "The Twins."

"These guys are not street punks," Berger told me. "Various law enforcement entities like them for a lot of different crimes, but they always skate. You got a special job to do in the Hispanic underworld, you call them." Berger looked at me with those cold eyes. "And you're telling me you don't know why these two came calling at your place?"

"No clue," I said. In retrospect, it wasn't the brightest move I've ever made, but I was still trying to put pieces together and wasn't ready to share my suspicions.

I don't think the detectives bought my claims of innocence. They just looked at me for a few minutes, saying nothing. Waiting for me to crack. I shifted in bed, moving my torso and feeling the click and stretch of muscle and bone. A cart rattled by in the hallway. Finally, Berger's partner pushed himself off the wall. "OK. Sure," he concluded wearily. He nodded at Berger and gestured with his head toward the door.

Berger stood up and handed me a card. "You think about it, Mr. Burke. What with all the excitement, I'll bet you're still a little foggy on things…" He tapped his business card. "You know the drill. Anything occurs to you, give me a call." He moved toward the door, and then turned slowly to face me. "Think about this, too. The Twins. They were inseparable. Word on the street was that they were lovers. When they came to your place, it was just a job. But you put a blade in Soledad's brain. And Martín is still at large…" He pushed open the door to the hallway and paused, the movement heavy with significance.

"Rest up, Mr. Burke. Think hard. Whatever brought the Twins into your world is not going to go away. Neither is Martín. It's personal now." Berger looked at me impassively. I looked back. We probably could have gone on like this for some time, but he was a busy guy. He winked at me, and the door swung close behind him.

I leaned back and shut my eyes. I could hear noise from the hospital corridor: the squeak of shoes on the linoleum, an intercom page calling someone, the rattle of metal trays. I sensed the change in air pressure as the door to my room opened again. I expected to see a nurse, yet had a sudden alarming thought: how good would the guard at my door be when a street psycho like Martín came calling?

Art's a big guy, and he pretty much filled the doorway. He smiled at me. "Hey, back in the land of the living, Connor. Pink, pretty, and patched up."

"Me in a nutshell," I agreed, relieved to see a familiar face.

Art gestured behind him with his thumb. "I ran into a coupla guys from the 68th who are not exactly crazy about you, though."

I shrugged. "They'll have to take a number and get in line."

Art sat down at the foot of the bed, resting comfortably and eyeing me with an odd, contented satisfaction. "They seem to think you're holding out on them."

I shrugged. "I'm still trying to sort things out myself."

"I bet. What do you remember?"

I lay back and stared at the ceiling. Faint water stains marred the acoustical tiles in one corner, the marks a reddish brown like old blood. "I remember the three guys coming in. Two with guns. One with a knife."

"Right," Art said. "One guy heads down the hall after Sarah and you tussle with the other two. Correct."

I nodded. "The knife came at me first. It was pretty crowded and we were moving a lot. The shooter didn't have a clean shot. I got the knife away and used it on the shooter…"

"OK," he nodded, recreating the scene in his mind. "But the pistol got away from you somehow and the other guy got it and started in on you?"

"I guess," I replied, squinting. "Things get a little jumbled after that."

"I'll bet," Art commented. "Let me fill in some blanks. One of the shooters— Martín—heads after Sarah. You shout out a warning to her and when Martín comes through the kitchen door, Sarah swings a plastic bag full of cans at him. It's a freak shot, but she catches him just right and down he goes like a sack of potatoes. She hears all the excitement from the front of the house, scoops up the gun, and heads your way." Art looked at me significantly. "Pretty impressive, Connor. There's screaming and banging and gunshots. She's just escaped an attack by an armed intruder. But your girlfriend heads *toward* the fight." He shook his head. "Most people I know would be running the other way."

I nodded in agreement. "Good thing she didn't."

"Oh yeah. 'Cause the third guy is, by this time, pretty pissed and about to empty a pistol into you. Sarah gets him first. The rest is history. She does what she can until the PD and EMT arrive. They slip you into a shock suit and away we go…"

"They ID the third guy?" I asked him.

"Nah," Art said. "Soledad and Martín usually didn't take on extra help. Whoever he is, he's not local. I've got some old friends keeping me up to date. They're running his prints now through the FBI's IAFIS system. We'll see what it turns up."

I nodded. "Speaking of turning up, where's Micky?"

Art frowned. "Your brother is out tearing a new asshole in the Hispanic underworld. Shaking the trees and hoping he can flush Martín."

"And you?"

He sighed. "You know how Mick gets, Connor. There's no stopping him, but it doesn't mean I gotta be a part of it. One loose cannon is enough…"

My brother pushed the door open as if on cue, and stood appraising me, his hands on his hips. He glanced at Art, who stared back, his face flat and expressionless. Then Micky walked toward me. "Well, you look a little better," he said. "What's the prognosis?"

I shrugged. "They make sure that the sutures are holding and I can get out of here." It's not exactly what the doctor had said, but it was what I was planning.

"Good," my brother told me. He looked Art's way. "I don't think the uniform they got on the door is destined for great things."

Art shrugged, but said nothing. It wasn't like them. My

brother and his partner had elevated banter into a minor art form. The silence between them now was not only unusual, it was heavy, and the atmosphere was like that of a bickering married couple being civil only out of consideration for guests.

"What is with you two?" I finally asked.

Micky waved a hand at his partner. "Nothin'. He's just being a pain."

"A pain?" Art said, standing up and moving right into Micky's face. I'll tell you what's a pain." He jabbed a finger into Micky's chest. "You, you moron."

"Don't gimme that…" Micky began in a snarl, but Art kept right on going.

"You're jumpin' all over an official investigation. You're steppin' on toes left and right and got nothing to show for it. And you want a pain? Wait until ACLU lodges a complaint."

My brother shrugged. "At least we won't have to worry about Internal Affairs."

"Internal Affairs," Art fumed, shaking his head. "You don't get it. We're not on the force anymore, Mick. You start pissing people off, they'll pull our contract."

"Hey," Micky spat back, his eyes narrowed, "Fuck the ACLU. And fuck the contract. Look at him!" He pointed in my direction. "Those three psychos almost got him. One's still on the loose."

"I know," Art shouted. "But we gotta work this smart."

A nurse peeked in the door, her face concerned. Both men stood facing each other like animals, their eyes locked. They never broke contact but simultaneously reached into their pockets. I had seen them flash their shields in situations like this before and the sudden realization washed across both their faces at the same time: they had no shields. It was almost comic, except for the look, bug-eyed and angry, on their faces. The nurse pulled her head back into her shoulders and wisely retreated.

"Fellas," I began.

Their heads swiveled toward me, their eyes bright and hard.

"Shut…" Micky began.

"Up," Art concluded. Then they faced each other again. Art took a breath as if winding up for more argument.

"You poke me one more time with that finger of yours and I'm gonna bite it off," Micky told him.

"Good," his partner replied. "Maybe you'll choke on it. Slow you down a bit." I couldn't be sure, but I thought I detected a slight smile on Micky's face. Art sensed something as well, and he pressed his case home. "We're on the outside now, Mick. We gotta work through channels on this. There's too much riding to let ourselves get screwed up 'cause we're pushin' too hard in the wrong places…" Micky stepped back and slouched against the wall, looking from me to Art and back again. He sighed.

"You worry too much about the business," Micky told his partner.

"One of us has to," Art countered.

"Wuss," Micky said.

"Moron," Art fired back.

It was the kind verbal ping-pong that could go on all day. So I spoke up, as much to stop the bickering as to get some information.

"Now that you're ready to kiss and make up, can either of you tell me whether Berger's right about Martín coming back for me?"

Micky squinted up at the ceiling as he thought. "Seems pretty likely to me. I mean, the guy's a psycho, so he gets off on killing people anyway…"

"And you nailed his partner," Art told me.

"Nice, Art," Micky commented. "No pun intended?"

Art ignored him. "You throw the fact in that Soledad was more than just his partner in crime, and I'd say that it's a pretty good guess that Martín will be coming back for a piece of you."

"How crazy is he?" I asked them.

"Dangerous crazy," my brother told me. "But not insane. He's coming to get you for sure. You killed his boyfriend, so it's personal. But he's also got a street rep to maintain. You take out one half of the *Los Gemenos,* there's gotta be some payback."

"Be bad for business otherwise," Art offered.

Of course. "So what's the plan?" I asked them.

"I get your brother hosed down," Art started.

Micky snickered. "You wish," he said, and continued Art's train of thought. "Then we hope the PD can identify the John Doe and try to figure out who's after you and why."

"And Martín?" I asked.

Art waved a hand. "Oh, he'll show up."

"They always do," Micky concluded and they both nodded sagely.

12
SHADOW

The air in any modern hospital is dry and clean feeling, scrubbed into an antiseptic wash that is meant to offer comfort. I wasn't buying it. The Burkes of older generations knew that hospitals were places where danger lurked. Their pale blue eyes were muddled with experience, superstition, and wear, but were keen to sense a threat. The hospital rooms and halls around me were permeated with an atmosphere that was dense with things unseen, yet real: fear, confusion, loneliness, the pain that pushes up through anesthetic like the limbs of a restless sleeper.

Our hug was awkward—at first I thought that it was because of my wound. But Sarah's kiss was dry and perfunctory, like a ritual leached of meaning and best finished quickly.

"Hey," I said as she sat beside me on the bed. "How are you?" I looked at her carefully. Sarah's eyes are big and dark, set in a heart-shaped face that was meant to smile. But she looked worn and tired. Her eyes glistened and she looked away as if seeking a distraction from what lay before her.

"Oh, Burke," she murmured, and reaching for a tissue on the table next to the bed, she got up to blow her nose.

I held my hand out, beckoning her closer. "Hey," I said quietly, "It's OK. We're all right." But she stood there, arms crossed in front of her as if in protection. She was folded in on herself, seeing something I didn't. My words weren't reaching her.

Sarah shook her head as if trying clear it. She looked up at me and smiled sadly. "Are we? Are we all right, Burke?" she demanded. Sarah closed her eyes for minute. "I keep seeing you on the floor this morning. The blood. The bodies..." she took a ragged gasp.

"Come here," I urged her, and she slowly sat next to me on the bed and let me hold her. But I could feel the tension trembling in her shoulders. We sat there quietly for a time and I searched in vain for words of comfort. But I couldn't come up with any. I hoped that somehow the very act of contact would offer solace, but I couldn't be sure.

Sarah was part of the collateral damage of all violent acts: the survivors bear wounds as surely as the ones who don't walk away. I've struggled with it and knew something of what she was experiencing. But each person deals with things like this differently. I'm harder. Not tougher, just harder. I don't know whether Yamashita has made me that way or whether his training just revealed something about me I never knew before. Sarah was a brighter, gentler person. For her to not only be attacked, but ultimately to have to kill someone, was going to press on her like a crushing weight. It wasn't that she ultimately wouldn't be able to stand the pressure, it was that the shadow of that weight would forever change the way she saw the world.

The world, I realized, had been a brighter place before she met me.

After a while, she seemed to relax somewhat. "Have you had any sleep?" I murmured. The light outside was fading and the morning's events seemed impossibly long ago. I could imagine her day after the shooting. The EMT's and the cops. Making a statement to the uniforms who responded. Answering the same few questions put a hundred different ways by the detectives. After a while, you just want to shut down, to close your eyes and drift away.

I felt Sarah's head shake. "No." She sighed. "There hasn't been time. I was at the precinct most of the day. Then they took me back home so I could… change." She shuddered and pushed against me to sit up. "They want me to go away for a few days. Out of town. For right now, they've got people watching my apartment." A note of urgency crept into her voice. "Burke," she said urgently, "what's going on?"

I let out a long sigh. "They think that the guy who escaped may come back," I began.

Sarah's eyes widened in alarm. "Come back?" she echoed. "Why?"

I shrugged, and I could feel the tug of the bandage on my side. "The police say that two of these guys were lovers. I killed one and the other one escaped. I don't know why they were after me in the first place, but now the cops think it's personal…"

"Oh my God." She sank back on the bed, unconsciously putting distance between us. "Who were they, Burke? What did they want?"

I had been turning possible answers over in my head since Berger left. I'd come up with very little I could say with certainty. And I wasn't about to scare Sarah any more than she was already. "I'm not sure," I told her, which was true. "I never saw any of these guys before. Maybe after they ID the third man, we'll get a clue." Sarah looked at me with a deep, sad skepticism. It was the same look I'd gotten from the detectives from the 68th as well as from Micky and Art. Nobody was buying my statements completely.

"Look," I said, wanting to change the subject, "for right now, what's important is that you get somewhere safe and get some rest. Stay away from my house. Can your sister put you up for a few days?"

She nodded tiredly. "The police helped me make arrangements."

"OK. I'm getting out of here as soon as I can. Micky and Art are working on things. We'll get to the bottom of this soon." She nodded hopefully and let me draw her close for a hug. A female detective had been waiting tactfully outside the hospital room. She stuck her head inside the door and I caught her eye and nodded. She led Sarah away.

"Sarah," I called, and they paused at the door. "Don't worry. It will be all right."

But all three of us knew that I was lying.

Dr. Weiss was reluctant to discharge me, despite the fact that the sutures were holding and I hadn't sprung a leak all night. But Micky and Art worked on him—no doctor likes the idea of a killer rampaging around his hospital—and, after I signed a bunch of release forms and promised to return in a few days, Weiss let me go. The bags under his eyes seemed to have deepened, and he watched me leave with both concern and relief.

Yamashita had no qualms. "Hospitals are for the sick, Burke," he told me. He was sitting placidly by my side in the back of Micky's car.

"What do you call this?" I asked, gesturing with the arm that Weiss had put in a sling.

"You are wounded," my *sensei* told me sternly. "You have been seen to. Time to stop taking up valuable space and come home where you can heal properly."

Art turned halfway around to face us. It was better than watching Micky drive. My brother is hard on cars and anyone around the one that he's operating. "You're better out of there for lots of reasons, Connor," Art said.

"Places like that leak like sieves," Micky commented as he gave the wheel a sudden jerk and we lurched across a lane of traffic, followed by the angry blaring of horns. "Probably a million ways Martín could get to you in there."

"You really think he's coming?" I asked him.

"Word on the street says so," my brother answered.

"We've got a twenty-four hour guard on your place and Sarah's," Art added. "We'll stash you with Yamashita while we run Martín to ground." I started to say something, but Yamashita jabbed me lightly in the side with one steel finger, his face immobile. I closed my mouth for the rest of the ride to Red Hook.

We watched Micky and Art drive off. Then Yamashita shut the metal door to his *dojo* firmly and we moved toward the weapons rack along one wall of the *dojo*. We had left our shoes at the door and our bare feet rasped dryly on the hardwood floor. The street sounds were muted, distant echoes from another place. Here, in the cavernous training space, we were in Yamashita's world.

He handed me a short wooden training sword known as a *shoto*. "We will assume that your arm will need some time to heal, Burke. But that is no reason to stop training. The *shoto* is a much-neglected weapon. We can use this opportunity to focus more intently on its use."

I hefted the small sword, the hard wood smooth and solid feeling. It wasn't a totally unfamiliar weapon: there are a number of training routines in the sword arts that use it. But in Yamashita's system, we tended to focus on weapons with a bit longer reach that require a two-handed grip to use properly. The *shoto* could be used to deflect and parry and stab. It was a close-quarters weapon. There seemed to be a lot of them in my life lately.

He worked me for a time and, as always, the experience was an odd blend of wonderment and terror. I was stiff from the wounds and inactivity. The bandage made me overly conscious about the need to protect my arm. Yamashita knew it and pressed me without mercy, feinting at the wound, forcing me to pivot and twist to avoid him. The handle of the short sword was slick with sweat. The perspiration made my scalp wound burn.

He came at me with the *bokken*—a long slashing strike to my head. I moved in and met his blade with mine, redirecting the cut down to my left and away from me. But Yamashita followed the flow and brought his sword back and around and at me again. I had to shift to my left and meet the blow again. Our weapons cracked together. I continued to pivot and forced his sword down to my right, keeping contact with the back of his weapon. I slid my *shoto* down and then back up to the hand guard of Yamashita's sword, snapping my weapon up against the hilt and moving in to lock his elbow with my left hand. It was a reflex action, and my arm moved out of the sling before I could stop myself. And to my surprise, it worked. It was awkward moving it, but it worked. I felt the slight tug of the sutures, but that was it.

Yamashita saw the surprise in my eyes and he smiled slightly. "Soo," he breathed. "Now we are getting somewhere." He backed away and bowed slightly. I did the same, wiping the sweat off my face with the back of my arm. Up in the loft section of the building where Yamashita had his living quarters, I heard the phone ring.

"I'll get it," I told him. But he was already on the move.

"No. I am expecting someone…" he murmured as he shot up the stairs. From my perspective, it hardly looked like he touched the steps: one minute he was moving toward the staircase, the next minute he was up and gone out of sight.

I couldn't hear his phone conversation. But in five minutes we were back on the street. Yamashita doesn't explain much—he leads and it's simply up to you whether you trust him enough to follow. And every time he does it, you know he's watching you, weighing your reactions, judging the quality of your fidelity. Beginning students find it unnerving and exasperating. I know I did. But more than a decade with him has changed me in some ways. The stubborn Irish in me still resents the call to obedience. But I've learned to narrow my eyes and follow, in part because, while I know he's watching me, I've developed the ability to watch him.

We walked quickly down the street toward the avenue. The men at the auto body shop eyed us warily. We once had a run-in with one of their more excitable employees. To this day, he finds it difficult to walk. Yamashita noticed the stares we got, but didn't react to them. We reached the corner and he paused. "You wish to know where we are going?" he said.

Aha! I knew I could wait him out. I shrugged. "That'd be nice," I told him, but I kept my voice noncommittal.

He turned his head and looked at me. "I have been thinking about this man, the one who escaped…"

"Martín," I supplied.

Yamashita nodded. "Just so. From speaking with your brother and his partner, my understanding is that both he and his partner were contract workers."

"Hit men," I corrected.

Yamashita waived a hand, dismissing this as a pointless

semantic detail. "The presence of the third man, who is as yet unidentified, suggests to me that their employer was not local." I started to say something, but he held up a hand. "And yet their... services... are ones that would be certain to call the attention of the police. And once that was done, the authorities would question... who?" His eyes glittered as he waited for my reply.

I shrugged. "The usual suspects, I suppose."

My teacher nodded. "Indeed. The usual suspects. And since these men are Hispanic, I assume that a great deal of attention would be focused on criminals from the Hispanic community."

"Sure," I said.

"I imagine it must be quite annoying, particularly if you had nothing to do with this attack, *neh*?" He didn't wait for my response. "The police questioning people. Disturbing your activities." Yamashita sounded almost wistful. "So if, for instance, the local crime boss could be made to understand that we only seek to locate this Martín and leave his... enterprises... alone, we might be able to secure his help."

"It's a theory," I admitted.

As we were talking, a big white Escalade pulled up to the curb. The passenger side door opened and a young guy, wearing wraparound shades, got out, opened the back door, and waited. He never once looked directly at us, instead his visor continuously scanned the perimeter.

"It is more than a theory, Burke," Yamashita told me. "Here is our ride." My teacher sounded pleased.

We ended up in a sun-drenched room in an upscale seafood place in Fort Hamilton. Our drivers—two men with extremely neat haircuts and thick necks—led us to the second story of the restaurant without saying a word. The room was almost empty of customers. It was too late for lunch, too early for dinner. A few members of the wait staff were arranging linen and setting silverware, but aside from the muted tinkle of knives and forks and their quiet conversation, the big room was quiet. Our escorts led us past a thickset man at the head of the stairs. He was older than they were, but appeared to frequent the same barber. He nodded and we passed on to the corner table where the room's only occupant sat.

He moved a long-stemmed wine glass back and forth in his hand, watching the play of refracted light on the tablecloth. He looked up when we reached the table, as if surprised to find us standing there.

"Ah," he said, getting to his feet. "Señor Yamashita, what a pleasure to meet *uno maestro del espada*." He regarded me with a tilt of the head. "And you must be Dr. Burke." He gestured at my arm in the sling. "I trust you are healing well?"

"Fine," I told him. Our host was a compact man with salt and pepper hair. His skin was deeply tanned with clusters of lines at the outer corners of brown and weary eyes. His suit was gray and it fit him well. Sixty, I thought, maybe sixty-five. In pretty good shape. His hands were manicured.

"Thank you for seeing us, Señor Osorio," Yamashita said.

Osorio closed his eyes as if dismissing the thought. "Please," he said, "it is my pleasure to finally meet you. But where are my manners? Please, be seated gentlemen. Some wine?" He made a small gesture and a waiter appeared with a bottle in a terra-cotta cooler. We sat down. The waiter poured carefully, Osorio sipped thoughtfully at the wine, and nodded. The waiter replaced the bottle in the cooler and retreated to the far end of the room.

Osorio regarded the wine in his class. "Crisp. Cool. I find

it just the thing on a pleasant, sunny afternoon." Yamashita picked his glass up and took a minute sip. He nodded in agreement with our host.

Osorio looked at my glass, untouched on the linen surface of the table. "Is the wine not to your liking, Dr. Burke?"

I didn't like the feeling I was getting from Osorio, his drivers, or the spooky atmosphere of the restaurant. I was worried that, in my current condition, the alcohol would affect me too much. I wanted to be ready for any surprises. But all I said was, "I'm trying to take it easy." I moved my arm in the sling.

"Ah. Indeed." Osorio looked at Yamashita. "It was an unfortunate event. I have assured the authorities that this was something done without my knowledge or my participation."

My teacher bowed slightly. "I appreciate that assurance. I imagine that the constant attention of the police must be... ." he frowned as if searching for a word.

"An inconvenience," Osorio suggested. "It is an unfortunate feature of the various enterprises I engage in that a police presence can depress commerce."

Yamashita nodded, as if in sympathy. "It would be better for us all if this matter were put to rest."

"Oh, I assume it will be concluded in time," Osorio said philosophically. "One way or the other, the police will lose interest..."

"We have a desire to put this matter to rest soon," Yamashita countered.

Osorio nodded in apparent sympathy. "I imagine the threat of Martín must weigh heavily on all concerned. But, as I have told the police, this attack was not of my doing. What can I do now?"

I spoke up. "The cops think Martín's still around. That he's going to try again. In the meantime, he's laying low. I'll bet that some of the people who are helping him are also people who have dealings with you."

My tone betrayed my annoyance and I saw the warning flicker in my teacher's eyes. He leaned forward. "It would be most helpful if you were to suggest to your associates that you would appreciate the withdrawal of any assistance to Martín," Yamashita interjected.

Osorio spread his hands out. "But what good would that do?" he asked.

"It would make it harder for Martín to hide," I told him. "It would force his hand and smoke him out."

"And then?" Osorio inquired.

"Then we will kill him," Yamashita answered primly. It wasn't boastful or said with the heat of anger, just a flat statement of lethal calculus.

Osorio nodded sagely. "*Claro.* It might be best for all concerned." His words sounded every bit like a man of the world regretting its ways. He sat back then and regarded us with half-closed eyes. It wasn't just the light pouring in from the windows that made him do it. It was a mannerism that showed you something of the real nature of the man. Beneath the custom suit and the polished fingertips was a hard and ruthless core.

Osorio sat quietly. Then he began. "I work in a world of favors dispensed or withheld, gentlemen. And all favors come with a price. If I do as you suggest, what benefit do I receive?"

"The cops would lay off you," I told him.

He shook his head. "They will be distracted soon by another crime. In seventy-two hours, the protection they have arranged for you will be revoked. It is simply the logic of budgets and overtime and the tax rate. However distressing this may be for you personally, Dr. Burke, it means that the momentary disruption of some of my enterprises will end relatively quickly as well. I can afford to wait."

Yamashita stirred. "In my country, too, we understand the nature of relationships, the importance of favors, of balance," he began. The concept of *on*, of an obligation between people of different statuses, was important in Japan. "And I would never consider requesting a favor from you unless I were sure that I could provide something of value in return."

Don't, I thought. *Don't do it. You put yourself in this guy's debt and he'll use you.* After all, I had seen *The Godfather*.

Yamashita looked at me as if he were reading my mind. His eyes betrayed little but I knew that look. You glimpsed it in the split second before he drove an attack home. Osorio watched placidly, thinking he had us in a bind. He couldn't read Yamashita like I could. I felt my stomach muscles unclench a bit.

Osorio gestured with an open palm, as if inviting a suggestion from my teacher.

"Some time ago," Yamashita began, "I was visited by a young man seeking instruction. At the time, I was unable to admit him to my *dojo*."

It happened all the time. In any given week, Yamashita is confronted by the impetuous, the ambitious, and the just plain deluded. His method of screening is complex and opaque. Sometimes he has me put the visitors through the most grueling workout I can. He likes it if I can make them vomit. That's when the real testing begins. At other times, people come with letters of high praise from teachers that Yamashita knows. He gazes at the applicants with silent intensity, searching their faces. I do, too, but whatever he sees eludes me. Sometimes he nods yes and admits them. Other times he says no and strides away. I get to walk the rejected to the door.

As Yamashita spoke of this particular applicant, I saw Osorio's mouth tighten. But he kept quiet and let my teacher continue.

"He was your nephew, was he not?" Yamashita asked. "I was surprised that you did not seek to… influence … my decision.

Osorio smiled, seemingly regaining his composure. "Ricardo, my sister's child. He is quite gifted, I understand, but young. Since his father died, I have tried to assist him with his life… . the advice only an older man can provide." He looked at me as he continued. "Ricardo does not approve of my activities, Dr. Burke. He seeks to make his own way in life. I admire him for it, but even the most determined young men sometimes need guidance. My sister, on the other hand, has a tendency to spoil her only child." He shrugged. "It is the way with women. We gentlemen, we know that sometimes allowing a young man to experience disappointment is a way to strengthen his will."

I wasn't convinced. I wasn't sure that a crime boss worried a great deal about character development. "And?" I pressed him.

Osorio sipped more of his wine and pressed a linen napkin to his lips. He smiled at me. "Ricardo has always been interested in the martial arts, Dr. Burke. He is, I hear, quite accomplished. But forgive me… this is something to be put aside as one grows older. I had hoped that your teacher's rejection would help him focus more on other pursuits."

"Did it?"

Osorio smiled ruefully. "I must admit, it has not. And my sister makes my life—uncomfortable."

Yamashita nodded. "Don Osorio, I understand the position of trying to keep harmony in one's family. I am also trying to bring harmony to mine." My teacher smiled tightly. "I remember that your nephew had some skill, and there is currently room for a new student. Unfortunately, with the threat of Martín hanging over my dojo, it would be unconscionable of me to take on a new student at this time.

Osorio looked skeptical, but finally said, "Yes, harmony is a blessing in all aspects of our lives. You have been kind enough to point out the disruption that Martin brings to my greater family. Perhaps it would be wise to have them withdraw from his presence."

The room was quiet, with faint sounds of rushing water coming from the kitchen. We sat silently in the sunny corner in the deserted room. Our host drained the last of his wine and gently set the empty glass down on the table. It made a muted thump on the tablecloth. Yamashita stood and bowed slightly; Osorio nodded his head in return.

My teacher and I made our way across the empty room, past the guard and down the stairs. Not a word was spoken. I watched Yamashita from the corner of my eye.

What are you up to?

13
TSUKI

"I have a message from your brother," Art told me. The *dojo* was closed that morning, but he had banged on the metal door like it was a drum. The sound let you know the person on the other side wasn't going away.

I cracked open the door, half expecting Martín to put a slug in my head. Art stood there instead, big and sandy-haired and quietly serious. Usually you could count on him to lighten the mood. He was the calm counterpart to Micky. If my brother gave you the eerie feeling of a human rocket poised for a random launch, Art was the guy placidly monitoring the buttons on the control panel. You always got the feeling that he was going to get things under control. But, as I looked at him in the doorway, I saw trouble.

"What gives?" I asked, moving aside to let him in. I took a quick, furtive glance up and down the street before closing the door. "Where's Micky?"

Art let out a sigh. "Your brother, my partner of lo these many years, is feverishly attempting to douse the many fires he has recently set."

I grunted. The acrimony between Micky and Art and their past NYPD supervisors was legendary. Their move to lives as independent consultants had been a godsend.

"What," I said, "someone new has learned to hate him?"

Art waved the thought away. "We should be so lucky. Last count, your brother had complaints lodged against him by the

ACLU, ASPIRA, the Brooklyn Borough President, and the Brooklyn Borough Commander. But the day is young."

My eyebrows shot up in silent inquiry. I waited.

"There are rumblings from the counter-terrorism unit that our contract may be cancelled. I think Mick's pissed off too many people this time."

"Oh boy."

"Yeah," he nodded. "I told him," Art said, clearly repeating a familiar litany. "Things have changed. You go shaking the trees, you gotta use a little restraint."

"Restraint—not Micky's strong suit," I commented.

Art shook his head wearily. "He was like a wild man, Connor. You were still out of it when we came to the hospital the first time. So we drove over to the crime scene. I could see the fuse start to burn. He wasn't gonna let up 'til he found the guys behind this."

I got a sinking feeling in my gut, a spasm of guilt. "I'm sorry, Art."

He looked at me and his eyes seemed hard. "We all got things to be sorry about, Connor. I'm not sure that having a brother who cares is what you should be apologizing for."

The tone in his voice made me jerk my head back a little. "What do you mean?" I got another guilty twinge.

Art didn't answer me. He looked around the *dojo*. It was silent, deserted. Yamashita was nowhere to be seen. It was a cavernous, dim space of diffuse light and hard surfaces. There was nowhere to hide.

"I've got a question from your brother," Art repeated, as if parts of our conversation hadn't taken place. "He wants to know what the hell you're up to."

I gave him what I think of as my flat face. I've developed it in imitation of the truly scary Japanese *sensei* I've crossed swords with over the years. Narrowed eyes. Skin frozen in immobility. It's an expression erected with great care to prevent others from seeing what you're thinking—part mask, part shield.

Art had been a cop too long not to see through it. It wasn't that he could tell what I was actually up to, but he knew something was going on. So finally I shrugged and let out a slow, hissing breath.

"I'm trying to put the pieces together," I admitted. "I never saw those guys before in my life." Art cocked his head as if weighing that last statement. "No, really," I assured him.

He wandered across the *dojo* floor to the weapons rack. Wooden swords and staffs of various lengths rested there. Art touched the shaft of one lightly.

"You get brained by one of these things, I'll bet it hurts," he mused. I nodded in agreement. "You think it makes much difference which one gets used?" he asked me.

It might have been a rhetorical question, but I shrugged and answered him anyway. "Choice of weapon conditions the attack, but the results are gonna be about the same."

Art grunted, and then turned to look directly at me. "So what do I care about the weapon? The real question is who wants to use it."

I saw where he was going. "So the identity of the attackers is beside the point?" I queried.

He held out a hand, palm down, and wiggled it. "Sort of yes. Sort of no. The three guys who came after you are important, but mostly because we can jump up the chain of association and maybe find out who hired them and who's behind this. And, of course, you've got a real issue if that freak Martín decides to come back at you…"

"Yeah," I admitted.

It was Art's turn to sigh. "You keep thrashing around, Connor, and all you do is get yourself in deeper and deeper."

Art waited for me to say something, but I didn't respond.

"What were you doing with Osorio?" he asked in exasperation.

"We went to see if he'd do us a favor," I said evasively, trying not to ask how he found out.

"The best favor he could do would be to drop dead," Art said. "The guy's a cancer."

"He's also a businessman of sorts," I said. "We all agreed that it would be best if the trouble with Martín could be wrapped up quickly."

Art cocked his head. "You making deals with a guy like Osorio? You're in way over your head, Connor. Lots of ways this could end to Osorio's satisfaction. Martín gets you, he goes away, and Osorio's happy. You get Martín, trouble also goes away, and Osorio's happy. "

"That's my preferred plan," I suggested.

Art snorted in a way that reminded me of my brother. These two men spent so much time together they were starting to share mannerisms. "Huh. There's a third possibility I'll bet you hadn't considered."

"Like what?"

Art smiled bitterly. "Here's Osorio merrily running his little crime empire. Someone not local sends some hired muscle who botch a hit and create trouble for him. So Osorio just wants things to quiet down, right?"

I nodded.

"So he's got a few options," Art explained. He held up a thick finger. "One, he can just hunker down and hope everything blows over. But it's not in his nature—he's a take-charge kind of guy. And whatever is drawing all this trouble is gotta be a concern to him." He paused. "That's you."

Up came a second finger. "He could try to eliminate Martín as the disruptive element. But he knows that it's going to be tricky and expensive. And besides, it's going to piss off whoever hired Martín in the first place. What you haven't considered is, Martín isn't the issue here. It's you."

The third finger came up. "Osorio could decide that the most efficient thing to do is to make Martín go away, end the disruption, and not annoy whoever hired the hit squad in the first place."

Art looked at me and saw the realization make its way to my eyes. So much for my vaunted flat face.

"You're right about Osorio being a businessman, Connor," Art concluded. "He didn't get where he is by not figuring all the angles. So the third option is probably going to be the one he'll take. He's gonna take the one action that will address all his concerns." Art was still holding up three fingers. He jabbed my chest with them. "He's gonna take you out, Connor. It's the best solution to his problem."

I said nothing. Art's idea hadn't really occurred to me before, but it didn't change much as far as I could tell. I knew I was in way over my head. I had been from the moment Martín and his two companions burst through my front door. But I also knew that there were rules Art had to follow that I didn't. If Micky were in trouble, it was because he had let his concern for me push him into actions that crossed a legal line. I wasn't going to drag these two men any deeper into this. There had to be a solution, but it was going to be one that I generated, not Micky and Art. At the end of the day, I could make deals and do things that they couldn't. I think Art knew that, but he didn't want to have to admit it out loud. If he acknowledged even to himself the sort of thing I was planning, he was going to have to have someone arrest me. And that would be hard to explain to my mom at the next family picnic.

We stood looking at each other in silence for a time. A slight noise from the loft made Art look up to see Yamashita watching us silently. My brother's partner gave my teacher one quick glance, then he focused on me again.

"The PD has a line on the third guy. Gangbanger from the West Coast. Explains the tattoos."

"I don't see how it connects with me," I commented.

"His record is pretty spotty, mostly run-ins with Immigration. He's an illegal and been back and forth across the border any number of times. Word is that he'd left California for new opportunities. Been working out of Phoenix." He put on a mock-thoughtful expression. "We know anyone been in Arizona lately, Connor?"

I just looked at him.

"You get yourself down to Berger's office at the 68th and tell them about your trip." He said tightly. "You obviously have pissed someone off somewhere. Don't try to figure this out yourself, Connor. Let the pros do it."

I let the advice marinate for moment. "Think about this, too," Art said. "Maybe if we can provide some assistance to the authorities, they might look a bit more favorably on us. Be the least that you could do, Connor."

I was in a bind. Art was right: maybe if I came forward with what I suspected, some good feelings might be generated and Micky would get out of the doghouse. But this wasn't something that was going to be solved with words. I felt the deep, intuitive tug that the Japanese call *haragei*. Blood was going to be spilled. If I could, I was going to shield Art and Micky from the repercussions.

So I just nodded in a non-committal way and walked Art to the door. But he wasn't finished.

"I been watching the Burke brothers at work for years, Connor," Art told me. "And I see a lot of similarities: the stubbornness…" Art stopped there, but you got the sense that his mental catalogue of similarities was more extensive than he was letting on. "But you know who you really remind me of?" he finally asked.

I shook my head no.

Art jerked with his chin toward the loft, where Yamashita stood, still as stone.

"Him."

14
WOLVES

The briefings were always scheduled for 1:00 AM, to leave Jackson and his men some final time to digest the information, formulate some plans, and check their gear. Of late, their Border Patrol supervisor looked more grim than usual. The small desk lamp that lit his notes threw shadows on his face and showed it drawn and remote, a specter practicing augury in a darkened temple.

"We've had reports of ambushes here, here, and here," he continued. There was a map projected on the far wall and the cherry light of a laser pointer touched in sequence at the ambush sites. "Units have also been sniped at with increasing frequency. It's been endemic down along the Texas border, now it's working its way along the line to us."

"Nuisance fire?" Jackson said.

"No. Precision sniping. Nobody's been killed yet, but whoever's doing the shooting is using it to slow pursuit. In some cases, they're taking out vehicles with their fire."

"Big rounds," someone commented.

"Fifties," the supervisor said, consulting his notes. Jackson and his men knew that a fifty-caliber sniper rifle was the mark of a professional. They had heard the intel about rogue elements from the Mexican special forces getting into the drug trade. They were pros. It changed the equation out in the field dramatically.

"That group we tracked that was ambushed," Jackson said, "the scene... it didn't strike me as the work of professionals."

"How so?"

Jackson remembered the sprawled bodies, the knife marks. He shrugged. "It seemed like too much... gratuitous. Know what I mean?"

"Someone sending a message?" one of his team suggested.

The supervisor looked up; the movement flashed light on his glasses, momentarily turning his eyes into flat, bright disks. "It's a mess. We've got local gangs in the mix as well. As both the Mexican and U.S. governments begin to squeeze, the various groups involved in the trade are increasingly at odds. What you saw with that group was probably the simple hijacking of a delivery."

"They killed everyone," Jackson noted.

"In some ways, not a bad thing," the Border Patrol supervisor commented. "... Let God sort them out." The room was silent. The view from a desk was different from the field. Jackson and his men knew that most of the "mules" used to transport drugs across the border were simply poor and desperate men. *Nobody deserves to die like that,* Jackson thought.

The supervisor cleared his throat self-consciously. "Well... headquarters is concerned that this is all spiraling up out of control. There's concern that the violence is going to spill over into the local communities more than it already has."

Jackson grunted. On the Tohono Reservation, that had already happened. Some tribal members had been co-opted by the allure of quick money. Many families had relatives on either side of the border, and some young men served as guides. Others had been forced into cooperation. It was not unusual for people living on the desolate reservation to have their buildings used as stash points for drug smugglers.

"Most of all, gentlemen," the supervisor continued, "we've

got some real and growing concerns for your safety. We've got some very strong intel that a rogue Mexican group is in the area, highly armed and making a play for domination of the local smuggling routes. We need to take them out."

The team sat, stunned. Eventually, Jackson stood up. "With all due respect, sir, we're happy to help. But we're trackers. It's not a combat unit. Some of my people have never even been in the military."

"Relax, Jackson. I've made it pretty clear to higher-ups just what our capabilities are and what we can and cannot be expected to do."

"What does that mean?"

"It means that we're getting help."

Jackson's head rocked back in surprise. *Help? What kind of help?* The supervisor picked up his desk phone and spoke a few words into the receiver. The door to the briefing room opened and a group of men filed in, dressed for the desert, and wearing combat harnesses.

"Who are they?" Jackson asked.

"Sierra Tango," the supervisor said. "A special tactical response unit of HSA."

Jackson looked at the men; the way they held themselves, the lean cut of their faces. They stared at Jackson and his team impassively. *These are hunters,* he realized. *A wolf pack.*

"They're not native," someone objected. "They can't go onto the Tohono lands."

"The regulation has been waived by executive order," the supervisor informed them. He motioned the new men to their seats. Jackson's people were silent.

"Let's get on with today's mission, people…" His briefing droned on. Jackson registered the salient details, but most of his attention was occupied with the implications of this new development and how it would shape their life in the field. Once again, he felt a sense of foreboding wash across him. Something dangerous in the wind.

"... tracker team drop will follow normal protocol," the supervisor concluded. "Sierra Tango team will follow at a distance by special insertion."

And then Jackson knew. He and his team were no longer being used to track prey. They had become the bait.

15
LOST BOYS

Yamashita sat, immobile. His skull was a weathered lump of ivory, his eyes slits, and his respiration was down so low that its tidal flow was impossible to detect. His thick hands were at rest in his lap, empty of weapons. But his fingers curled slightly as if gripping an invisible haft—the body memory of a swordsman's life.

I sat and meditated with him, waiting. I should have been a hollow reed that permitted my surroundings to ebb and flow through me. Clear. Calm. At peace. But even the best of students is imperfect.

I sensed pressure building somewhere out there; the psychic energy of a violent threat pulsed like a living thing seeking a target. My teacher has worked with me over the years to enhance my sensitivity to vibrations unseen. What the Japanese call *ki*, an invisible force that permeates the universe, can sometimes be harnessed and often be sensed. But it takes some doing. Recently, Yamashita had become even more insistent that we both work to strengthen this skill. I knew, in part, that it was a reaction to his wounds; as his pure physical ability deteriorated, he sought to enhance his more esoteric powers. But my master is a complex man and always blends things of mystery with those of practicality.

For psychic energy is real: it pulses off an opponent and is conducted down a blade as you cross swords. If you're paying close attention, it can tell you many things. In *kendo*, they speak of *seme*, a type of aggressive energy that can be used to intimidate an opponent. It's one facet of the larger phenomenon of *ki*. Yamashita has honed my acuity to such a point that I am increasingly aware of the wash of *ki* in the air around me. The only problem is that, once you become receptive to it, it's hard to block out. Now I was being battered by a feeling that danger was closing in.

I sighed and Yamashita's head swiveled slowly in my direction. The light in the room was dim and his eyes were fathomless, dark things. It was hard to tell what he was seeing and what thoughts were slowly swirling in his head. He seemed remote, otherworldly, and dangerous.

I sat, immobile, and we regarded each other in silence: two very different wheels linked to the same cart.

Yamashita stirred. "You can feel it," he said, and it wasn't a question.

"Yes," I admitted.

His hand came up and swirled in a small circle. "Multiple points. Different motivations."

He's reading my mind again. But I had grown used to it. I had been thinking about just this idea. All this violence could not have been generated merely by Lori Westmann's latest literary hoax. By this time, the publishing world was used to frauds of various types. There was something else going on.

"I believe so, *sensei*," I said.

He grunted. "This is what comes of such ventures. Better to stay in the *dojo*, Burke." There was a fleeting tone of recrimination in his voice, but then he smothered it. He began again. "Each time the warrior crosses swords, the odds against him increase. Remember the rule of three."

I sighed. In the Japanese tradition, samurai knew that they

had a one in three chance of coming through a duel unscathed.

"We have a duty to the *dojo*, Burke," my teacher said. "Who will succeed me when I am gone?" He looked at me, eyes and face rigid. When he spoke again his voice was rough. "The other students depend on you... I depend on you."

The words hung between us, their truth difficult to admit but unassailable. Then Yamashita shrugged his shoulders, a man ridding himself of a burden. "Yes, the *dojo*. But first, there is danger that must be addressed."

I cocked my head. "How so?"

"Burke," he said and smiled slightly, "sometimes I do not think you are aware of how much you yourself already know." He came forward off the *zabuton* and moved slowly to his feet. The motion was a ruse, the elegant slowness designed to disguise the stiffness of old wounds.

He gestured at me. "A multiple-threat attack in the *dojo*. You are surrounded. What do you do?"

I shrugged. "Take the initiative. Break the circle and stack 'em up in line. Work fast."

"So," he nodded approvingly. "This is good. To remain in the center of the circle is to merely be a target."

I rubbed my healing arm and nodded ruefully. "I know, I know. The problem is that I can't *see* these attackers. Unless I can identify them, I can't stack them up."

Yamashita moved into the kitchen. I heard water being poured as he prepared to brew the coffee he loved so much. It was a curious enthusiasm that made him seem more human and more complex at the same time. I got up and followed him into the narrow galley kitchen that was always kept immaculately clean.

My teacher poured beans into a hand grinder. His moves

were measured and precise, the expectant look on his face that of an alchemist, perpetually alive to mysterious possibilities. I did the grinding; his elbow joints give him trouble.

"The *kagemusha* is a formidable opponent," he said. A shadow warrior. Someone who can conceal intention, who gives nothing away before the fight is joined."

"How do I coax him out into the light?"

The water boiled; he let it sit for a time to cool slightly, and then began to brew the coffee. The aroma filled the narrow space.

"You can move and hope that your action creates a response that pulls the opponents out of the shadows. Or you can wait and watch until something gives your opponents away."

"But you said waiting wasn't good in a situation like this," I responded.

He looked at me blankly. "Life is complex, Burke. Solutions are not always automatic."

Or available, I thought, with just a hint of annoyance.

Yamashita poured the coffee in a carafe, set it and some cups on a wooden tray, and ghosted into the sitting area. He sat gratefully on a sofa, poured for us both, and brought the cup to his lips, letting the aromatic steam wash over his face before sipping.

"For now, we will wait," he told me, "and enjoy the coffee." He could sense my consternation and gestured for me to sit. I obeyed grudgingly. Yamashita gestured at my cup and I took it up.

"There are many things at play here, Burke. Perhaps you have sensed some of them. But there are other more subtle currents..." His voice trailed off for a moment, then gained strength once more. "You will not have to wait long."

He nodded his head slowly as if responding to some inner voice. Then he held up one thick finger and seemed to listen to something far away.

"Your brother," he said.

The phone rang.

"How badly did you get burned?" I asked Micky.

He snickered, and even though we were talking on the phone, in my mind I could see the defiant cast of his face. "A few of the bosses in the counter-terrorism bureau got some juice with the commissioner," he said. "And we've done good work for them. Me and Art will survive."

"That's good," I said.

"Yeah, sure," he said and his voice got harder. "But fun time's over now, buddy boy. You gotta get your head straight on this one and we gotta nail it all down. Fast."

"Hey," I told him, "point me in the right direction and I'll bring the hammer."

My brother grunted. "Connor," Micky said, "some of the pieces are coming together... We need to talk. And not on the phone."

"I'm on my way," I told him

These days, the actual location where Art and Micky work is not generally accessible to civilians. It's a nondescript brick building in the outer boroughs, just one more squat cube in a desolate industrial zone of body shops, welders, and junkyards. Despite its nondescript exterior, Micky and Art tell me that the inside of the counter-terrorism bureau's headquarters is like nothing they had ever experienced in their lives as cops: hi-tech and state of the art. The glass in the windows is bullet-proof and the walls are covered in ballistic sheetrock. They have secure communication lines and backup power generators to keep the servers humming and the walls of display monitors in the Global Intelligence Room flickering.

After 911, NYPD realized that the City was going to be a high priority terrorist target for a long time to come. And no New York cop trusted the people they called "the three-letter guys"—CIA, FBI, NSA. So the NYPD decided it was going to build its own anti-terrorism capabilities. The bureau that Micky and Art consulted for collected and disseminated intelligence from all over the world, while operatives simultaneously worked the streets of Manhattan, watching, listening, and cultivating informants.

It's cop work that is equal parts brain and muscle. Geeks write algorithms and sift cascades of electronic data. Personnel conduct threat analyses, but the bureau also has its ops people to train public and private personnel in streetcraft. And at the far, hard end of the unit's spectrum, the black clad Hercules rapid deployment teams wait to be unleashed.

The counter-terrorism bureau is an odd mix of ex-intelligence types, seasoned detectives, and bright young cops with competency in languages like Arabic, Pashto, and Urdu. But because the organization is still young, many of its people are as well. As Micky once noted, they're smart, but not yet street smart. Which is where he and Art come in. Reading documents can be learned in a classroom; reading people takes years of hard life experience. My brother and his partner have a knack for observation, for sifting information to find just the right points of leverage when dealing with suspects. The bureau values the skill and wants them to pass it on to the greener members of the team.

The bureau doesn't like visitors. So Micky and I arranged to meet at One Police Plaza in downtown Manhattan. My brother was waiting at the entrance: a thin, intense man with a cop mustache and a stripe of white in his dark hair. Micky looked at me without comment as I came in the door, his expression one of weary annoyance. A silent uniformed officer stood next to him.

"Nice suit," I said and meant it. Micky had spent much of his career in an unmarked car, a rolling trash bin of empty coffee cups, old newspapers, and greasy, wadded-up sandwich wrappers. His tired, rumpled clothing fit right in. But now he was actually presentable.

My brother looked down at himself and seemed almost amazed. "When you're a consultant you gotta dress smart," he mumbled. Then he recovered his cynicism somewhat. "It gives clients the illusion we've got all the answers."

The uniformed cop moved us through the formalities of signing in and getting the visitors' passes we would need. Then, without saying a word, he wheeled around and headed toward the elevators. Micky and I followed.

We ended up on the eighth floor. "Where are we going?" I said.

The doors slid open and we stepped out into a hallway. "RTCC," Micky said.

"Which is?"

My brother sighed in annoyance. "Real Time Crime Center."

I put my hands on my hips and stood there in the middle of the hallway. "Which is?"

He pulled me aside, his voice low. "Connor, stop being such an asshole. Just shut up and come with me. The RTCC's a networked data center for the PD. Lets you access all kinds of stuff. For our purposes, it's the next best thing to the bureau's center. And I go back a long way with the inspector in charge. So he's doing me a favor and letting us use one of his analysts."

"But why?"

He poked me in the chest with a finger. "Look, technically, your little incident is not of immediate interest to the bureau. They got a mile of things that take priority over that. I have a personal interest in the case, but they're not gonna let me tie up their resources. So I made some calls."

"Why?"

Micky squinted at me and sighed. "Because you're my brother. And because you, you moron, have kicked over a full bucket of shit."

The RTCC looked like Mission Control. It had maybe a dozen computer operators with headsets sitting behind paired flat screens. The air was filled with the staccato plastic clicks of people working computer keyboards. The operators' passive faces flickered with light as images expanded, shrunk, or were arranged in tiles in rapid succession. There was a constant, muted hum of conversation as requests came in and data was fed out to the laptops of detectives in the field. One entire wall of the room was taken up by a screen that contained photos, data, what looked like flowcharts, as well as streaming video.

"Wow," I said.

Micky nudged me toward the giant wall screen. A small, muscular looking cop with a shaved head was standing there, arms crossed, and eyes focused on the huge display.

"What you got going, McHale?" my brother asked.

The man turned and smiled in recognition. "Burke. How's

life on the outside? I knew you said you needed some help, but I didn't think you were so desperate you'd be by today."

Micky shrugged, "I'm between things..." Then gestured at me. "My brother."

McHale extended a hand. "The other Burke," he said mockingly. "I've read about you."

"Hello Inspector," I said as we shook hands. His grip could crush stone. I tried not to let my voice waver as McHale tried to see how much pressure I could take before my knees buckled and my bones popped.

Micky came to my rescue. "What gives on the screen, McHale?"

The Inspector, distracted, released his grip. He looked back at the wall and squinted at the mug shot in the center of the screen. "Liquor store robbery. Perp shot the clerk in the face, but he'll survive. Local surveillance camera caught him fleeing in an '87 Civic. They streamed the video here, we enhanced it for the plates and cross-reffed it to DMV. Registered to a kid by the name of Kwame McPatrick. Ran him for priors, wants, and warrants. Hence the mug shot. He's gone to ground and we're running cross-checks for family and known associates..."

"In the old days, we'd have to pound the streets for this kind of thing," Micky told me.

"Now, we're moving a bit smarter and a lot faster," McHale said. "We ran checks on income tax returns, credit reports, parking tickets. Plus whatever we've got in our own database: known associates, MO, identifying marks. He's got a mother living in Ithaca and a sister in Brooklyn. At least three old girl-friends. We got addresses out to the field on all of them, and prepped the responding units on the locale details."

"On all the addresses?" I asked. "You did that from here?"

"Sure," he said simply. "We use Google Earth."

The three of us were clustered around one of the analyst's stations. Her name was Park: high cheekbones with sleek dark hair pulled into a tight ponytail. She asked the occasional question, but her eyes rarely left the dual screens in front of her. Her fingers flew across the computer keyboard as we talked McHale through the problem.

"You got a incident file number on this case?" Park asked. Micky fished a rumpled slip of paper from his pocket, handed it to her and the report appeared on screen. Park dragged it to a corner with her mouse, then popped up mug shots of the three men who had tried to kill me.

"*Los Gemenos*," McHale whistled in recognition. "Bad news comes in twos."

Park moved one of the pictures to her left-hand screen. "Xavier Soledad. Dead on the scene."

McHale looked at Micky. "What happened?"

My brother jerked his chin at me. "Him."

McHale seemed incredulous. "*He* took out one of the Twins?"

Micky nodded. "Stuck a knife in his eye." For a split second, Park looked up at me.

McHale shook his head. "Burke, is everyone in your family a complete maniac?" But it was a rhetorical question, and he returned to scanning the data on the screen before him. "Seems we got another dead guy, but Martín got away?" We nodded. "Whoa boy," McHale continued, "I would not want Martín on the loose and after me."

"You begin to see the dimension of our problem here," Micky said. The remaining Twin's mug shot stared out at us from the center of the screen. He had a thick neck and pitted skin. People rarely look their best in arraignment photos, but Martín's picture did him justice. He looked like a homicidal toad.

Micky continued. "I need whatever you can pull on Soledad and Martín: known associates, places where Martín might go to ground."

"Sure. Who's the other stiff?" McHale asked.

"That one took a while," Micky said. "He's not local. The bureau ran a search, and the guy's name is Ruiz, a gangbanger. In and out of trouble. Bad rep on the street. Moved from LA to Phoenix two years ago. On the surface, nothing really out of the ordinary."

Except he almost killed me. I remembered this man, the smell of him as we fought that day, the odd horn-like designs inked on his head, the cruel look of satisfaction on his face as he watched me start to bleed out.

"So why do you need us?" McHale asked.

"I was describing Ruiz to an operative I know," Micky said. "I mentioned his tats and he said that we might want to do a bit more research on that angle."

McHale nodded. "Tattoos can tell us all kinds of things: where someone did time, gang membership. We've been amassing quite a series of data sets on these things."

Park spoke again. Her ancestry was probably Korean, but her accent was pure Queens. "We'll need more detailed descriptions of his tattoos. Did the coroner get some shots?"

Micky gave her another file reference number and a series of digital photos stacked up on the screen. Park's fingers flew and windows began flashing open and closed. "I'm running an image recognition program against a series of files we've developed on tattoos," she explained.

"It may take a few minutes," McHale commented. "In the meantime, we'll dump a file for you on what we've got on *Los Gemenos*."

He looked at Micky and then at me. "Basically, the info on Ruiz is not the problem here."

"No shit," Micky said. "The real mystery is why he showed up in Brooklyn with the Twins to off my brother."

McHale nodded. "It does seem like overkill. The Twins were usually more than enough to get a job done." He looked shrewdly at Micky. "More than one reason for the visit?"

"That's what I'm thinking," my brother said. "The Twins were experienced local talent. Ruiz didn't need to be there. Unless something else needed to be done…"

"Like what?" I said.

"From what I picked up from that operative, I'm starting to get a pretty good sense," Micky said. "But I need it corroborated."

Park's program was spitting out information. She was watching as line after line of information began flowing across the screen. She sat back in satisfaction. "Ah," she said.

"Ah?" I couldn't help myself.

"Ruiz had a lot of tattoos," Park said. "Any stick out?"

"He had horn tattoos," I said. "Devil's horns."

Park nodded at the screen and highlighted a line for McHale. McHale seemed suddenly tired. "Nice job, Sue," he told Park. "Dump this stuff in a folder and keep trolling on known associates of Ruiz."

"Whatta we got?" Micky prompted.

"Your visitor from Phoenix wasn't just involved with any gang," McHale said. "He was a member of TM-7, *Todos Muertos*."

Micky looked at me. "Oh. Shit. I was hoping I was wrong."

"About what?" I asked.

"TM-7 is one of the fastest growing and most violent gangs out there," McHale said.

"Worse than that," Micky said. "There are plenty of TM-7 members in the New York area. The fact that the gang sent one of their own all the way from Phoenix to visit you does not bode well, Connor."

"If it was just a hit, they could have handled it locally," McHale chimed in. "It's bad enough to have pissed these guys off, but this…"

"What?" I said. "I don't get it."

"If they sent Ruiz, it was because they wanted something from you, Connor," Micky explained. "Something important. Something they didn't want to have to reveal to anyone local…"

"But I don't have anything like that," I protested.

"You may not know you have it, but you do," McHale said. "And if I were you, I'd wrack my brains to figure that out. Because these guys are not going away."

16
FADING THINGS

"It gets better with time," I told her. I would have liked to say that the dreams go away, but they never do. At least not entirely. Yamashita's worked hard with me, but even still the images return, unbidden.

Sarah's voice sounded shaky over the phone, even as she tried to be upbeat. "That's good to know," she said. But she didn't sound convinced.

"The cops say that Martín is gone."

"Gone where?" Her voice rose slightly in concern.

"Gone, Sarah," I said, trying to be soothing. "Away. Out of our lives." I wasn't sure that this was entirely true, but she needed some safe space and a sense that normalcy was returning. "The cops say you can come home," I added.

She took a ragged breath. "Burke... I'm not sure I can."

"Sarah..."

"I keep seeing you, covered in blood... What I did... The bodies."

"I know," I told her. It's a hard thing to experience. The sensations are bad enough: the sight of blood splashed on walls and pooling in rubbery spots on the floor. The metallic scent of it. The animal grunts, the seeping of air. The fluid rip of a blade or the crash of a gun. And the stunned silence that gets slowly overwhelmed by the growing wail of a siren. But it's the realization such sensations bring that's worse: that we're vulnerable, violent, and mortal despite all our striving.

I wished that I had been with Sarah instead of just a voice over the wire, but her sister had told me how fragile she was and that she didn't want any visitors. I thought that just holding her might have been enough to help keep the demons at bay.

There was silence on the line for a time. The she spoke. "How do you stand it, Burke?" she asked in something close to desperation.

"Yamashita says… ." I began, but she ripped into me with ferocity.

"I don't care about Yamashita! How do *you* stand it? How do you live with it? How do you live with yourself?"

I wasn't sure I had an answer to that. Or even if I did that it could be explained. I took a breath. "You put it in a box," I said. "You push it away… The situation is not who you are." It sounded lame, even as I said it. The truth is that some things don't bear too much scrutiny. I try not to think about them too much. You fight the fight and, if you come out the other end, you don't look back. Some wells are too dark and too deep to peer into. If you do, the dense force of the depths will pull you in.

Yamashita had worked with me for years, teaching me to walk across a landscape studded with pits, aware of the danger, yet focused instead on a distant light. It took patience and discipline and the light was often a thin beam, bright enough, but with little warmth to it. It was an odd, cold type of hope and not what Sarah was looking for.

"What if the situation *is* who you are, Burke?' she pressed.

"What do you mean?"

"What I mean is… Look at your life. What you do. And the things that keep happening…"

"I don't create those situations," I objected. I felt my ears flush.

"No?" she demanded. "What if, deep down, you do? What if you set yourself up for them? What if you *need* them?"

"Sarah…" We were heading toward the pit. It's not that her ideas didn't merit some thought. But you fight one fight at a time.

"Look," she said, "I'm sorry. I'm upset. But I need some time."

"Sure," I answered quickly. I think even then that I could sense what was coming and was trying to head it off. "We could take some time and go somewhere."

Again the ragged breath over the phone. "Connor," she said quietly. "I need some time… on my own… to think things through."

The rest of the conversation was a blur. When we were done, she said goodbye and the link between us clicked apart. I sat in the quiet of approaching night, still and cold and confused.

At dawn, the lights from the Verrazano Bridge still twinkled in the distance. I stared out at the approach of day, wondering where to begin. I had already stretched and worked through the basic sword forms that I had learned years ago, old lessons forever new. I tried to lose myself in the action, but last night's conversation with Sarah kept running through my head. Eventually, I set the sword aside and let my thoughts cascade through me.

I didn't know whether Sarah's questions bothered me because of what they said about her or because of what they suggested about me. Either way, I felt oddly defensive. She had come late to the martial arts, but Yamashita saw something in her. Perhaps it was that she had an instinctual knowledge of where to stick the blade.

I sighed and rose from the cold floor. I would need to think about the things Sarah had said. Part of me knew that. But I also knew that I had other things to do as well. Perhaps they weren't as significant as Sarah's questions, but they were much more urgent. I set my face, blank and expressionless, as the milky dawn sky brightened over Staten Island, and got dressed.

Martín's whereabouts were unknown to the NYPD, but the word on the street was that he was gone from New York. Osorio left the same message. I thought that Martín would be back without a doubt. The types of people who hired him react poorly to disappointment. In addition, he had an image to consider as well as a lover to avenge. I figured I had some breathing space, but eventually I was going to see his toad face again. I hoped it would be on my terms.

I knew about Martín—McHale had been nice enough to let Micky spend some time with the file he had generated. So I set him aside for a time. He was just a link in the chain. What I had to figure out was why TM-7 was on my case and what I could do about it.

I teach sporadically as an adjunct instructor at NYU. My schedule is always changing, and after a while the IT people got tired of turning my computer access on and off, so when the head of the history department vouched for me, they left me connected and I could log on to the university system whenever I wanted.

I sat at a cluster of terminals in the university library and did some basic Web searches on the gang known as *Todos Muertos*, TM-7. It was a grim story. Civil war in Central America sent millions of refugees into the US during the 80's. The barrios they ended up in were crowded and violent. Crack cocaine and gangs shaped existence there, a nasty Darwinian world where you learned quickly or died. In LA, TM-7 was the mutant product of this hothouse—a nasty, ruthless thing that mirrored the environment.

Over the years, gang members had been deported back across the border and recruited new members among the destitute and desperate in Mexico and Central America. In time, these new recruits made their way north and the circle continued. The beast was thriving.

And it was no longer just a local issue. Today TM-7 is reported in at least five countries and some thirty states north of the border. Membership is always difficult to determine, but some sources put it as high as one hundred thousand, with instability and desperation adding to the rolls on a regular basis. More good news. I may have inadvertently trimmed the gang population down somewhat, but there was no shortage of replacements.

I read on: highly violent, heavily tattooed. Drugs. Murder. And it got better: as they grew more successful, TM-7 was also becoming a more sophisticated organization. The gang had hired paramilitary experts from Mexico to assist them, rogue members of another border organization known as the Alphas. They were reputed to have come from an elite federal battalion known as the Special Mobile Force Group. They brought increased firepower, sophistication, and ruthlessness to the mix in the dry lands of the Southwest between Mexico and the US.

The members of TM-7's cells had adapted and expanded their range of activity. They were now heavily involved in working the border, moving dope and guns and anything else that pays. The Feds even worried that they may have ties with Al Qaeda.

And McHale said that they were after me.

And I knew why. Sort of. My explanation was fuzzy, but it provided the only link. How could I have possibly run afoul of TM-7? The only thing I could think of was my trip to Tucson. What had I done? I annoyed some mystery writers, but all their mayhem was confined to paper. I ticked off Lori Westmann, but it had all worked out to her benefit in the end. Little people like me got used and discarded on a regular basis in her world. I doubt she even gave me a second thought.

I did have a fight in the desert with a bunch of guys who seemed to be waiting for something. But thinking back, they didn't appear to fit the TM-7 mold. They were working men, not gang-bangers. They may have been smugglers, but they were small time.

What had been important enough to send someone after me in Brooklyn? What did I have that could be of any possible interest? I sat back and closed my eyes. I could hear the clicking of other people tapping on keyboards to either side of me, the shuffle of footsteps and distant conversations. My hands rested, palm up, in my lap. I slowed my breathing and waited for the sensation of simultaneously sinking and rising to take hold. Images flickered across my mind: Sarah's face floating above me as she tried to staunch the bleeding, Yamashita standing in the *dojo*, a rock worn and pitted by time. My brother's smirk.

And the appalled, fearful expression of the desert guide Xochi as he saw the copies of Eliot Westmann's most recent journal spill out of my bags as I headed for the airport.

"You gonna use that terminal?" a voice asked. I opened my eyes, momentarily startled. He was just a college kid: lean and bearded with the intense eyes and shapeless suit jacket of a graduate student. I never even heard him approach.

Nice work, Burke. An army of psychopaths is after you and you're napping in a public place.

The kid had a copy of Spengler's *Decline of the West* under his arm. *Oh boy. Danger is all around.*

"No," I told him. "Knock yourself out. I'm done."

When I had returned from Tucson and before the attack at the house had knocked me off balance, I wondered about Xochi's concern about the copy of the Westmann manuscript. Lori Westmann's agent hadn't even mentioned it when I had visited, so it couldn't have meant something to her. I wondered again whether Xochi had kept its existence secret. Something about it must have caught his attention.

He was a desert guide and advocate for traditional Southwest culture. It was clear to me that Elliot Westmann had been milking Xochi for all kinds of information. The author's notes gave a pretty clear sense of the old faker collecting odds and ends of cultural minutiae that could be used to dress up a new book. Westmann was working on some kind of Eco-Indian-New Age scheme. It was structurally similar to what he had done with his earlier *Tales of a Warrior Mystic*, but designed to be sold in a different era to a different clientele. There's a sucker born every generation.

It was, I thought, pretty transparent. When I had originally scanned Westmann's notes, I made a rough allocation of elements to different categories—local color, religion, ritual, ecology. But there were also chunks of material that combined hiking narrative with odd little numerical references in the margins—Paired strings of five digits. Westmann did not strike me as a numbers guy, so they stuck out in my mind.

But then *Los Gemenos* came calling and there were other

things to worry about. Yet now I wondered again about the numbers and what they could tell me.

The university has a nice map room, with expansive blocks of document cases in natural wood. Clusters of soft chairs were spread here and there, with the occasional napping students sprawled in them, but it was mostly deserted. No skulking hit men, students of German intellectualism or other dangerous types. A young, gum chewing reference librarian showed me how to access the relevant data files at yet another bank of computer terminals.

I yearned for the musty card catalogues of my youth. But it was not to be. The room was cool and angular and high tech. The only real maps immediately apparent were behind Plexiglas and mounted on the wall like archaeological exhibits from a bygone age. The librarian, however, fit right in with the contemporary decor. She had short spiky hair that was dyed black. A small jewel of some sort was set in her nose. Her skirt was short and her long, thin legs were encased in nubby tights. The only makeup she wore was an odd maroon lip gloss. It created an unfortunate contrast with the purple of the laminated ID card she wore on a lanyard around her neck.

"How do you feel about the ideas of Oswald Spengler?" I asked on a hunch. She looked at me dismissively. "This," she said, "is the map room. Crackpot philosophy is on the first floor."

"OK, so we're safe," I replied. She tilted her head and looked at me. I could see the wheels turning as she wondered whether to call security. I waved a sheet of paper at her. "I'm an adjunct in the history department and I'm doing some freelance research," I explained. I put on my most pathetic face.

"I'm looking to see what these coordinates can tell me. Got a globe?"

She rolled her eyes, sat down on a wheeled chair, and bumped me away from the keyboard. "Just numbers?" she said, "no indications of direction?"

"Is that a problem?"

She shrugged. "Nah. Just a process of elimination. You've got some idea of the general location, right? Please?"

"Surprise me," I told her and showed her the numbers.

"Ah," she said, "a test." She closed her eyes and pulled data directly from the cartographic fissures of her librarian's brain. "East latitude, north longitude puts you… in south-central China. South longitude somewhere in the Pacific Ocean east of Australia."

"You can do this from memory?" I asked.

Her eyes opened. "This," she repeated with some emphasis, "is the map room."

"Of course. And it's impressive, but not what I'm looking for."

"Flip the latitude and you're south of the Tropic of Capricorn, again in the ocean." She eyed me for a reaction.

"Nope."

"OK. Last variant is west latitude and north longitude. Somewhere in the American southwest?"

"Bingo," I said.

She fired up a software program and began plugging in the string of numbers that I had copied from Westmann's journal.

She typed and thought and frowned. "You copied these down sequentially, right?"

"Uh, yeah, they're samples from a document I'm working on." She looked at me as if wondering who in their right mind would let me work on something like this unaided.

"OK," she said and blew a slow, steady stream of air out as she backtracked and adjusted her entries.

"What?"

"They didn't make sense at first, but I can see now... these are multiple readings in more than one series and you just ran them all together..."

"Almost as if I didn't know what I was doing." She looked at me. "Hard to believe, but true," I suggested.

Again the testy exhale, but I thought I saw a suppressed smile. Her pale fingers clacked across the keyboard. She moved a mouse with the smooth precision of long practice. The nails of her fingers were cut short, but carefully colored to match her maroon lipstick. Finally, she was done. She rolled the chair back and stood up. "I'm running a printout from the office laser," she told me. "It's got better resolution and you won't get charged for the printout."

She came back with a fistful of papers: a record of the data entered and maps of various scales showing the plotted courses suggested by the coordinates. I shuffled through them.

"Interesting stuff," she said.

"Why so?"

She spread the sheets out on a table and started pointing things out. "Notice the routes being suggested. I overlaid them on maps with both terrain and manmade features."

"Lots of terrain," I said. "Not many roads."

"Not much of anything," she said. "Except this little feature." All the routes were, at one point or another, bisected by a dashed line. "You know what this is?" She asked.

"The border between Arizona and the Mexican state of Sonora," I said, proud of at least that much knowledge.

"Yes. All of these routes cross the border. At locations far from anything, including, I assume, anything remotely resembling a Customs inspection."

"I wonder," I said innocently, "what that's all about?"

She looked then as if she suspected new and unpleasant things about me. Life in the library was probably pretty tidy. I was not. Then the momentary suspicion faded, routine reasserted itself and she shrugged. "We supply directions, not motivations."

"Of course," I agreed, "this is, after all, the map room."

17
FLIGHT

The mean streets of the old Red Hook have changed. Gentrification has arrived in the form of small bistros, coffee bars, and microbreweries. The stolid nineteenth century warehouses are being rehabbed into apartments with big windows and open floor plans. It's all very civilized, but not always pleasant.

"Don't even open your mouth, you asshole," the voice said with a venom that was potent. We sat in the dim recesses of a microbrewery, the brick walls arching over our heads. It should have felt safe and comforting; vaguely old world. Instead, I felt like I was sitting in a vault where they store gunpowder.

My brother Micky was about as angry as I had ever seen him, and that was saying a great deal. His partner Art sat next to him, facing me across the dark wooden plank table. He's usually the affable one, a man naturally disposed to play the Good Cop in the same way that my brother emerged from the womb fully formed as the consummate Bad Cop. Today, Art's face was a tight mask; he watched me with eyes that were remote and uncaring. It wasn't like him, but I seemed to be getting this reaction from him a lot in the last few days

I opened and closed my mouth, and then opted for the smart move and just sat there.

"You are so deep into this wormhole, Connor... I can't even begin to..." Micky's anger seemed to briefly choke off his ability to speak.

"Bad enough you run afoul of TM-7," Art said. "And, by the

199

way, we're still waiting for you to come clean about that."

"I can explain…" I began, but Art held up a stern hand.

"Little late in the game for confidences. Let me finish." He looked like he would rather finish me. "We go from bad to worse. You manage to get *Los Gemenos* on your case. And we warned you about Osorio…"

My brother found his voice. "What the *fuck* were you thinking?"

The waitress came over with our beers. I didn't answer Micky's question, just watched mutely as she set the pint glasses down in front of us. When she left, I shrugged. "We needed some sort of 'in' to the Hispanic underworld."

Art made a deep harrumphing noise. "Hispanic underworld. You been watching too many movies."

Micky picked up the thought. "Osorio's a jackal, Connor. He may like to pretend he's Ricardo Montalban, but in the end he's just another thug."

I couldn't object to the characterization. Osorio was the one who'd told me that Martín was gone. Maybe he was mistaken. But maybe he'd decided to do someone a favor and set me up. Time would tell. It was yet another complication that I decided not to think about right now. I hefted the glass of beer, taking small comfort in the familiar smooth curve of the glass in my hand. I lifted it to my lips and let the aroma of the hops wash over my face.

Neither of the two men sitting opposite me touched their glasses. They watched me with an unblinking patience, waiting for me to crack.

"Look," I finally said, "I don't have all the pieces put together yet. And I was trying not to get you guys involved."

My brother snorted. "A little late for that."

"Connor," Art said with real pain, "you are in way over your fucking head."

Micky sat back and glared at me. "This has nothing to do with you wanting to protect us, Connor. I know you. When are you gonna realize that this is not about you and some fucking test of skill? It's not about measuring up to Yamashita or some assholic warrior code. This is the real deal."

"I know that," I protested. "But I'm pretty sure that this isn't the kind of thing that you can afford to be involved with. I may have to do some things..."

"Things?" Art said.

I nodded. "They might arrest me before it's all over."

"Arrest you," my brother demanded. "Arrest you?" He started to rise from his seat, but Art held him down. "I'm gonna fucking kill you if you don't level with me and tell us what's going on!"

So I did. The odd job for Lori Westmann and the manuscript copy I made. The suspicious fire at the Westmann estate that destroyed the original. The notes and coordinates in the manuscript copy that detailed a host of clandestine trails for border crossings.

After my story we all sat for a moment, saying nothing. Micky ordered a Jameson. Art and I joined him.

"When did you finally fit the pieces together?' Micky said. "After the attack?"

I shook my head. "No. I wasn't really focused on the manuscript then. But once you got the information about TM-7, I started thinking about that guy Xochi in Tucson and the expression on his face when he saw me with a copy of the manuscript. Then, when I ran the GPS coordinates, it began to dawn on me."

"You coulda brought us in, Connor," Art chided.

I sipped at the gold and smoke of the Irish whiskey. "Art. You guys aren't cops anymore. But you still have to play by the rules." Micky started to say something, but I held up a hand. "Yeah, I know, not all the rules all the time. But the big ones? Please. It's what you do…"

The two cops sat in grudging agreement, looking into the whiskey for answers it couldn't provide.

Micky grimaced. "Here's your problem. TM-7 is like some beast with multiple heads. Someone in the organization wants you taken out. You blew away a few of them and Martín has disappeared for the time being. It gives you some breathing room, but they're just gonna send someone else."

I swallowed and asked the big question. "Now what?"

The eyed each other, sending silent signals back and forth, an ocular cop semaphore. My brother seemed uncomfortable. Art leaned forward, his big hands resting on the table.

"The rumble over the networks is that something big is going down on the border. The various cartels are jockeying for control over smuggling routes. TM-7 is just one of the players. They want what you have and are not gonna stop 'til they get it."

"So what do I do?"

Micky shrugged. "The good news is that these guys are busy and that if you can find whoever is really pissed at you and placate him, the organization itself will move on."

"Bigger fish to fry," Art observed.

"So?" I prompted.

"So you give it to them."

"Huh?"

"Hear me out," my brother said. "Someone wants what you have. They also want you in case you know what you have. For them it's a two-part problem. They want the info on the smuggling routes, and they don't want anyone else to have it.

"Why not just ask that guy Xochi?"

Art waved a hand. "They may already have him."

"They could ask him, of course," Micky mused. "And it's our experience that people like this are terrible liars."

"There are, of course, more vigorous ways to question someone," Art added. "But there are issues…"

"Such as?"

Art smiled smugly. "Contrary to whatever wet dream some politicians have had, torture doesn't yield such great information. Besides, even if they got the info, they tend to—get rid of the source. Makes things much tidier. Although not a great deal for your pal Xochi. That still leaves the problem of you having a copy of the coordinates."

"So the manuscript is important to them," Micky said. "They want it back."

"Of course, you have also read it," Art added. "Bad news for them, since now there's another loose wheel in their little scheme."

"Even worse news for you personally," my brother added with a perverse tone of satisfaction. "'Cause now they have to eliminate you."

Art leaned back and smiled broadly. "Of course, we have made a career out of seeing the silver lining in black clouds. This problem is no exception"

"I'm overjoyed," I told them.

They looked at each other and leaned in over the table simultaneously, the wheels in their heads spinning. I waited, openmouthed.

"Simple, really," Micky said. "We provide the bait—in this case you and the manuscript. It would be really surprising if whoever is in charge down there, the guy funding the hit on you, doesn't surface."

"And then?"

"The details need a little fleshing out," Art admitted.

"But the big picture is simple," Micky said. "You find whoever is behind this…"

"And have him arrested?" I asked hopefully.

Art looked guilty. "Well, no…"

"Guy like this is gonna be able to put a hit on you whether he's in jail or out," Micky said.

"Which means?"

"You know what it means," my brother said quietly. He spoke slowly, tapping the scarred planks of the table for emphasis. "Bait gets set. Big man arrives. You take him out."

I had known where they were going, of course. But part of me hoped that they had an alternative. This was crossing a line for all of us. I wanted to find another solution. We all did. But life is what you get, not what you wish for.

I sighed. "So we go down there?"

"Well, technically, no… you go down there," Art said with a half smile. "The two of us are still under something of a cloud."

"They're not gonna let us anywhere near the border anytime soon," Micky explained.

"You're going to send me alone?"

"Who better?" Art shrugged. "You're already up to your eyeballs in this thing."

I stared at Micky. "You two just finished telling me I was in over my head!"

He smiled tightly. "Yeah. But at least now you know it. Besides, we can pull some strings and get you some backup."

Art took a letter-size manila envelope out of his jacket and slid it over to me. "Four thousand in cash. It's all we could come up with. Plus a plane ticket to Tucson."

"You got a few good days," Micky instructed. "You get down there and find who's after you…"

"How'm I gonna do that?" I protested.

"We know a guy out there. Former INS inspector named Steve Daley. He owes me. He'll meet you at the plane."

"Keep a low profile, Connor," Art said. "Stay off the grid. No credit cards, nothing that will leave a trace." He looked at his watch. "Clock's ticking. TM-7 will be back. They'll be looking for you, so you gotta move quick."

They let me think about it. I heard the faint tinkle of ice in a glass, the murmur of distant conversation near the bar. I thought of Sarah and the things I could lose if I went. Then I thought of what I might lose if I didn't.

"OK," I sighed.

They nodded, but neither man seemed particularly happy.

"Listen up," Art said quietly. "There's no telling who's watching you or watching us at this point in time. We're gonna walk out of here and drive away. There's an overnight bag for you up front with the cashier. Don't go back to Yamashita's. Take the bag and use the subway to get to JFK. Get on a plane to Tucson. Get this done…"

"One more thing," my brother interjected. He handed me a black cell phone. "Take this."

"I have a phone, Mick."

"I've seen your phone. It's a piece of shit. Take this, Keep it charged up and on at all times. If I find out anything, if I can do anything, I will." But his voice was terse and devoid of any comfort. I'm not even sure that he believed what he was saying.

I took the phone and sat there while he and his partner

stumped away, grim, unhappy, and vaguely guilty.

"This is what happens," Yamashita told me with deep displeasure. I had gone back to see him before leaving, of course. There's something deep in the Burke DNA that makes us congenitally incapable of obeying orders.

We were seated on the floor in the *dojo*. It was dim and silent, a vast clean expanse of space. I could hear my heart thudding as I tried to explain.

"I don't know any other way out of this," I told him.

His eyes were hollow slits in a rigid mask. My *sensei* doesn't leak much energy, but when he does, you can feel it. It washed over me, a tide of anger and disapproval. I had spent more than a decade with this man, accepting his guidance, working for his respect. Now I felt as if every move I made was both inevitable and unacceptable to him.

I bowed slightly. "*Moushiwake arimasen.*" It's the most formal way to say that you're sorry to a superior. But Yamashita wasn't buying it; he didn't even blink in acknowledgement.

"Contrition is beside the point," he said tightly. "Do you know what you are doing?"

"I do," I began.

"*Bakka!*" he cut me off. Idiot. "You have no idea!" His rebuke stung: I rocked back on my heels. I opened my mouth to continue, but he made a chopping motion with his hand to silence me.

"This is their world, Burke, not ours. It is without rules. It… compromises your honor."

"I didn't mean for any of this to happen, Sensei."

He looked to one side as if seeking patience in another location. "Please. You are like a child. What you meant to do and what has been done are two different things. It was why I warned you against getting too involved."

I swallowed. I thought of Sarah and her dreams. I knew that something had to be done, even if Yamashita objected.

"But I am involved" I told him.

Yamashita sighed. "You are. As are others. And now, you will place yourself in danger…"

"It's what you have trained me to do." It was an almost involuntary comment, but I flinched; the relationship between a teacher and pupil in the martial arts isn't one that encourages a free exchange of opinion.

Yamashita's nostrils flared. "I have spent years training you. And now—to run the risk of throwing it all away…" His voice trailed off and we both sat in silence, stunned at the rare admission of concern.

We both knew about the danger I faced. The warriors of old Japan knew that every confrontation was more than likely to end in disaster. The dispiriting rule of the *samurai*: a superior opponent will certainly kill you; an equally matched opponent will probably kill you even if you manage to kill him as well; only someone vastly inferior in skill will permit you to emerge unscathed.

"It's something I have to do," I said quietly.

Yamashita fidgeted slightly. "I know," he answered, his tone bitter. "But these are thugs… they are animals…"

"I have to stop them," I added. "For Sarah."

My teacher squinted at me. "There is *on* here, Burke, I know. *On,* the tug of human relationships. "But what of *giri*, your duty to the *dojo*?" He licked his lips as if the next question took some effort. "What of your duty to me?"

And I saw him with new eyes: an old battered man, sitting

there in the dimness, wondering what the future was for his school and his pupils. His anger was for the possibility of a legacy squandered as much as it was generated by concern for me.

"Sensei," I began, "you know what you mean to me…"

"And yet there is this rebellious streak," he said coldly. "The *dojo* is your world, Burke. Not this other place…"

"How can you say that? You worked for the *Kunaicho*!" In years past, Yamashita had been deeply involved with the more clandestine activities of the Japanese Imperial Household Agency. The details were fuzzy and he didn't like to talk about it much.

His bullet head nodded slightly and he sipped at the air. "Yes. And at the time, I thought I was doing what was right… but it brought only pain. You know some of this, Burke."

Yamashita was gazing at the floor, avoiding eye contact or perhaps lost in painful memories from his past.

"And yet you did it," I prompted gently. "Because you thought it was the right thing."

"It brought only pain," he repeated, as if to himself.

"Sensei…"

Yamashita waived me to silence. "Go. You will do what you will do." He rose to his feet and, since we were alone, he did not mask the pain involved in the movement. "I had hoped…" he said, but paused as if something was caught in his throat. "I had hoped that as a teacher I could save my pupil from the same mistakes I had made—that I would find someone wise enough to heed me." He looked up and his voice was old and raspy. "It was not to be."

Before he turned away, I saw his eyes: glittering with regret and dismissal.

18
INTO THE WEST

The junkie's skin was brown from the sun, but looked as if it had a faint covering of ash on it. His eyes were red-rimmed and furtive. There was a restless animal prowling inside his head, simultaneously wary, distracted, and frightened.

I watched Steve Daley work him. It wasn't the questions he asked so much as the way they were delivered that made him effective: words that emerged like random gunshots from unexpected quarters, elliptical, phrased differently each time. His voice disoriented his victim and its tone demanded a response. Daley lightly pinched the back of the junkie's stringy neck between the thumb and fingers of his hand as they talked. The touch transferred an oscillating current: alternately avuncular and menacing, a soothing touch or the prelude to a shake that could rattle what was left of the junkie's brains around his skull like a stone in a gourd.

This was the last in a succession of informants he'd interrogated. It was always the same. And it wasn't pretty to watch; this type of interrogation is about breaking people down. There wasn't much left of a junkie like this one; the questioning felt needlessly cruel, one of a final series of humiliations that would dot the dizzy downward spiral of his life. Daley was oblivious to this, or perhaps he was just jaded. He ground at this latest junkie informant mercilessly, testing and probing for lies or inconsistencies, flaws in the answers. In the end, Daley wrung the junkie out. You would have thought that there was nothing left in that jumble of ashy skin and nerve but a consciousness that winked on and off like some distant, failing light, powered only by the need for its next fix.

"They all know things," Daley confided to me. We were back in his car, letting the air conditioner wash the heat away from our bodies. He was tall and lanky, with long graying hair pushed behind his ears and a goatee that, along with the Hawaiian shirt and cowboy boots, completed an odd image: Jimmy Buffet channeling Buffalo Bill Cody. "But they all lie."

"So what's the point?"

"You see what they lie about—then you start comparing stories. And then you start drilling." Daley slipped his sunglasses on and pulled the car out into traffic. His hands were freckled and the muscles on his forearms were long and ropy. Daley had been baked by the desert into a taut machine; most of the softness in him had been desiccated and worn until it had simply blown away. What was left was wiry and functional and supremely competent: sinew, bone, and the bright eye of a predator.

He had met me at the airport, standing at the end of the chute where arriving passengers were funneled like cattle away from the gate area. At the screening complex, the serious people from the TSA were warily searching carry-on luggage, alive to the possibility of exploding toothpaste tubes. Daley stood slightly apart from the other drivers, men in dark suits who held small whiteboards with the names of their fares written on them. Daley slouched in isolation and held up a ragged piece of cardboard with the single word "Burke" scrawled on it in bad handwriting. As I got closer, I noticed that he had used the top from a discarded pizza box.

I stopped in front of him. "I'm Burke."

Daley had obviously spoken to my brother: he knew what I was up to and regarded me with weary skepticism He didn't say hello and didn't offer to shake hands, just jerked his head to indicate the direction we needed to go. He spoke quietly as we moved. "I can provide you with some support and information, Burke. I owe your brother that much. I can help you set this thing up, but it may take some time. And it may get dicey. I can't guarantee how it's going to work out."

"I got it," I said.

Daley looked at me with those washed out eyes. "You're trouble, man. I can sense that. Know this: things start to fall apart, I'm out of there. End of the day, it's your problem, not mine. We clear?"

I nodded. *Great help, Mick.* "I need to see about setting up some contacts. The Westmann Resort..."

He cut me off. "Forget it. Your man Xochi has gone to ground."

"Whaddaya mean?" My basic plan was to get to Xochi and tell him that I was willing to trade the Westmann manuscript to whoever was trying to have me killed if they would just stop. You'd think that the long flight would have provided me with enough time to develop a plan of more elegance, or at least a part two.

I stopped in consternation, however, wondering what my alternatives were now that Xochi had disappeared. Daley never paused and I hurried after him as he turned right, heading past Ike's coffee shop toward the parking garage.

"He's dropped out of sight," Daley continued. If he sensed my distress, he didn't show it. "From what I hear, there are any number of people looking for him." Now it was his turn to pause. He stopped for a moment and looked directly at me.

"Angry people, Burke."

But I was beyond the point where someone was going to scare me. "Any idea where he could be?"

Daley gestured toward the glass doors we were approaching. "Lots of space out there to get lost in. He could be up in the Santa Catalina Mountains. He could've high-tailed it down to the Papago Indian reservation. Then again, we're only sixty miles from Mexico. Take your pick. But if I were him, I'd be burrowed somewhere way under the surface, waiting until all this blows over."

"All this?" We moved out into the bright white light, across the blinding expanse of concrete, to the parking garage. His car was a dusty black Chevy Blazer. It had oversized tires and rust was eating away at the wheel wells. The interior was hot and stuffy; it smelled of dust, stale coffee, and old apples.

We settled into the car. My seat was lumpy and I could feel springs trying to sprout up through the fabric.

"You read the papers, Burke? We got quite a circus goin' on down here. The drug cartels are at war with the Mexican government. The local gangs are at war with each other, trying to get control of the cross border trade. And the U.S. is on the losing end of a war on so many things I sort o' have a hard time keeping track: a war on illegal immigration, a war on drugs, a war on terror… It's mess. But it does keep us all busy one way or the other." We left the airport and headed north toward Tucson.

"My brother said you had retired."

Daley's head turned slightly toward me. He was wearing wraparound sunglasses with dark lenses that shimmered blue and bronze and green; it was impossible to see his eyes, and I think he liked it like that.

"Partner," he instructed me, "I worked long and hard to get as good as I am. It's true that I left government employ. But the situation down here is so fluid that there are ample opportunities for someone like me to make a little side cash."

"How entrepreneurial," I said.

He grinned at that; his teeth were yellow and long. "That's me," he said happily. "An en-tre-pre-neur." He spaced the word out like he was savoring the sound.

That was when we went looking for some junkies to question.

Mercifully, the sun was setting and Daley was done with his informants. We sat in the Blazer, parked in the shade of a Wal-Mart. I could feel the skin on my face, tight from the light and heat of the desert. Daley watched me for a minute.

"You reach on into the back seat, Burke. I got a few jugs of water stashed. You get some of that into you right now. The weather out here'll kill you." I realized how dry my mouth was. I twisted around to get the jug.

"Here's what I think you got," Daley told me as I got the jug. He waived the proffered water away with a hand. "Interesting situation. The street people say that the smack supply is—sporadic. Some dealers are scrambling to supply product, others have so much they're discounting it."

"What's it mean?"

Daley reached into a sack and pulled out an apple. He sunk his ivory teeth into the fruit and I could hear the sucking sound as he pulled the juice out before he completed the bite. He chewed for a minute, then continued. "If I were still writing reports for our government I'd say that there's a shift in distribution taking place. But that doesn't really get to the meat of it.

There's a turf war taking place, Burke. Coupla different groups fighting to control the trade. Old gangs being pushed aside or rolling over. New ones coming in. It'll be a mess for a while."

"TM-7?" I asked.

Daley nodded, biting the apple. "That's one crazy bunch of inked-up motherfuckers," he said. "Your brother likes them for the attempted hit in New York." He lowered his sunglasses and peered over them at me. "Hard to believe you walked away from that one."

"The world is full of surprises," I told him. Not that I really walked away.

Daley snorted in amusement. "Border's always been a crazy place, Burke. Dangerous enough as it was. But now we got various cartels working hard at controlling a huge expanse of highly profitable activities. And the greater the money to be made, the crazier they all get. You're a case in point. Why in God's name did they put a hit out on someone like you?"

"I stumbled on a manuscript with some pretty detailed descriptions of old trails that crossed the border…"

He snorted again. "Lots o' ways across the border, my man. Every *chollo* with some ambition and a connection knows that."

"These are ancient Indian trails," I explained. "Long forgotten. They're not used very often…"

"So theoretically they're off the Border Patrol's radar," Daley commented, although he sounded skeptical. "Nice, if it's true. I suppose that fraud Xochi was involved in this?"

"What do you know about him?"

Daley slid his sunglasses down the bridge of his nose and peered at me. "I made some inquiries. He's a man on the make, my friend. Workin' more than a few angles. He's pushing all that Native American desert mysticism bullshit with the tourists. Though I hear his backcountry skills are real enough. He's also been known to help out with a special border crossing now and then. And lately, he's been trying to peddle his alleged knowledge of secret trails to the highest bidder..."

"TM-7?"

Daley pushed his shades back into place and stared out through the windshield. "He was originally talking with some other group, but I guess the negotiations got ..." he licked his lips, "co-opted by our friends from *Todos Muertos*. I don't think he knew what he was getting into. If he's snowing them..." He shrugged. "My guess is that Xochi promised that he could provide them with some cherry routes across the desert. And the kicker is that supposedly he's the only one who knows. 'Knowledge of the ancient ones' and all that horseshit. I don't know how he conned them, but he did."

Daley sat for a while, pausing in admiration of Xochi's accomplishment or appalled at his stupidity. Then he stirred and tapped me on the thigh. "Then you come along and complicate things. Ha! TM-7 are a bunch of lunatics, Burke, but they like a nice tidy package as much as anyone. You, roaming around with a manuscript that contains info on their allegedly secret trails, most certainly would have pissed them off. They thought our man Xochi had a monopoly on that knowledge." He grinned tightly, an unpleasant wrinkling of leather skin and teeth like old bone. "Imagine their—disappointment. So they went looking for you in the wilds of New York. Obviously, from what your brother tells me, complications ensued. Xochi realized he was probably next on their list and did a fast fade."

"Do you know who he was dealing with?" I asked. Ultimately I had to get to whoever was directing the hits.

He shook his head slowly, ruminating. "Nooo," he said,

drawing the word out as he pondered. "There are a few likely suspects. Guy known as El Carnicero is a big man with the local TM-7. He's a bit of a freak. Enjoys working on people with a blade. Hence the nickname: the Butcher. Likes to keep things personal, ya know? But if you're going into harm's way, it would be wise to make sure that it's gonna solve your problem and not just piss off a new set of gang bangers. This particular circus is filled with freaks. It could take some time to narrow down the list to anything actionable."

"Be quicker to just find Xochi," I said. "Ask him."

He nodded. "I agree. Quick is good, Burke," Daley said. "I got this feelin' that you're running out of time…"

I felt a spasm of alarm. "Did you hear something from my brother?"

Daley looked at me. "Huh? No. That's not what I mean. You got bigger issues to deal with."

I sat there, saying nothing. Waiting. The daylight was going, and the line of mountains in the distance was a black, jagged mass, backlit by the orange flare of the sun as it burned its way across the rocky expanse of the Southwest and into the distant Pacific Ocean. I worked my way through Daley's information so far, weighing it, seeing how pieces fit together. I didn't try to force a solution; the effort of doing so would probably just push it away.

I had few, if any, options. I knew that. But that made whatever I did that much more important. It was like the intensity of a sword duel with live blades: each slight twitch of muscle pulsed into the ether, an expanding ring of possibility that opened a path to some gambits at the same time that it closed off others. Each step held within it the potential for victory or the seeds of your own destruction. So you push that awareness down deep, smother it so that the animal pleading for deliverance doesn't echo in the back of your head. There's no time for that; it's a fatal luxury, because if you succumb you'll be a split second too slow when the blade is arcing toward you for the decisive cut.

I sat in Daley's car and slowed my breathing. I tried to concentrate on nothing, let go of intention, of urgency, and to be in the moment. All that Zen stuff. But, of course, it was futile. Yamashita's students try to set themselves as still, empty vessels, but life pushes at us and fills us as it will. I was no exception. A lifetime of training hasn't made me invulnerable; sometimes it just makes me resigned.

So I sat, simply waiting for the other shoe to drop, and determined not to let Daley enjoy the experience.

"Here's the kicker," he finally said. "You got the different cartels all jockeying for dominance: Tijuana, Sonoma, Juarez. They got local offshoots all along the border. Xochi probably had feelers out to the local families, then TM-7 dropped by and rewrote the rules. But now someone else is pushing at *them*."

"Who?"

"You heard of the Alphas, Burke?" Daley took off his sunglasses. His eyes were a pale, haggard blue. "Alphas take this to a whole new level."

I was getting impatient with Daley's act: the world-weary expert sent to keep tabs on me, the local informant with a wealth of knowledge that he was doling out drop by drop, the Old Scout squinting out along the ridge line, searching for hostiles.

"Daley," I said. "Lose the drama. I don't need the color on your play-by-play. I need some concrete leads and an accurate assessment of what I'm going to face. That's it."

It seemed to me at that moment that I spent my life among men who never gave you the complete picture. Maybe it was because they somehow didn't take you completely seriously, like my brother Mickey. Or they harbored some secret kernel of doubt that you'd ultimately be unable to meet the coming test. I used to think Yamashita eyed me skeptically, scanning me for the telltale signs of the germinal flaw that slumbered deep within me. Over the years those feelings had faded, but the experience still left old wounds that could flare into life.

Daley didn't flinch. He stared off into the distance and just started talking.

"The Alphas are renegades, Burke. Anti-drug commandos trained in Mexico who realized they could make more money working for the drug cartels than against them. They've been involved with killings and kidnappings all over the place, although until recently they were concentrating their activities on this side of the fence to Texas." He snorted. "There are mayors of Mexican border towns down there scared so bad that they hide out in the U.S. The Alphas protect the drug corridors. And anyone who gets in the way," his head swiveled to look at me "and I mean anyone, gets taken out. Cops, Border Patrol agents, you name it. These guys are killing machines. The freaks from TM-7 are psychos. They like the rush of power they get from scaring people or hacking them up with a blade. Alphas could care less about that shit. They're pros. Some of them have been at Benning at the School of the Americas. You know what that means?"

I nodded. I had been to Fort Benning and seen the Special Forces training at work. There's a special school there, the Western Hemisphere Institute for Security Cooperation, which trains military personnel from Latin America.

"Well, the Alphas are expanding their reach. The word I get is that they're here. And they're even scaring our pals from TM-7. My guess is that you've got more than one problem and soon the Alphas will be on your case as well."

His voice was somber, almost reflective in the dim recess of the car. Then he stirred, prompted by a new thought.

"You're not carrying a weapon, are you, Burke? My professional opinion is that you're gonna need one." He dropped the Blazer into gear, seeming relieved at the prospect of concrete action. "Fortunately, here in the West, that's something that's easily fixed."

19
GROUND

Distant hills washed pink in the early morning light. Small birds fluttered in the bushes. I could smell water and cut grass. The golf course itself was an expanse of lush, dark greens. It was as if all the moisture had been sucked down out of those far hills, leaving them to ring the horizon like the fossilized remains of ancient monsters.

Parties of golfers dotted the course; men and women in brightly colored sportswear and sunglasses, tanned and intent on the game. Noises were subdued: the distinctive *whuck* of someone hitting a ball, and the faint snippets of conversation across the fairway. I stood in the shadow of the clubhouse, waiting.

Charlie Fiorella spotted me as he approached the final hole, walking with Lori Westmann. A good cop never loses the knack of scanning the environment for threats, and Charlie had been a good cop. I saw him look my way, once, but other than that he didn't react. His movements on the green were smooth and unhurried, focused. When he was done, he spoke quietly to Westmann. She looked up sharply, her head turning in my direction. Fiorella touched her on the arm, a reassuring gesture. Then he came my way.

"It's a private club," he told me. "She wants to have you arrested for trespassing." There was no greeting or handshake. He stood about five feet away, his tanned face professional.

"What if I were just here to see you?"

"Then maybe *I'll* have you arrested." But his body language was relaxed and there was a hint of levity in his voice.

I shrugged. "You'll probably have to wait in line."

Charlie took off his sunglasses and looked at me carefully. He jerked his head. "Come inside, I'll buy you a cup of coffee."

Another nice view, another table with clean linen and heavy silverware. There was the aromatic scent of coffee and bacon. It was surreal. In the subdued and civilized clubhouse dining room, I was oblivious to comfort, conscious only of the dangerous world stirring with another dawn, of time ticking away and the need to be moving.

The waiter was Latino. His dark, sunburned skin made a nice contrast with the elegant white jacket he wore. He wordlessly delivered a stainless steel carafe of coffee to our table, flashed Charlie a knowing smile, and left.

Fiorella sat across from me, waiting.

"Ever get to the bottom of that bogus attack with the *shuriken* when I was out here, Charlie?"

"What makes you think it was bogus?" he said.

"You never followed up. I never heard anything. It's not like you."

Fiorella swung his head back and forth, mulling over what to say. He finally decided. "Westmann put him up to it. Her boyfriend, Xochi. The Chief. I didn't know it at the time. It was a harebrained stunt, but Lori was looking for something to spice up the negotiations about re-releasing her father's books. She figured resurrecting the old man's bullshit fantasy about Asian assassins would help drive up her advance."

"She was probably right," I said. "Ever wonder why her boyfriend was so eager to help out?"

He shrugged. "You'd have to ask him."

"Xochi," I said. "I'll bet he has all kinds of information."

"He might," Fiorella said noncommittally, "but he seems to have disappeared."

"Convenient."

"For him," he told me.

"I hear that he's laying low, Charlie. He may have gotten in over his head and needs to hide out until things blow over."

"Things?" His voice sounded skeptical, but Fiorella didn't smile. He also didn't seem to care whether I went on or not. He poured some cream into his coffee and meticulously stirred it with a spoon. The act didn't fool me: there was watchfulness in his eyes—they were the still eyes of a man looking hard at hostile terrain.

"He knows a lot about the desert, Charlie," I began, "about the border. And before he died, Elliot Westmann was writing down the lore that Xochi proffered. Westmann didn't know it, but some of that stuff was valuable information."

"What makes you say that, Burke?" He didn't betray any interest, but he was letting me talk to see where this was going to go.

"That stupid project I started for Lori Westmann," I said. "I ended up with copies of some of her father's notes on a new book."

"All of which is property of the Westmann estate," he instructed. "I'll want them back."

"You're not alone."

Charlie carefully picked up his coffee cup and sipped at it, like someone working very hard not to react. "What's that mean?" he said.

I leaned back in my chair. "Let's say that perhaps Xochi,

who is, I think we can both agree, a man on the make, was looking to cash in on some of his knowledge about the desert."

Fiorella shrugged. "Let's say that."

"Elliot Westmann takes an unfortunate spill and that potential gravy train gets derailed. Xochi's sleeping with Lori Westmann, which is nice for him I suppose, but he's looking for more. Maybe he wants to impress her; maybe he suspects that theirs is not a long-term thing. So maybe Xochi, who is not hindered by too many scruples, puts some feelers out to the sorts of people who are interested in little known, relatively unused trails across the desert. He wants to sell them his maps."

"Wouldn't surprise me," Fiorella commented. "Wouldn't be a brilliant move in my opinion."

"Unfortunately for Xochi, he didn't ask you," I concluded. He said nothing, but tipped his coffee cup in acknowledgment.

I sat forward in my seat. "Problem is, Charlie, that these people are very committed to the idea that Xochi's trails stay their little secret. And when they learned I might have inadvertently stumbled onto this information, they were not pleased."

Fiorella's face went slack; he set his cup down on the table and waited.

"They sent someone after me, Charlie," I hissed. I tried to stay calm, but my voice was tight. It trembled with memory. "They tried to kill my girlfriend Sarah. They tried to kill me." I could feel the anger starting to spiral out of me. The implications of what I was going to do sparked to life inside my head. *They made me more like them than I cared to admit.*

He looked down at his hands, dark and thick things against the expanse of clean linen. His eyes came up and met mine. "I didn't know," he said simply.

I pushed the anger down and got some control back. "If I

thought you did I wouldn't be here," I finally said.

Fiorella took a deep breath and gazed out the window. He exhaled slowly through his nostrils, shaking his head. "Idiots."

He could have meant Xochi and Lori Westmann. He could have meant the people who came after me. It could have been a global comment on humanity. I didn't respond to it.

"I'm not sure what they told you, Charlie. How much you know."

He looked back at me. "My job," he said with mild disdain, "is to know only the things I need to, and not too much more. Makes it easier on everyone and keeps me out of trouble."

"Nice theory," I told him. He didn't say anything, so I continued. "Let me fill you in on some of the things you maybe don't know. Xochi sold the maps to his secret trails to the local members of TM-7."

"Oh, for Christ sake," he muttered.

I held up a hand. "Wait, it gets better. Now a new group is moving into town and they want to take over. Xochi by this time is smart enough to realize that he doesn't want to be anywhere near this dogfight. And he needs to go to ground. He could hide out in the desert, of course, but that's where all these very angry new people are. He could maybe hunker down in the *barrio*, but it wouldn't take long to find him there either. He needs to go somewhere that they can't. My guess is that he turns to Lori Westmann. But my experience of rich people, Charlie, is that they are not particularly good about saying no to themselves. And hiding out takes some discipline, involves some discomfort."

Fiorella grimaced. "They were both pretty clueless," he admitted.

I nodded. "They needed a pro, Charlie. A fixer. Xochi,

I think, was realizing that he was getting expendable. He figured he'd lay low until all the shouting ended. Works out for him, I suppose. But what he didn't tell you was that the local head of TM-7 was still looking to kill me to keep the desert routes secret."

Fiorella clasped his hands on the table, leaning in on his forearms. "Burke, I had no way of knowing this."

"I know Charlie, a round of golf every morning." I poured some more coffee into his cup. "You owe me nothing, but I'm asking for some help; something very simple."

Outside the sun was climbing. The sky was a bright, hard blue. The expanse of the golf course shimmered in the rising heat. Far away in the distance, the image of rocks and scrub and hills danced in the thermal pulse of desert air. In the restaurant, Charlie Fiorella was very still, dreading what I might ask.

"Tell Lori Westmann I can help her. TM-7 is gonna clean up by eliminating anyone who knows about it, including her. So, she's got to convince Xochi to serve as a go between for me. I need to meet with the man he sold his secrets to."

"You sure?" Fiorella could read between the lines.

But I didn't answer him. I wasn't sure, just in motion.

Later, Daly had listened to my description of the ideal meeting place: secluded, away from the city, with a high enough rise to create a field of fire and enough cover on the ground to give a reasonable chance of escape. He thought for a while, took out a map, and checked some coordinates. Then we were off.

Southwest of the city along Route 86, he pulled off at a town called Three Points, heading north toward the Ironwood Forest National Monument. He made a series of turns onto increasingly poor roads. On our final turn, the gravel gave out quickly and we bounced along the packed dirt road through the dusty scrub brush toward our final destination.

The road didn't end, it simply dissipated. A single-story adobe building sat along the northern edge of the fan-shaped clearing. The windows were blown out and there was no door remaining. Some blotchy fifty gallon drums were scatted around the side wall of the building. Odd pieces of old metal laid tangled in sporadic clumps around the area.

Hills rimmed the clearing. I squinted into the sun, checked my watch, and mentally noted due west.

"When will the sun be hitting the hill line over there?" I asked. Daley told me. I nodded. "That's when we'll set the meet."

I strode across the clearing and up the western slope, working my way around rocks and through the scrub until I thought we were high enough. At a jumbled cluster of rocks, I looked down on the clearing and the building for line of sight. Then I came back down. Daley watched me silently and said nothing.

"When we meet, I'll ask him to come alone. How likely is it that he'll comply?" I asked him.

Daley snorted. "Not likely at all. These aren't the boy scouts. One way or another, he'll bring backup."

We were down by the building. "Could we get him inside the building?"

"I wouldn't go in, why would he?"

"So it happens here," I said, standing in the dusty wash where the road ended. I poked around. "There's a gulley behind the house, trending north and west. If we had to scramble, we could get in it and head uphill to those rocks."

"It would take some real scrambling, Burke." Daley sounded doubtful. "And what do you mean, 'we'?"

I ignored him. "We'll need to distract them, pull them off balance."

"I can get my hand on some flash-bang grenades," Daley said. "Work better indoors, but they're loud as hell."

The interior of the house was a shambles. It smelled of heat and dust and old paper. I looked out the front windows. "Someone could cover me from here." I turned around and walked to the back wall. A wooden screen door sagged in the back doorway. "Out here if things got tough, into the ditch and off and over the western hill. Sun'll be in their eyes."

I turned around and walked out the front. "This'll work."

"I don't see how," he said.

So I told him.

"And this," the voice on the cell phone said, dripping sarcasm "is your big plan?"

I took a breath. "Hey, it's best to keep things simple. And you told me to keep in touch."

"Yeah," Micky said. "I feel much better now." He may have been concerned, but his sarcasm was still in place.

"You got anything for me?" I demanded. "Otherwise I can hang up and we can argue when I get back."

Daley's apartment was a box, a place where he waited. Nothing more. The walls were painted with the flat, off-white color contractors buy in five gallon tubs. The carpet was cheap and grey. My voice echoed in a room that was largely devoid of any sign of real human habitation: Daley decorated it with a folding lawn chair, some upended plastic milk crates that served as tables and a small television set. Laid upon a bare mattress on the corner of the floor, a rumpled sleeping bag looked like the covered body at a crime scene. Daley sat in his cheap aluminum chair sipping a beer and watching me as I paced in front of the windows, phone to my ear.

"Burke," he whispered. I looked over at him as he gestured at me. "The windows. Get away from them."

The sun was setting, but there was still daylight outside. The lights weren't on in the apartment, so I doubted I was being silhouetted. I thought Daley was being a bit paranoid.

"What, you afraid of snipers?" I said, half joking.

He wasn't smiling. "A surveillance team with a parabolic mike can pick up the vibrations of your phone conversation through the glass. Get away." I humored him and left the broad window at the front of the apartment.

Micky heard the conversation. "Is Daley there?" he demanded. "Put him on." I handed the phone over and Daley wandered into the galley kitchen. I had been in there earlier and it was like the rest of the place: the occasional signs of life only served to heighten the sense of emptiness. The kitchen featured cheap cabinets, a metal sink with a curled yellow sponge, and a case of Bud Light in the refrigerator along with the seemingly inevitable bag of apples. The fake butcher block counter was the resting site for the gnawed remains of half a loaf of stale Italian bread, now the shape and hardness of the head of a medieval war hammer.

Daley's voice reached me as a murmur. I stopped trying to listen and sat down, facing the wall. Sinking into the meditation posture of *seiza* is a movement I have repeated so often in my life that it brings its own sense of comfort, a muscle reminder of who I am and what I do. I needed that centering now.

I began the cadenced series of breaths that would slow the body and calm the mind. My thoughts were jumbled, a racing, disconnected montage of images and ideas. My emotional state wasn't much better. I knew what I had to do. I had an idea of how I would do it. But any fight is a thing of angles, probable moves, and possible permutations. If you dwell too much on the endless ways in which an attack can occur, your focus is shattered. You spend more time dreading what might happen than you do being watchful enough to see what is happening.

Breathe. There were so many ways this could go wrong.

Let the thoughts bubble off. I wasn't sure I could go through with it. And if I did, would Sarah ever speak to me again?

Breathe. I was so exhausted.

I sat, eyelids barely closed, and the warrior's meditative discipline began to take hold. I was sinking and rising, a stone centered on itself, both intensely aware of everything and completely out of the moment. And in that space, I heard Yamashita's voice. Not a memory of him, but his actual voice in striking clarity.

"A battle is won by many things, Burke. Weapons and skill. Terrain. Planning. But most important of all is spirit. Do not give in to doubt or fear. You think you are tired. You are not. Your mind is troubled and uses your body as an ally. Ignore it. Hakka yoi, *Burke."*

My pulse jumped. *Hakka yoi,* the samurai's stern admonition to endure. I opened my eyes, seeing nothing but the blank wall in front of me. At that moment I didn't know what I was more afraid of: what I would have to do or the possibility that I'd be able to do it.

20
SHINKEN

I stood, the warm rays of the sun at my back. The dust swirled in front of the old adobe house. Near the souped-up Hummers that El Carnicero and the other members of TM-7 had driven to the rendezvous, silent men in dark clothes and sunglasses were methodically forcing gang members to their knees and shooting them through the back of the head.

I was frozen, hands up, while a man with a gun watched me intently. Thought was gone; sensation ruled. There was the sight of the reddish wash of light from the setting sun, the glinting metal surfaces of vehicles and weapons. Shadows were growing long. I heard weapons popping and the squealing and the scuffling sound of bodies as they spasmed on the ground. I could smell my own sweat, the resinous scent of creosote bushes, cordite. And the sharp, coppery smell of blood.

I knew then that my plan had gone about as wrong as it could go.

After he finished his hushed phone conversation with my brother, Daley tersely said he needed to go out for a while. It suited me fine. He dragged a heavy duffle out of an otherwise empty closet, kneeled on the floor, and began to remove a trove of weapons from the bag. He laid them side by side in front of him, with a methodical care that reminded me of Yamashita tending to his swords.

"See if anything here looks familiar," Daley told me.

"Whether you might be able to handle it. You've used these sorts of things before?" I nodded, but he didn't seem encouraged. Daley stood up and looked at me with his washed-out eyes. "They're unloaded. Keep 'em that way until I get back with the flash-bangs."

I sat slumped on the floor with my back against the wall, watching him. I didn't move toward the weapons. When he left, I made a phone call of my own.

Steve Hasegawa met me on the fringe of the garden apartment property where Daley kept his lair. There was a meandering pathway ringing the complex, studded with decorative cactus and large rocks. It was supposed to strike you as aesthetic, but I suspected that there were less elevated motives at work. I had seen the shoddy nature of the apartment buildings close up. The rocks were there because the contractor had simply not wanted to bother with the expense of removing them. We walked for a time in the night. Steve listened to my story without comment, but hesitated when I asked for help.

"I saw the pictures on the wall," I urged. "You used to be a pro." The framed picture on the *dojo* wall had showed a leaner, younger Steve Hasegawa, cradling a sniper rifle and wearing the tabs of an Army Ranger.

He smiled sadly. "Long time gone, Burke."

"The skills don't go away," I said.

He looked at me with a type of bemused tolerance. "No, but the attitude does. All that 'hoorah' stuff and the feeling that you're invincible. And maybe the skills don't go away, but they do get rusty." His voice trailed off to get lost in some interior reverie.

"But you *could* do it," I prodded. I had described the layout of the meeting place and what I had in mind. He nodded reluctantly, sighing. "Probably. The distance isn't that great." A faint smile appeared. "I'm rusty, but I'm not that rusty."

"I'm out of options, Steve."

"I know," he said. He looked off into the west where the sun had dropped down out of sight behind the mountains. The distant hills were outlined with a bright line of gold. Above us, stars were coming out.

"It's a pretty night," he began. He stopped walking and looked at me. "You know that my father died?"

I remembered the old man in the wheelchair entering the *dojo* and the tender solicitude that Steve had shown him. There was pain in his voice.

"No," I stammered. "I'm sorry…"

He waved my sympathy away. "It was no way for him to end his life. Strapped in that chair, a prisoner in his own body. In the end, it was a blessing." He walked along the path and I followed.

"You should have seen him in his prime, Burke." The pain in his voice had given way to a sad, gentle pride. "Nobody on the mats could touch him. Nobody, not even your Yamashita." I wasn't going to dispute the claim. We'd be like two overgrown kids arguing about whose father could beat up whom. Steve's memory wasn't about the facts, but about the power of love and the way his father's presence was woven into his life, filling it almost to bursting.

"It was no way for him to go," he repeated. He stopped and looked at me. "We train all our lives, Burke, always trying to get a little better. And for what? Most of us are never going to use these skills in a fight."

"I know," I said. "We strive for perfection," I said, quoting an old article I had written once, "but to what end? We train to be brave, but in what service?"

"Fancy stuff," he grunted.

I shrugged sheepishly. "I have a Ph.D. Sometimes it gets out of control."

"Sure—and what you said was true enough. And, in the end, life will wear us all down."

"Relentless as fire," I agreed, remembering his parting comment the last time I had seen him. My stomach muscles were clenched with tension. I knew the effect my own decision to act had on me; I could imagine Steve Hasegawa's state of mind.

"I know what I'm asking you to do isn't legal," I began.

"Yeah," he grunted, letting out a breath. Then he was silent.

"It's got to be done," I prodded.

He squinted at me. "Not legal, just right?" I nodded.

"Man, Burke," he sighed, "who are we to judge?"

I shrugged. "Two *bugeisha*. Who better?"

Steve Hasegawa nodded thoughtfully, staring at the dirt. Nothing happened for what seemed like a long time. Then he looked up to the fading line of hills and finally craned his neck to take in the stars.

"*Mono no aware*," he told me. "You know the idea?"

"Sure," I said. The sad, powerful beauty of transience. The Japanese insistence that the most beautiful things are, by nature, fleeting.

"I used to think all that old samurai stuff about *bushido* and the glory of death was nuts," he confided. "These days… I dunno. I wouldn't want to go like my father." We walked for a time and then he halted, turning to face me. "So maybe— maybe for once we can *be* the fire, Burke." His rueful smile flashed faintly in the growing dark. "I'm in."

The next day, they came right on time. I had dragged some dilapidated chairs from the house and set them out in the clearing facing each other along an east/west axis. I placed an empty fifty gallon drum between them and put Westmann's manuscript on top. It was, after all, why they were coming. I sat with my back to the western slope where Steve Hasegawa waited with a long rifle, a laser-sighted Bushmaster Predator. The setting sun would be in their eyes. They would, of course, probably all be wearing sunglasses, but I hoped the placement would give me some small edge. I had a wireless earphone on and Steve's voice was clear and calm through it: "They're coming."

I stood up. Daley was right: the Butcher, El Carnicero, wasn't coming alone. The two big Hummers jounced along the road, the wide tires throwing rocks and kicking up the dust. The adobe building was to my left. Daley had placed himself deep in the interior shadows near a window, cradling a snub Heckler and Koch MP5. He took one look at the approaching vehicles and faded away into the building. Part of me wanted to listen for the telltale bang of the back door as he hightailed it into the gulley and away, but I forced myself to face what was coming.

A real fight, a fight to the death, is called *shinken shobu*. There are no rules, just stratagems. You study your opponent, scanning for danger, probing for weaknesses. You know your own faults well enough. Or you should if you pick up a *shinken*, a live sword.

The man who was coming was ruthless. I had thwarted him and he would be angry. He wasn't mentally stable to begin with; being called the Butcher was a tribute to a savage anger and the inability to control it. I could use that.

What did he know of me? Little enough. I was some sort of

scholar who'd stumbled on a manuscript that was valuable for reasons I didn't realize at first. I was also some sort of martial artist, but he was a man who lived in a bloody world. I could imagine his dismissive idea of martial artists—delusional people in exotic pajamas pretending to be warriors. He knew that I had somehow survived the killers he had sent to Brooklyn, but probably believed that it was an accident, a fluke. Now I was on his turf and he would be eager to end this and prove his worth to his gang.

He would think I was naïve. That I would want to make a deal for my life. He'd let me try. He'd play with me for a time. But then he'd take the manuscript and, no matter what deal I'd offer, he'd kill me.

Or he'd try.

There were ten of them, arms and necks dark with the winding stain of tattoos. A few cradled shotguns; many had large, nickel-plated pistols stuck conspicuously in the waistbands of baggy pants. El Carnicero approached me empty-handed. He had thick black hair that was slicked back from a high, narrow forehead. His eyes were hidden behind wraparound sunglasses. His face was lean, and when he smiled you could see the play of muscle and tendon along his jaw line.

"Dr. Burke," he said, with a sarcastic emphasis on the title. He glanced toward the building on his right and made a quick gesture with his head. Two of his men peeled off and checked it. They came out and reported.

"*No hay nadie, jefe,*" one said.

I felt a brief surge of betrayal and remembered Daley's own description of himself: an entrepreneur. The fact that he was gone spoke volumes about his assessment of the situation: there was no profit to be made here.

"You came alone, as promised," el Carnicero said, incredulous. His speech had only the slightest trace of an accent. "Man, you are always a surprise..." He leaned back and said loudly. "He came alone!" His men laughed. The snakes writhed just under skin as he smiled once more. He looked at me, raising his chin up to one side as if critically appraising an object. "Hey, you're not quite what I expected."

The story of my life. But Yamashita has taught me that there are advantages to being more than you seem. To keeping your true nature in the shadows.

"That's what *Los Gemenos* thought," I said.

His chin came down and he faced me directly. The setting sun flashed on the surface of his sunglasses. He raised his arms to indicate the men standing behind them. They formed a rough arc, their backs to the vehicles. "*Mira.* I'm not stupid, bro. I've got backup."

"I told you to come alone." I tried to sound angry.

"Oh, *si...* but I have been doing this too long, man. And rules are meant for games." He turned slightly to his men. "And we're not playing fucking games, eh?" A few of the gang members laughed scornfully at me.

He sat down with a sigh of contentment in one of the chairs. "Hey, think of it as a sign of respect, Dr. Burke. Maybe I think enough of you to believe that you might be dangerous."

I sat down as well. The chairs were far enough from the metal drum that we could see each other. I had measured the distances carefully. It's what all good swordsmen do. The ability to gauge distance and use it to your advantage is a critical skill. Living or dying can be measured in a matter of inches. El Carnicero had a reputation as someone who liked to use a knife. I wanted him far enough away from me to make a deadly lunge difficult.

The dark sunglasses hid his eyes from me, but I could imagine the small darting movements they would make as he assessed the situation.

He leaned forward and placed a hand on the manuscript in its package. Or he could have been shifting his body a few inches closer in preparation for an attack. I felt the air crackle with nuance and dangerous possibility.

"So," he said, "this is the book with Westmann's notes? The lists of the trails?"

"Yes."

He opened the package and leafed through the pages, his lips pressed together as if doing something distasteful. "*Claro*," he said, "but let's be sure, get another set of eyes on this…" He leaned back and turned toward the Hummers.

"Xochi!"

A door opened and Xochi slid out of the vehicle. He looked much as he had that day I met him on the trail: dressed in hiking clothes, his long, dark hair in a loose ponytail, his eyes hid by high-tech sunglasses. But his gait as he approached El Carnicero was hesitant, stiff. Xochi seemed fearful of being near the man. But he came.

Xochi inspected the package, moving carefully through the pages and examining in depth the section with the trail. He avoided looking at me. When he was done, he glanced furtively at me, then nodded to his master and murmured something.

"*Todas las paginas?*"

"*Si*," Xochi answered, "*todas.*" He backed away from the two of us like someone desperate to escape a booby trap, but fearful that his haste might detonate it.

"This book is mine," El Carnicero said, sitting back comfortably in his chair.

"I am willing to return it to you," I said.

Again, the unsettling smile. "Hey, nice. But you know, in my world, you don't get things like this without a price tag."

"Consider it a gift," I said.

It intrigued him. He sat up and leaned forward. "*Un regalo*... this I understand." He wagged a finger at me. "You are a clever one, Dr. Burke. In my culture, gifts entail obligations, *no?*"

I nodded my agreement.

The smile flattened out. The jaw line quivered. "And what would be the obligation that comes with this gift?"

I felt the impulse to mimic his settling back into a relaxed posture in the chair, to appear confident as we dickered. I didn't do it. The position would put me off balance and vulnerable to attack. This is the draining aspect of the high-tension period before a fight is joined; the thousand and one shifts of position and balance and attention, the cascade of sensations that need to be sorted and evaluated for threat.

"Simple," I said. "Leave me alone. Leave those I love alone."

"Simple?" he countered, "I don't think so..."

"I don't care about what you're up to," I broke in. "I live a world away. Take the package. Walk away. I'll do the same."

He laughed then. "Oh, Dr. Burke, man, you don't have the fucking slightest idea about my world, do you?" He gestured and one of his men started to come forward, drawing a pistol.

I held up my hand in the signal Steve and I had agreed on; the green dot of a laser sight flicked on the book in front of us, then onto El Carnicero's chest, then onto the torso of the man with the pistol.

"I understand your world better than you think," I told him.

I wished I could see his eyes, notice whether they widened with fear or tightened with anger. But I couldn't. Was there a slight hunching of the shoulder muscles? El Carnicero stood and I did the same. I could almost sense him tensing for an attack, noting the placement of obstacles, the length of my arms, and just where he would stick the knife.

"Hey, pretty clever, Dr. Burke. You're not so innocent after all… What's next?"

"You take the package and walk away. You never bother me again and I forget we ever met." I knew that I was going to have to kill him, but part of me still hoped I could get him to just walk away.

"*Ay, Dio.* If only it were that simple. For me, you see, there's more at stake…" He gestured at his men. "They follow me because I am a man who achieves what he sets out to do."

"You got the book…" I started, but he grunted in derision.

"Dr. Burke, I sent men to get the book back and punish the one who took it. Only one of my goals has been achieved. So, bro, I'm afraid that I've really got to finish what I started."

One of the gang members near a Hummer started to sidle away into the brush, perhaps hoping to be able to flank me. The echoing crack of the rifle came at the same time that the round punched into the hood of the vehicle near him. The man froze in his tracks.

El Carnicero nodded. "So. You know what they call this in the movies, Burke?" I noticed that the title was gone. He was getting angry, getting ready.

"A Mexican standoff," I said. "Seems appropriate."

"I have more guns than you," he told me.

"My shooter is under orders to kill you first," I told him.

Even through the rifle's scope, the intensity of the situation was clear to Steve Hasegawa. His voice buzzed in my earpiece. *Got you covered, Burke. He's in my sights.* The green laser dot was on El Carnicero.

"Take the packet and walk away," I urged the gang leader. "You get what you want, I drop out of sight and never bother you again." I gestured at his men. "They'll buy that."

But I could tell from the tension in his frame that El Carnicero was not going to take the deal and that I was going to have to follow through with what I had come to do. The anger started to leak out of him, like fluid seeping through cracks in a surface, straining his ability to control it.

The snakes wiggled. He smiled. "Man, you still do not get this…"

Hasegawa's voice. *Movement on the perimeter, Burke.*

"I don't need to understand," I told El Carnicero.

Burke! I got a string of men coming through the brush to the south.

"I just want to walk away," I assured him. But by then we both knew that I was lying.

"You're not walking anywhere, Burke."

Pull out of there, Burke. Hostiles in sight. I'll meet you… Then the transmission was cut off.

I whirled to look behind me up the hill toward Steve's position and El Carnicero lunged at me.

I felt a momentary jolt of fear, and then a perverse relief as experience took over. After all, Yamashita had been launching attacks at me for more than fifteen years. But a real fight is different from the *dojo*. There's a certain crazy intensity at the core of someone who's really trying to kill you. I stayed low, minimizing the target for El Carnicero, letting him enter into my space and turning him slightly so his energy blew past me.

I needed the momentary break in the action so I could spot the knife—a butcher's weapon of choice.

I hate fighting with knives. They can punch into you or slice you up. If they're configured right they can cut you on the thrust or on the backhand withdrawal. It's hard to walk away unscathed. There's an old exercise that's used in karate *dojo* to show just how lethal a knife fight is. The attacker takes a red Magic Marker and uses it instead of the weapon. The defender's job is to disarm the assailant without having the white surface of the *gi* marred by the red marker. Invariably, even in a successful disarming technique, the defender's sleeves and even his torso is slashed with crimson ink that shows where the cuts would have been.

El Carnicero was quick; he arrested his momentum and managed to slam into me. We sprawled in the dirt. *The blade. Watch the blade.* This is where it got tricky. When you were in close and couldn't immobilize the knife. *Finish this quick.* Otherwise, he'd slip the thing in me and it would be all over.

I could hear voices that were raised in alarm all around me, but they were distant, unimportant things. I was collapsing into a dense, frantic organism totally focused on one thing and one thing only. *The knife.*

The boot slammed into me from behind, knocking me breathless. The only reason I survived was because someone else had kicked El Carnicero in the head, stunning him. We were dragged apart. I stood bent over, lungs frozen in momentary nerve paralysis. Then they gave a painful heave and I started breathing again.

The people Steve Hasegawa had spotted now swarmed over and subdued the members of TM-7. They moved with smooth, brutal efficiency; Latinos in camouflage clothing wearing weapons, harnesses, and carrying machine pistols a lot like Daley's. They weren't dressed like gang members. They were young and fit and looked like soldiers.

A man pointed a stubby, black pistol at me. He had a broad, impassive face and a heavy Mexican accent. "What is your name?" he asked. He didn't seem particularly interested in hearing the answer, but I told him anyway. Another man was rolling the stunned El Carnicero over, frisking him, and making sure he had no other weapons. The man with the pistol jerked his head. "And he?"

"He's the one I told you about, Capitán," Daley said, emerging from behind the adobe building. "El Carnicero."

The broad-faced captain smiled. "Ah, *bueno.*" He looked at me. "He doesn't like your friend much, Daley." Then he reached behind him and pulled a thick manila envelope out of his waistband. It looked about the right size to hold a thick wad of money. He tossed it to Daley, who caught it with a grin.

Behind the Capitán, the men with the machine pistols were making gang members kneel in the dirt. Some of the TM-7 people tried to put up a fight. That's when the pistols staring popping and the executions began. The sun was setting; the weapons flashed in the dimming light.

"OK, I delivered them to you," Daley said. It was as if the shooting of young men not thirty feet from where we stood was taking place somewhere else; he was completely disinterested. "Now we boogie out of here. Me and Burke."

The broad-faced man shook his head. "*Lo siento*, Daley. I am afraid he knows too much."

Daley's eyes narrowed. "The deal was that we both walk."

"Deals change," the Capitán sighed. "If I were you, I would go." He began to raise his pistol toward me. As he did, Daley tossed a flash-bang grenade toward us. The man who was about to kill me glanced at the thing rolling toward us for a split second.

And at that exact moment, the scrub all around the perimeter rippled with noise and light and high velocity rounds began slicing through the air.

21
SCRAMBLE

Some kind of rocket or RPG arced in and blew up a Hummer. The detonation made us stagger; the Capitán was already squeezing the trigger of his gun and the shot went wild. Then I heard him grunt, twisting under the sudden force of multiple bullet wounds. I was already moving, and out of the corner of my eye I noticed that El Carnicero was trying to scramble away from the killing zone as well. I stumbled backwards, momentarily incapable of doing anything but taking in the chaotic scene. The smoking Hummer listed, broken backed and pocked with bullet holes. There was someone inside, but he wasn't moving. *Xochi.*

The Capitán's men had been surprised, but they didn't panic. They scuttled into positions, setting up a defensive perimeter with what cover they could get. They were well armed and began returning fire. The surviving gang members, on the other hand, were scrambling in every direction. The meeting place was being lashed with gunfire. The trucks were riddled with bullets, the dust jumped under their impact, and the occasional ricochet zinged through the air.

I finally tore myself away, lurched toward the adobe building and dove through an empty window. Daley was already on the floor there, his face smudged with dust and sweat. His washed out eyes glowed an eerie blue, as if excitement was providing some internal light. From outside, we heard muted yells, shouted orders in Spanish, and the more piercing crack of weapons. Rounds punched in through the walls of the building, showering us with dust.

"We gotta move, Burke," Daley grunted, jerking his head toward the rear doorway. "Get to the arroyo, follow it west; when it forks, take the north branch and hunker down in the rocks up there. You with me?" He didn't wait for a reply. "Let's go!" He cocked his machine pistol, slid across the floor, and shot out the rear door. I hesitated for a moment, not sure that this was what I needed to do. Bullets began gouging larger and larger chunks out of the walls. Splinters of wood mixed in the air with the dust and dirt. I took a deep breath and followed Daley's path out the back.

The arroyo was about five feet deep, a twisting gouge in the earth lined with spindly brush and studded with rocks. I glanced around. Twenty yards to my right, a few gang members were hunkered down in the depression, sticking pistols up and firing blindly in the directions where they thought targets might be. They were cursing and sweating, loading their pistols with frantic, jerky movements and simultaneously casting about for an escape route. The firefight whipped all along the clearing, with muzzle flashes and small explosions everywhere. I glanced along the arroyo bed to the west, but Daley was already out of sight.

I should have followed him. I didn't know what was going on, who was out there in the bush shooting at the Capitán and his men, but I knew that if El Carnicero somehow got away, he'd blame me for this ambush and hunt me down later. I thought of *Los Gemenos*, of the toll already taken on Sarah, and I knew I couldn't let it happen again. If El Carnicero was still alive, I had to get to him and make sure he didn't escape.

It was a crazy idea; I was unarmed in the middle of a roiling gunfight between three armed groups. And perhaps I should have followed Daley's lead and tried to escape myself. But you don't think very clearly when bullet rounds are ripping the air all around you, when you can hear cries of pain and fear and anger even through the din of battle. You're running on impulse and emotion, your mouth dry and your eyes wide. The brain is scanning the environment for danger, not mapping out possible actions three moves ahead.

At this point, it was all body think. I dragged myself over the lip of the arroyo and wormed my way across the hard ground and back into the killing zone. The few surviving TM-7 members had scattered. They were isolated and ineffective, and like the two in the arroyo, appeared to be focused mainly on escape. The Capitán's men, on the other hand, had taken some casualties, but even with the loss of their leader they didn't panic. They were putting out rounds, seeking targets, and calling to one another to coordinate fire and movement.

These were soldier's skills. I realized with a chill that they were the Alphas. It all fit: their jumping the meeting with TM-7 and their animosity toward the gang, their interest in the manuscript with its cross border trails, and their paramilitary appearance. The hair on the nape of my neck rose. I was chilled with the awareness of just how dangerous a place I was in.

I inched my way along the base of one of the building's walls, trying to get a glimpse of the last place where El Carnicero had lain. I tasted dirt and could smell the heat leaking from the rocks as the day waned and the air cooled. The light was fading and the air was filled with a blue mist, but I could see that El Carnicero was gone. Someone spotted my movement. I heard rounds impacting into the wall near me, and the little animal I had become scuttled behind the building and back into the arroyo and relative safety.

I looked to my right. The two TM-7 members down the gully were down, crumpled in the awkward stillness of the dead. And leaning over them was the lean form of El Carnicero, rifling the bodies in search of a weapon.

I went for him without thought or plan. My hands were extended with the urge to break him. I was panting with the effort of bringing all that I had to bear on the attack. The Japanese speak of *kime*, a type of integrated focus that yokes intent and capability, the will of the actor with bone and sinew and muscle memory. But don't be fooled; it's an elegant fiction, far removed from the reality of heat and impulse and blind fury of the battlefield.

There was no *kime* here, or at least not something most people would recognize as such—No elegance—No coordination—just a battered, dusty animal, eyes wild and bloodshot, with every part of his body on fire to do violence.

Even so, it was hard to get much velocity up. The arroyo's floor was uneven and I was ducking the rounds that seemed to be angling in from all directions. But I dug in as hard as I could and set my legs pumping. I needed to get to him before he got a pistol in his hand and spotted me.

El Carnicero turned at the last moment before I got within striking distance. His eyes narrowed, the jaw line writhed, and he raised a pistol, racking the slide, aiming it at me and pulling the trigger, but the magazine was empty. He snarled in fury, but it was too late. I was on him.

There's a trick to generating maximum force for a hit, to slam into another body at high speed: a coiling down of the muscles that pulls your body together into a solid mass before the last, sudden surge into the target. Most people make the mistake of anticipating the impact and unconsciously slowing down. But to really hit someone like this, you've got to tighten together and drive through.

I gave it my best, filling the strike with all the fury I felt for him and what he had done to me, but mostly for Sarah. I heard him grunt with the impact and he went down. But the footing was bad and I lost my balance as well, lurching to my knees a step beyond him on the arroyo floor.

The Butcher was tough, I'll admit that. He was still clutching the pistol as he rolled upright. I spun toward him. His brown hands reached out for me, desperate claws. He slammed the weapon against the side of my head; pain and a ringing in the ears, a spreading warmth that felt like I was bleeding. He scrambled closer and dragged me up against one side of the arroyo wall. There was no attempt to hit me, he was simply driving with both hands to get me upright. I heard the crack of a high velocity round go by my head.

He's propping me up. Hoping someone out there will take a shot at me.

And they did. I slammed down on his forearms and twisted away to get below the lip of the gully where the bullets couldn't reach. He was on me in a flash.

We rolled and lurched around on the dry ground. Rocks dug into my back. I was reaching for the soft tissue of his face, hoping to get a strike in to the eyes. He grunted as he drove repeated knee blows at me, trying for the groin, but I deflected them. He ended up battering my thigh muscles instead. *Rectus femoris. Vastus lateralis.* It's odd the things that shoot in disconnected bursts through your mind when you're fighting for your life. I knew that these muscles were big and strong ones, but I also knew that they weren't going to take this much pounding indefinitely.

We jerked and slammed each other, searching for a point of entry, a gap in defense—a place to land a killing blow. But grappling doesn't work that way. It's more cunning than brute force. It requires you to harness the fury into something that could be fluid and patient, but ultimately more deadly in its relentless search for an opening.

Maybe that's what brought me back to myself—somewhat. I hadn't completely slipped the reins of years of training. Something about the fight was familiar, and even in the heat of the struggle, I experienced a type of clarity and detachment, even as I tried every trick I knew.

A good, experienced ground fighter will keep tight contact with his opponent. The fight slips and morphs in a thousand subtle ways. You need the broad tactile input of contact to sense an opportunity, a shift in position or leverage that flashes the potential for a counter. But El Carnicero didn't know that. He wasn't a ground fighter, he was a butcher used to hacking his way through his victims. He reared back to get more force into one of his knee attacks, and I used the gap as well as his momentum to turn him, pushing with the force of his windup. It was enough to create the opening I sought, and I slipped around behind his back.

I circled his waist with my legs and managed to get him in a choke hold. It was a variant of *hadaka-jime*: nothing fancy, but effective. You put your left forearm across the victim's throat, push the head forward with the right arm, and pull back with the left. El Carnicero knew he was in trouble; he bucked and slammed me into the arroyo floor, trying to break the hold.

I wasn't letting go. He pounded me back onto the rocks and

my breath left me, returning only in a feeble, ragged flow. He sensed that he had hurt me, and writhed to escape the hold, swinging back with furious elbow jabs. But he didn't know enough to drop his jaw down to blunt the choke. If I could hold on long enough…

My ears were ringing and I was totally focused on the goal of choking him to death. But, for a moment, the outside world broke in and I sensed that the firefight above us was slackening. Time was short.

I finally got it right. He arched his back in panic. I heard the juttering breath just before he blacked out. His body went limp.

Finish it. I knew how: a slight readjustment of the arms to align force on the vertebrae, set up the angles, then a quick, hard jerk.

Yamashita would do it. After all, he had shown me the technique.

But I'm not Yamashita. I couldn't bring myself to do it. Maybe it was foolish, but I couldn't do it, not like this. Not with him unconscious and at my mercy.

I lay there for a minute, sensing new voices and sounds. The shooting had grown sporadic. I needed to get my brain working again, get working on a plan. *What now?*

Then someone tossed a flash-bang grenade in the ditch with us and the world was filled with a roaring flash, a paralyzing wave of light and noise designed to overload the neural circuits.

I was laying there stunned, mouth open, gaping at the darkening sky, when a figure loomed over me. His skin was dark and weathered, the corners of his eyes crinkled with lines from years in the sun. He was wearing desert fatigues and pointing a CAR-15 in my direction.

He looked at the two of us. "You a bad guy or a good guy?" he asked. His English had the unique inflection of a Native American.

I had to swallow a few times. "Good guy," I croaked.

He nodded, rolled El Carnicero off me and extended a hand. Behind him, other men looking much like he did were checking out the bodies of the gang members in the arroyo.

He hauled me to my feet. I was a bit shaky and my thighs burned. I bent over, hands on my knees and gagged. I spit into the dust. The man waited patiently until I had straightened up. He gestured at the unconscious gang leader on the ground. "Him?"

"Bad guy."

He turned from me for a moment to scan the clearing. He had a radio handset clipped to his harness and he spoke into it. It gabbled back and he nodded.

"That your friend upslope with the sniper rifle?"

Steve. I had completely forgotten him. I nodded.

"He's OK," he told me. "One of my men is bringing him down."

A lean, younger man walked toward us along the rim of the arroyo. He was dressed in the same desert wear as the others, but was no Indian. He stopped and looked down at us.

"Who are you?" he demanded.

"Burke," I stammered.

He nodded as if mentally ticking a point off some list. Then he grunted, shifting mental gears. "Jackson, can you have your people work the perimeter in case some of these characters got away into the bush? Use the night vision gear."

The Indian named Jackson shrugged. "Won't help much in cutting sign. But it's sandy enough here. Should be no problem."

"Night's coming on. Watch for rattlers."

Jackson bridled at that. "We know our job, and we know our land."

The man above us pursed his lips for a minute then nodded. "Point taken," he said, and then asked who was lying at our feet. When I told him, he gave a low whistle.

"El Carnicero. The Butcher, huh? So how'd he end up like this?"

"I choked him out," I said.

"You tussled with this guy?" the man asked.

"He has it in for me," I explained. It was simplistic and lame, but only too true.

"Yeah, but you…" I was obviously not looking too impressive. Then he continued. "Well, it's a shame you didn't kill him. Guy like this has got a long rap sheet and plenty of wants and warrants. He'll do time, for sure, but it's not gonna faze him, ya know? He'll run the gang from inside, recruit some new members…" He snorted in amusement. "Get some new tats, build on his legend." He squinted down at me. "I wouldn't want to be someone he had it in for, though." His voice had a thoughtful tone.

A voice called and he turned toward the sound, waved, and then looked down at us from his place on the lip of the arroyo. "Jackson, why don't you take Dr. Burke here over to the other side of the clearing? We got a medic who can clean him up and check for wounds." I realized that blood was caking in my left eye, pulling the lid down, and gluing it shut. "Then get your men out along the perimeter to look for strays. We need to police the area and arrange for a dust-off. We don't want our guest here wandering around—one more loose end, ya know?" He winked at me as we climbed up and moved past him.

"What about him?" Jackson said, gesturing at El Carnicero.

"I got it," the young man said.

"What's that mean? You want him secured or what?"

The lean face clouded. "Jackson, you people are here in a support capacity. I'm calling the shots. Just get the men out into the brush like I told you."

I could sense the older man's resentment swirl up for a moment. The he took a breath, sighed, and shrugged his shoulders. "Come on," he said, "let's get you cleaned up."

There were men in desert camo everywhere checking the bodies that were humped in random spots around the clearing. Voices crackled over radios. A medic had set up near the adobe building and was swabbing a wound on a man who leaned, grimacing, against the wall.

But my thoughts were still in the arroyo. "What's going on?" I hissed to Jackson.

Jackson held my upper arm and propelled me forward. His grip was gentle, but it was firm. "Not your worry. Not mine either."

"Whattaya mean? The Butcher— we've got to make sure that he doesn't get away." I turned, arching my neck to try to see what was happening. But Jackson prevented me from getting a good look.

"You just keep moving, mister," he advised. "Nothing you want to see back there." His voice sounded sad and resigned, but calm.

The desert was hushed with the arrival of twilight, a quiet pause before the true dark arrived. It was a false tranquility; in the desert, darkness and danger were linked together. Nighttime was when the predators ruled.

The sound of the muffled shot from the arroyo, the metallic

clink of an automatic pistol's slide was unmistakable. After a few seconds, the lean man strode past us, holstering his pistol and giving orders. The man named Jackson set his face like stone and propelled me away.

22
DEPARTURES

The hangar was a vast cavern. Helicopters slumbered in the shadows like immense prehistoric insects. They had dumped us here after the dust off. Steve Hasegawa and I sat in a small, partitioned office with metal chairs and too much paperwork on the desk. There was a small lamp that gave little real light but seemed to feed the shadows. We slumped in the chairs while Jackson's men and the other team bustled around in the dim hangar.

"Well," Steve told me quietly, "that was something."

"You ever see anything like it?"

He thought for a moment, reliving memories. "Not stateside."

"Me neither. Who are these guys?"

Steve got up and peered out a window into the hangar proper, cautiously moving the blinds with his fingers to spy on the goings on.

"The guys who picked me up on the hill are part of some all-Indian team of trackers—Jackson's team. They work for the Border Patrol on smuggling interdiction."

"What about the other guys?"

He sat back down, closing his eyes, and rubbing his face with both hands. "I don't know who they are. But I know the type. Jackson's guys are trackers. These other people are hunters."

"What's the difference?" I said.

He took his hands away from his face and looked at me

like I was a simpleton. "Trackers follow things. Hunters follow things to kill them."

In the stillness of that room, I could once again hear the muffled report of the shot and the clank of the pistol receiver as the lean man had finished El Carnicero in that arroyo.

We both sat in silence for a time.

"Did you ever actually get a shot off with that rifle?" I asked.

"No," he said, shaking his head.

"Are you sorry you didn't?"

"Me? No. I figured I was there for insurance…"

I nodded. "That part at least worked out. When you lit them up with the laser, it gave me a little more time to negotiate. I was worried that they were going to dispense with all small talk and just shoot me."

"As it turns out, there was lots of shooting anyway, Burke."

I said nothing, and Steve continued. "Those Indians snuck up on me pretty good, I gotta give 'em that."

"The red man is notoriously stealthy," I said. For a moment, I got a mental image of my brother Micky and Art. It was the kind of comment either one might make. I wondered what it would be like with them when I returned. I hadn't actually pulled the trigger on the weapon that killed El Carnicero, but we were all complicit.

Steve broke in on my thoughts. "I think the politically correct phrase is Native American. They got the drop on me good and ghosted me down the hill just as hell broke loose."

The door opened and the lean man with the pistol entered. He grimaced at the cluttered desk and slapped a new folder on the pile of papers that was already there. He leaned one hip against the desktop, crossed his arms, and stared at us.

"Gentlemen," he said without preamble, "you managed,

through ways that we need not detail, to get yourself into the middle of a classified operation that was targeting some high-profile border smugglers. How you are still alive is anyone's guess, and your good fortune."

"I can explain," I began.

The man shook his head. "Dr. Burke, when I said that we need not go into any detail on your involvement, I mean that we don't need to go into any detail." The words were spat out with emphasis. "Am I clear? It is buried so deep that, officially, it doesn't even exist."

He addressed Steve Hasegawa. "I ran a check on you. You were in the 75th. You know the drill."

Steve nodded. His voice sounded tired. "We were never there."

"What about Daley?" I asked. I had glimpsed him in the gloom of the site of the desert shoot-out, so I knew he had survived. But he hadn't been in the chopper with us.

"Dr. Burke," the lean man said, "Daley is another detail we don't need to discuss. His involvement is completely off the record."

I looked from one man to the other. "So," I said cautiously, "we're off the hook?"

The lean man removed some documents from his folder. "The Patriot Act outlines any number of situations where citizens are compelled, under force of law, to maintain absolute silence about anything they may or may not have seen in the course of classified security operations, foreign..." he paused for emphasis, "... or domestic.

"I'll need each of you to sign this acknowledgment form, binding you not to reveal any of the events you witnessed, under pain of prosecution." He clicked a pen. We signed. When it was over he looked us up and down.

"Hasegawa, there's a ride waiting to take you home. Burke, you're going to be escorted to the civilian side of the airport and put on the next available flight to New York." He put this folder under his arm, gave us one last look, and disappeared into the hangar.

When a Border Patrol agent came for Steve, he stood up and extended a hand. "Good luck, Burke."

"Thanks, Steve," I said.

He nodded. "Come visit some time when you're not in trouble."

I smiled sheepishly. "Might be some time."

He nodded and shrugged. "I'm not going anywhere."

A dour uniformed Border Patrol officer escorted me to the civilian portion of the airport. He handed me off to an equally charming guy in the white uniform shirt of a TSA agent, then stood with folded arms to ensure that I didn't set the metal detector off and make a break for it.

I had hours to kill until the flight. I like airports: the suspension of the normal routine and surroundings, the muted wash of crowds flowing up and down the corridors, the endlessly fascinating parade of people in all their varieties. I sat for a time in one of a series of white painted rockers by a huge window and watched planes take off and land. I wandered the aisles of the bookstore and scanned the magazines. The usual suspects smiled at me from the glossy covers: golfers and movie stars and thin, surly-looking musicians with names I didn't recognize. I browsed the skimpy philosophy section: no *Decline of the West*—probably not a fast-moving title out here in Arizona, or anywhere else, for that matter.

Back out on the concourse, I moved aimlessly, filling the time with random observations. I had a mediocre sandwich and a nice beer. I had another drink and watched the television. I didn't want to have to think too much. Watching the cable station they had tuned in at the bar would probably actually kill some of my brain cells and solve this problem for me.

Walking back to the gate area, something caught my attention. It was a peripheral glance at a lanky form waiting for his seat number to be called on a flight to San Diego. I took a second look: tanned, clean-shaven, with freshly cut hair and very pale eyes behind rimless glasses. He wore a summer-weight, tan suit and woven leather loafers. His blue shirt made his eyes almost glow. He was finishing an apple.

Daley watched me as I approached, a crooked smile on his face.

"On your way back east?" he said.

I nodded. "And you?"

He crossed his legs, hiking up the leg of his trousers to preserve its nice crease. "Heading west."

"Of course."

"Of course," he echoed.

"Who are you really, Daley?"

He shrugged. "I work deals, Burke. Angles. I generate—innovative solutions to thorny problems." He smiled at that, his long, yellow teeth showing in pleasure.

"But who do you work for?" I persisted.

Daley took off his glasses and wiped the lenses while looking at me with those pale eyes. "Probably not a detail you need to concern yourself with, Burke."

I sat down next to him. "Know what I think?" He turned toward me, a small gesture of polite interest. "I think you set up that whole ambush."

"Now, why would I do that?"

"The opportunity was too good to pass up," I said. "You had the manuscript as bait…"

"And you," he said, "don't forget you."

"And me. Once I arranged the meet with TM-7, you contacted the Alphas and arranged for them to be there as well." I paused for moment, remembering the envelope the Capitán had tossed Daley just before everything went haywire. "How much did the Alphas pay you, Daley?"

He smiled briefly. "Given the situation, not nearly enough."

"And you brought in the Border Patrol people."

"Slick, wasn't it? Like icing on the cake."

I shook my head. "So what you do, is it just for money?"

"Burke," he said quietly, "it's never just about the money. But if a little extra happens to come my way in the course of my activities…" he shrugged. "I told you. I'm an entrepreneur."

The gate agent called his seat and he stood up and offered a hand. "You take care, Burke."

I looked at his destination. "San Diego."

"Border town," he said, then winked at me as he headed toward the gate. "Opportunity calls."

He ghosted through the entranceway and was gone.

I spent the flight alternately pretending I was asleep on the one hand, and sleeping and dreaming I was awake on the other. It made for a tremendously restful experience. The cabin was crowded, the engines loud, and my mind was like a vast floor where the pieces of the past few days had been shattered, leaving jagged and disconnected memories.

He was waiting for me at the airport; I knew he would be.

I exited the concourse and walked up to him, saying nothing.

"Bag?" Micky said.

"No."

He grunted and gestured for me to follow along.

Outside, he had parked the car in a no-parking zone—old habits die hard. Micky waived to a transit cop on the pavement when we emerged.

"How'd it go?" he asked. He pointed his remote at the car and its locks chirped open.

"You know how it went."

"Do I?" He moved around the car as if to get in. We looked at each other across the roof of the vehicle.

I slide the cell phone he had lent me across the car top. "It's GPS enabled, Mick," I told him. "You were tracking me every step I took."

He shrugged. "So?"

"And your pal Daley— he's not some retired INS guy, is he?"

Micky looked at me and said nothing.

"You used me," I said. "Me."

He smirked. "Connor, don't be an asshole. Like you weren't using me?"

"It's not the same."

"No? Lemme fill you on a few things." His finger jabbed angrily at me. "You had those lunatics from TM-7 on your case. What was I gonna do? Nothing?"

"I thought we had agreed that I would handle it."

He cut me off. "Connor, you were so far in over your fuck-ing head, it was a miracle you could see daylight at all!"

"So you used me," I repeated.

"I cut a deal! If we could work a way to nab some high-profile smugglers, I could get you some backup."

"Nab 'em? Mick, it was a fucking free-fire zone!" Now I was getting hot.

He shrugged. "Like your plan was gonna be any safer? Connor, when you get involved in these things, it's always a little iffy."

"You could have told me!"

Micky shook his head. "Nah. You're not a good enough actor. And we needed an outsider with no connections to the local scene. I needed you strung out and working on the edge for this thing to work."

"And did it?" For a moment I was back there, the bodies in the desert, the night falling and the lone sound of a silenced pistol going off.

"Oh yeah," he said.

"I don't believe you did this…"

He snorted. "Don't be so fucking high and mighty. You were going out there to kill someone."

"You know why I did that!"

He waived it away. "Doesn't change the facts."

I slammed the roof of the car in anger. The Transit cop began to drift over, but Micky waived him away.

My brother's eyes hardened. His face was tight and focused and cruel in a way I'd never seen before.

"What is it you don't like, Connor? The fact that all your martial art skills weren't enough? That I had to rig something to get your ass out of a wringer?"

"I didn't ask you for any help!"

· He snorted. "Bullshit. Every time you need information, you come to me. Every time you need help, you come to me. So accept it and shut up. You take a good fucking look at yourself, you asshole," he said. "Think about what you're really mad at. Is it me? Or you?" I started to say something, but he kept right on. "You think this world is so cut and dry? Black and white? Grow up!" He glanced around in fury, gathering more steam.

"You decided to get into this stuff, Connor. You walked in, eyes wide open. It's my world, and let me tell you, everyone cuts deals. Everyone uses everyone. Once in a great while, like now, it works out. But nobody walks away clean or comes out whole." His voice cracked. "Nobody."

What was there to say? We glared at each other across a car's roof, snarling animals, bodies in rigid postures familiar since boyhood. Around us, the bustle of the airport created a jumbled, jerky background, both prosaic and surreal.

I turned away. Angry. Resentful.

"Where ya goin'?"

"Home," I said.

My brother said nothing. No plea to stop or get in the car—to think things through. He watched me with distant, cold eyes. But his heart cracked for a moment.

"I gonna see you again?" he croaked.

I turned toward him, walking backwards for a minute.

"Now who's being the asshole?" I said, and left him.

23

SHELLS

Part of me wanted to head to the *dojo* in Red Hook, but I wasn't sure what kind of welcome I'd get. So I headed home to the empty house in Sunset Park. I was weary and hoped things were over. But I was wrong.

The red message light was winking, and I played the series of phone calls that Sarah's sister Deborah had left for me since that morning, increasingly frantic with worry. By the time we spoke, Deborah was almost incoherent. Sarah was gone. A simple trip for groceries that shot her down a wormhole. Her car empty in a local shopping center, and the cops advising the family that they'd have to wait the usual forty-eight hours before an official search could begin.

We didn't have to.

"I have her," he breathed. Even on my cell phone, I could hear that his voice was thick, as if the excitement were choking him.

"Martín?" I asked. He didn't answer. He didn't have to.

"Anything, "I said then, a jet of adrenalin arching through my chest but my voice as dry as dust. "Anything you want."

"I need the manuscript," he said. "You deliver it. Alone. No cops."

They always warn you about the cops. In a kidnapping, the experts say that going it alone is the worst thing you can do. But I knew deep down that this was more than just a kidnapping.

And the ransom was simply an excuse: he didn't even realize that the people who had initially paid him were all dead. And he didn't care; Martín would want me there by myself for his own reasons. So, it would turn out, did I.

Martín told me what he wanted me to do. I stalled, trying to figure out my options. "I'll need a car," I explained.

"Call this number when you get it," he said, reciting the digits. "Hurry. I think your woman needs you." He laughed and then hung up.

I went first to the *dojo*, of course. I swallowed my pride and Yamashita knew it. He sat, immobile, as I told him what had happened. He pursed his lips, thinking for minute, then rose to his feet; smooth and powerful, a wave swelling and gathering momentum.

"I'll get my weapons," he said.

We were on the road for twenty minutes before I called the number I had been given. The voice that answered was not Martín, but it told me what to do. Yamashita sat beside me in the car, watching me with the merciless intensity of a tiger.

"You know this place?" he asked.

I nodded tightly. "Port Jefferson. North Shore. Suffolk County. With luck we'll make it in an hour and a half."

"You told the man on the phone two hours."

"I lied," I said.

Yamashita nodded approvingly. "And you are not telling your brother." A statement, not a question, but I answered anyway.

"They said no cops. If I let Micky know, he'd probably have to let them know. It's probably best that he's not involved." I didn't mention that we weren't talking.

My teacher was silent for a time. He gazed out at the concrete flow of the road. I swerved around the traffic, frantic to reach a destination where I would in all likelihood die. I was like a man on a flimsy raft, desperately avoiding the jagged rocks of the river, even as the distant roar of the falls thundered ultimate disaster.

"This man Martín is the contract killer?" Yamashita asked. I nodded. "And you have killed his lover." I shrugged. Yamashita swiveled his torso in my direction, his eyes intent. "So he has no real interest in the manuscript, Burke."

"No," I admitted. We sat for a while in silence, working through the implications in our own separate ways. The tires hummed.

"What will you do?" my teacher asked.

"I don't know," I said evasively. I didn't want to go through this again. There's a big distinction between self-defense and premeditation. I knew I had almost stepped over that line in Arizona; it was only my brother's machinations that had saved me. I had gone there to kill El Carnicero. Perhaps it was too fine a distinction, but I was holding on to it, it made me feel a little less cold-blooded. I could still feel the sting of Sarah's accusations. Was I just a good man who ended up in these situations by accident, or was I some kind of adrenalin junkie who sought them out? What I was thinking now was too close to the things she had accused me of.

"Burke!" Yamashita's voice was low and intent. In the close confines of the car, his energy was startling, a shaped charge detonating in a tight place. "You must do what you must do!"

I drove the car in silence—My mind, not so silent. As the miles reeled off, Yamashita's quiet voice prodded me through other terrain. He had done this before, a patient teacher herding an ox of a student into painful awareness. He has never promised me a life free of pain, only one free of delusions.

At the point where we passed the exit for the Seaford-Oysterbay Expressway, he stirred and broke into my thoughts.

"Beat the grass and surprise the snake," he told me.

I grunted. It's an old Zen saying that means something along the lines that it was better to hurt one thing a little than have to hurt something else more.

"You recognize it?" my teacher prompted.

I let out a stream of air. "Yagyu Munenori," I said. A master swordsman of the famous Yagyu family, he would have been good to have along on this trip, but he's been dead for almost four centuries.

"Indeed. A complex man. He used the adage in a way that can be interpreted in various ways."

"How so?"

"Think Professor," he smiled tightly. "The motto of the Yagyu…"

"*Katsuninken, satsuninto*," I replied, ever the dutiful student. The life giving sword can also be a death dealing sword.

"So…" Yamashita breathed. "Martín wishes us to think we are engaged in a ransom attempt."

"We are," I protested.

Yamashita waived a hand. "Stop hiding. You know it is other than this. This man wishes to kill you. His plan is to lure you into a trap and finish what he started—to avenge himself on you and Sarah."

"I know," I admitted. "I've been wracking my brains for ways to get Sarah away, safe, and sound."

"Of course," Yamashita said, "but you are thinking about

the wrong thing. A focus on rescue clouds your mind. It prevents you from grasping what you must really do."

"Which is?"

My teacher sighed and settled back in his seat. "The only way to save Sarah Klein is to not try to save her. You must let Martín think you are on the defensive for a while and lull him into a sense of control. Then do the unexpected."

"How so?"

"He wishes you to come alone. He will expect you to try to bargain with him—to talk your way to a solution. Part of him will want this. He will, I think, enjoy the spectacle and the secret knowledge that, when all is done, he will kill you both.

"There is a rhythm to a fight, Burke. You know this. Move and countermove. An expectation of how events will transpire." He nodded to himself. "We can use this."

"OK," I said. But I wasn't quite clear yet as to what he was proposing.

Yamashita could sense it; he peered at me for a moment, reading my agitation and my uncertainty.

"I will be there, Burke. My presence will be unexpected and it will distract him."

"And then?"

"And then," he said brightly, "we will avail ourselves of an old *ninja* trick; very ancient, very reliable."

"Which is?"

"While I distract Martín, you will sneak up behind him and kill him." He sounded pleased with the tidiness of the solution.

At that moment, I resented him. It's not the first time I've felt this way. In the past, the psychic tug of war of training had often left me sullen and angry. But Yamashita has a way of battering through your defenses, of shredding your delusions until you stand, trembling yet clear-eyed, in the place to which he has led you.

I realized that I had always clung to Munenori's idea of a life-giving sword, and believed in the training as a way to somehow make me a better person. The science of how to cut and where, of the vulnerabilities of the human body, had always seemed arcane and exotic knowledge. They were things of a bygone era; knowledge that was dated and rendered impractical. I thought the sword a symbol and suppressed the knowledge of how fearsome the blade could be. Now I would be asked to fully engage in the killer's art. I could not hide behind the justification of self-defense as I had in the past. Yes, Sarah's life was the bait but the truth was that I wanted Martín dead. It made me doubt myself. My motives. My ability to stay whole.

He has always been amazingly perceptive, but lately Yamashita's ability in this regard had increased tremendously. It's as if the wounds and injuries that are slowing him down physically, have simultaneously channeled his energy in new ways.

He touched my arm, a rare instance of intimate contact. His hands are still thick and strong looking, although the joints swell with arthritis, and residual damage from torture makes his left hand weaker than it has been, but the flow of something powerful yet intangible was in that touch. It was as comforting as it was terrifying.

"Burke," he said, "the sword's blade has two faces, *ura* and *omote*. They have been forged together for a purpose. Sometimes the sword is a thing of beauty, at other times it is put to other uses."

"How can you be sure that the uses—that you're doing the right thing?" I croaked.

He smiled contentedly. "Burke, you know the purpose behind this."

"To save Sarah. To stop Martín."

"Yes. And you know that the police will not be able to do this in time. And Martín must be killed."

"I know," I admitted.

We drove in silence for a short time, and then I pulled off onto Rte. 110 South.

"A detour?" Yamashita sounded more interested than alarmed, a scientist watching his newest experiment bubble.

"Big snake," I told him. "I need a bigger stick."

The squat building had firearms lining three walls, with counters separating the merchandise from the buying public. The salespeople were friendly, informative, and all had small pistols clipped to their belts. In this world, everyone was courteous and contained, but clearly the clerks would shoot you if you got out of line. Different tools, but not so different from Yamashita's *dojo*.

The purchase process itself didn't take long; the salesman was informative and enthusiastic in a creepy sort of way. I settled on a Remington 870 Express 12-gauge shotgun.

"The eighteen-inch barrel makes it easier to use in home defense situations," the salesman informed me. I had confided that I was worried about crime in my neighborhood. He nodded in sympathy, but his eyes lit with enthusiasm. He set a few boxes of shells on the counter as we processed the sales paperwork.

"You'll want these," he informed me.

"Number one buckshot," I read. "Not double-ought?" My gun knowledge is not deep; I was relying on jargon I'd heard in movies.

"Nope. The International Wound Ballistics Association says number one buckshot is the superior choice for home defense. This shotshell has the capacity to produce 30 percent more wound trauma than other shotshell loads." He nodded to himself with satisfaction. This was obviously a conversation he'd had before. "Plus," he added with the flourish of a conjuror producing yet another amazing item, "it's less likely to over-penetrate or exit the target. Reduces the risk of collateral damage."

"Deadly and yet safe," I said. "It's good to know." He looked at me sharply, sensing sarcasm. I kept my face expressionless and waited to see if his gun hand was going to twitch toward his holster. But the moment passed.

I bought a duffel bag to carry the gear and he cashed me out. I tossed it in the trunk of the car, got back in, and told Yamashita what I'd been up to.

"And they sold you this weapon— just like that?" he said, incredulous. He's spent a lifetime developing lethal skills and I imagined it disgusted him that it's possible to accelerate the process with a clean record, a driver's license, and a credit card. Where was the sweat, the discipline, the process where the character was forged into something new and tensile and beautifully lethal? But the day's events reminded both of us that the world is as it is, not as we wish it to be.

I slipped the car into gear as we headed back to the Expressway. I checked my watch. We were good. I'd make Martín's deadline.

"Sometimes your country alarms me," my *sensei* said.

When I hit Exit 64 for Port Jefferson, my cell phone rang. "Burke," I said.

"Where are you?" the thick voice of Martín asked. I could hear him breathing.

"I'm just getting off the Expressway onto Rte 112," I told him.

"The ferry to Bridgeport leaves in forty minutes. There is a reservation for you. Take the car. Go to the terminal in Connecticut."

"And?" I demanded. "What then?" But the voice was gone.

"They're leading us along," I told Yamashita. "Probably to make sure that we're not being followed by anyone. And crossing a state line means that it would make it that much more difficult for us to involve the cops."

"He has thought this out," Yamashita told me. "You will be watched to ensure you are alone. We must maintain an element of surprise. Drop me off before the ferry terminal and I will board as a passenger. Leave the car unlocked and I will hide in it just before we disembark."

"What if they spot you?"

He smiled tightly. "Burke, they will be looking for plain-clothes policemen. A broken down, old man will not attract their attention."

The crossing was smooth—the Long Island Sound an expanse of gray water and the low coast of Connecticut a hazy smudge on the horizon. I leaned on the rail in the cool wind and watched the froth that was churned up by the boat's passage. I thought of what I would do and how I would do it. After a time I sat down, slightly queasy. The trip seemed to take a long time.

When I got to the terminal in Connecticut, my phone rang and another voice told me to look on the bulletin board by the restrooms. An envelope had been tacked there with my name on it. Inside was a menu for the Golden Mountain Restaurant in Bridgeport. *Comidas Chinas,* the banner said. Someone had circled the address and written "Go here."

It wasn't a nice part of town, but then Bridgeport has seen better days in general. The streets were dirty and old cars sagged and rusted along listing curbs that were slowly surrendering to time and neglect. Most of the storefronts had signs in Spanish. The Golden Mountain was no exception.

I took a deep breath outside the restaurant, marveling that the world seemed so prosaic and worn and normal looking. But it was an illusion, or at best a blurry backdrop, glimpsed fleetingly as I hurtled down a tunnel that was getting tighter and darker with every second.

Less thought, Burke. More action. Was it Yamashita's voice I heard in my head, or my own?

It was a classic storefront Chinese takeout place, with a few wobbly Formica tables and industrial strength chairs set by the plate glass windows for diners who were not overly concerned with ambience. A chest high counter was at the far end, with stacks of takeout menus, a can of pencils, and a backlit menu overhead, with bright pictures of Chinese food. A short hall led to the right, away from the dining area. Signs on the wall promised a fire exit and a restroom. An old woman, her face puckered with decades of work, sat behind the counter. In the kitchen behind her, woks clanged and sizzled, manhandled by thin Asian boys with scraggly facial hair and grease-spotted baseball caps.

Two Hispanic men were draped over some chairs. Tattoos dotted their hands, circled their wrists, and climbed like black vines up their necks. When I came through the door, one of the men looked at the woman. She slid off her stool and disappeared from sight. The kitchen noises faded. At the counter, a phone rang and nobody answered it.

They stood on either side of me, muscle and dark ink and hostility. They wore baggy street clothes and one had a nickel-plated revolver dangling from his hand. The other man gestured at me. I showed him the plastic bag I carried that was filled with a bundle of paper I had doctored up to look like Westmann's manuscript. It was long gone, but this guy didn't know that. It was wasted energy: he peered in at the bundle, but didn't seem interested in any real way. I put my arms up and he patted me down, searching for a weapon. Satisfied, he stepped back, flipped open a cell phone, and had a short conversation, staccato vowels in a Latin rhythm. But I heard my name mentioned. He nodded me toward the narrow hall that led off to the restrooms and the fire door.

While we were doing this, an old Asian man limped in, lugging a duffel bag. The one with the gun looked at him, annoyed.

"*Oye, Viejo! Esta cerrado!*" But the old man obviously didn't understand. He gestured helplessly, mumbled something, and started toward the counter. They propelled me toward the fire door. The guy with the gun went for the old man, and I got shoved along the hall by his partner so I couldn't see what happened next.

But I heard the sound of the strikes hitting a body, the whoosh of air as it was forced out of the lungs, and the sound of the gun hitting the floor. My escort heard it, too. He turned back, his eyes leaving me for a moment. It was a mistake.

I'm not sure whether he really registered what had happened in the restaurant; I hit him so hard he blacked out briefly. But there Yamashita stood over a crumpled body, holding the shiny pistol in his hand like it had germs. He came toward me, still lugging the duffel.

Time, Burke. Move fast.

My escort's knees had buckled and I took him down to the floor. I put him in a basic armlock and set my knee on his neck while I searched him for a weapon. I pointed with my chin to the other man.

"Dead?"

Yamashita feigned shock. "Dead? No. But he will be unconscious for a while."

"What happens when he comes to?"

"He will have other issues to deal with. I broke both his collar bones. It will make using something like this," he dangled the pistol in front of him, "difficult."

The man beneath me was stirring: I could feel the muscle tension build in his arm and neck. I found what looked like a .45 automatic stuffed in his waistband. I put the muzzle against the base of his skull and released the arm lock. His eyes rolled back as he tried to get a glimpse of me.

"Get up," I told him.

Time. Don't give them time to think. It cuts both ways.

He was wobbly, but he managed to get to his feet by sliding up along the wall.

"Where are we going?" I asked.

He shrugged sullenly. I pulled the slide back on the pistol, the movement of metal loud in the little hallway. I ground the pistol up under his jaw and jerked my head in the direction of his friend.

"You wanna end up like that? My friend here can make it so you never walk again." He lived in a world where the threat of violence was not an idle one. He knew danger when he saw it. He could hear the fury in my voice.

"The repair shop," he mumbled grudgingly. His accent was thick, but it was clear enough.

"Where?"

His eyes moved to the fire door. "Out the door. Down the alley."

"They're expecting me?"

His eyes flickered from side to side as if searching for options, calculating his chances.

I pushed the pistol so he gagged slightly. "Don't," I ordered. His eyes came back to me and he nodded in surrender.

"I am to take you."

"Let's go, then."

The alley featured a few battered dumpsters, shattered remnants of wooden loading pallets, and broken glass. It smelled of old cooking oil and the acrid grit of city air. At the far end, I could see the rolled steel doors of the bays of the auto repair shop. There was an entrance door to the right and a narrow drive leading down the left side of the building to the rear. We halted in the cover of a dumpster and I slid the shells into the shotgun. I racked the pump and put a shell in the chamber. Our escort had gotten some of his color back and that worried me.

"Here's the deal," I told him. "You get us in the door and then leave. Don't try to warn him. Don't look back." I gestured with the shotgun. "I see you again, I'll kill you. Understand?"

"*Claro*," he answered.

The three of us scuttled down the alley. Nobody spoke.

Yamashita made a faint whistling noise to get my attention.

"*Ura*, Burke." he told me.

"The back way? You think there'll be a door?"

"Burke, it is repair shop. It was not designed as a fortress. There will be a rear entrance."

I slipped down the narrow drive. There was a gate, a high chain link fence with plastic strips woven through it to block the vision of what was behind the building. I swung it open just enough to get through. I whipped around the corner, shotgun up.

The kid leaning against the car was in the process of lighting a cigarette. When he saw me, his mouth opened and the cigarette fell to the ground, but the hand holding the lighter hung in front of his face for a moment. His eyes were wide.

I kept him covered and tested the back door. It opened.

I jerked my head toward the street. "Get out." It took a minute to register, and then he nodded gravely, his hands held up in surrender, and scooted around the corner. He was still holding the lighter.

I slid into the building. It was a dim storeroom lined with metal shelves filled with the jutting angles of auto parts. There was an old desk covered with papers. The few small windows were covered with pebbled glass and crossed with bars to prevent break-ins. I picked my way carefully across the floor to the door that led to the main area. It was wide open and I could hear voices.

"*Jefe!*" Our escort's voice announced himself.

"*Ven' aqui.*" The voice was thick and phlegmy.

I scanned the sight before me from the gloom of the storeroom. Two bays with hydraulic lifts, the rails fully up like strange metal mushrooms. Walls lined with workbenches. The smell of old metal and oil. And in the stained cement strip in the center of the room, a woman tied to a chair, a small work spotlight shining on her and casting shadows in the dark shop.

Even from behind, I could tell it was Sarah from the shape of her head and the slope of her shoulders. She had been stripped to her panties and t-shirt, barefoot and bound and gagged. I couldn't tell whether she was conscious or not. I couldn't even be sure that she was alive.

That was when I almost lost it. But an internal voice cautioned me. *Easy Burke. Go fast, but don't rush.*

And I could not see Martín yet. He was there in the shadows somewhere, perhaps behind a pillar. The hydraulic shafts of the lifts broke up my line of sight. A deadly man. A cautious man. *Wait.*

The front door opened and Yamashita came in, holding the plastic bag with the manuscript in it.

"Who are you?" A voice came from the shadows, somewhere to my right. But I couldn't pinpoint his location.

Yamashita raised his arms from his sides as if to show he was harmless. He limped into the room, completing the picture of a broken down, old man.

"I am the go-between," my teacher stuttered, like a man afraid. His eyes barely moved, but I knew he was scanning the space, looking for our target. He didn't react to Sarah's presence, although I was sure that he had seen her. He shuffled another few steps forward.

"Enough," Martín ordered, and came into sight. He held a large, black automatic in his right hand "Where is Burke?" He was at the far right of the room, about halfway along the wall. From where I stood, Sarah Klein was directly in my line of fire. And Martín would be able to see me if I came through the door.

Yamashita shuffled to his left to come closer to Martín. "He is waiting with your young men," he explained. It appeared as if he was merely eager to talk, but I knew what he was doing. He was changing the angles. It's what a good swordsman does. By coming left, Yamashita would force Martín to move out from the wall to free his gun hand to be able to continue to cover him. And if Martín turned, even slightly toward Yamashita, I'd be outside his peripheral vision. The Japanese call it the dead zone.

Come on. I raised the shotgun and drew a breath.

Behind me, the rear door clanged open and I knew that I had waited too long and it was all coming apart.

The kid with the cigarette was back, and he was armed. It was some sort of machine pistol, with a long extended magazine jutting down from the handgrip. He came through the door wide-eyed and started firing before he even saw me. "Martín!" he screamed.

I whirled toward him as rounds clanged off the metal doorjamb I was leaning against. The shotgun went off with a roar, but I didn't stop to see if the first round hit him. I pumped another load up and shot him square in the chest. Behind me I heard a pistol shot. I wheeled back to the repair bay, hot and sick with fear for what I would find.

Yamashita was nowhere in sight. Martín was moving toward Sarah. Bound and gagged in the chair, she was squealing in terror at the sight of his extended gun arm, a questing, ugly thing. But Martín moved like a man carrying a great weight, one who was no longer sure he could remember what he was doing.

It gave me the time I needed. I moved into the room and he saw me, but it was too late. The shotgun blast caught him high in the chest; he spun around and down, the pistol spinning away into the grimy shadows. I shot him again.

I ran to Sarah and pulled the gag off. "Oh God," she sobbed.

Yamashita ghosted up to the body on the floor. He rolled Martín onto one side and pulled at something. It was then that I noticed the throwing knife jutting from his neck.

My teacher saw my surprised expression. "This one was not easy to distract. I used a more direct method."

"Oh God, Burke," Sarah moaned.

But I'm not sure He exists in Munenori's world.

24
GARDEN

The faces on the line of blue-clad swordsman were different, but all the same: stolid, remote. Some were still flushed with recent exertion, the skin sweat-slick. Their eyes were dark spots, markers of hidden thoughts. They were still recovering from the endorphin wash of hard training and the pull of the lesson's final meditation session, where the respiration and heartbeat are slowed and you are pulled down and away, deep into your core.

"*Sensei ni rei!*" I ordered, and we bowed to Yamashita, a dolmen set among a field of polished wood and indigo uniforms. He set his palms forward and inclined his torso toward us, a grudging acknowledgement.

"*Otaga ni rei!*" I called. We bowed to each other. "*Domo arigato goziemashita.* The polite, formal phrase of thanks. But it was mechanical, routine, a ritual murmur that did not connect us. Or perhaps it was that my mind was elsewhere.

Sarah's sister Deborah was pale with relief when we brought Sarah back, but her eyes widened with concern when she saw Sarah's condition, and I told her some of what had happened. She took her from me, steering Sarah gently to a bedroom.

Yamashita and I had sat quietly in the suburban kitchen. It smelled of coffee and the refrigerator was decorated with a child's drawings—Sarah's niece. Small magnets held notes and receipts, coupons, and the other detritus of everyday life. Mail lay unopened on a counter. From a distant room, the murmur of conversation as Deborah conferred with someone on the phone, probably her husband. Other calls followed and arrangements were made. I heard a shower start up.

After a time, Deborah came into the room. "I've called some people," she began. "The doctor will want to see her—a counselor I've got connections with…" she bit her lip and looked past me out the window.

"The man who did this…" she began.

I shook my head. "He won't ever hurt her again."

"How can you be sure?"

"Deborah," I answered bleakly. "I'm sure." She saw the look on my face and awareness filled her eyes.

"Good!" she said with a touch of vehemence, but then her hands flew to her cheeks in horrified surprise. There's a dark beast in all of us, and it's never pleasant when it breaks the surface.

"Can I see her?" I asked.

Deborah shook her head. "She's very fragile, Burke. I can't imagine what she's been through." She paused. "It might be best to wait awhile."

I stood up. "Deborah, I'm sorry." I went to touch her, but she backed away. The look in her eyes told me that she held me responsible for the abduction and the assault, the trauma. But there was more. She knew what I had done and approved of it some way; in that she was complicit and it frightened her. Her face was stiff with anger and concern and confusion. Blaming me wasn't a completely rational reaction on her part, but I understood it. She lived a tidy life and now it was as if I'd yanked back a curtain and the wild forces that churned just out of sight were brought into shocking view. She had to blame someone. Might as well be me.

"What can I do to help?" I asked her.

Deborah swallowed. "Leave," she told me. You can leave."

"Burke," Yamashita said. I focused once again on the broad, wooden floor of the *dojo*, students bowing out, racking weapons. I was still in *seiza*, the formal seated posture. My *sensei* loomed above me like an angry god. "You are not focusing."

I felt a deep surge of anger. "I am focusing," I answered. "Just not on what you want me to."

I didn't know what to expect from Yamashita when I answered like that. He doesn't show anger; the most you notice is a faint narrowing of the eyes, an unnerving stillness. A warrior who leaks emotion is not much of a warrior.

Surprisingly, my teacher sighed audibly and sank down next to me. He sat sideways, gazing across the front of my body, looking intently at something only he could see. In the West, direct eye contact is often a sign that something important is being said. For the Japanese, it is just the opposite. I waited as the students unobtrusively, but quickly, left us alone, my eyes lowered to the floor.

"I know that Ms. Klein occupies your mind," he said quietly. He cocked his head to one side as if examining a complex object from a different angle. "She has suggested some things about you that you find troubling." He nodded to himself, but whether it was in agreement with Sarah or for some other reason I couldn't tell.

"I worry I'll lose her," I told him.

"It is a real fear," he agreed. He held up a hand, finger pointing in the air. "But is this the thing that bothers you most?"

I took a deep breath. "I worry…" I began. But I paused.

"Yes?"

"I worry some of what she says about me is true."

He dropped his hand to his thigh and shifted slightly, the type of centering move a swordsman makes before starting a technique. "So. There is this strange conflict always with you, Burke. You tread the Way and value it. But it is the Way of the *Sword*. You know this in some sense, but…"

"Am I a violent man?" I interrupted. My voice trembled slightly with emotion.

Yamashita grunted. "You are a man. A good man. It should be enough. You Americans—why this fixation on violence as something good or bad? It is a tool. Nothing more." He paused and rocked slightly on his heels, thinking. "The world is full of violence. It is the way of nature." He gestured with his hand around the *dojo*. "Here we see the world for what it is. We take the chaos of the violent act and channel it. We forge ourselves into people who can bend violence for better purposes."

I sighed. "How do we know what is better?"

For the first time, Yamashita's voice grew cold and hard. "Burke. It is a child's question. It is why I wished to shield you from the world beyond these walls. At least for a time, until you grew stronger. But the world comes upon us when it will." His voice was reflective and sad. Then, he seemed to push down an emotion deep and away from himself, sat up and waved his hand in annoyance. "All this speculation—it is pointless now. Was there another way to deal with that man Martín?"

"Maybe," I began.

"Do not be a fool. If you had gone to the police, Ms. Klein would be dead. If they arrested Martín, he would bide his time or simply send someone else. The evil would live on."

"Is that how you see it," I asked, my eyes rising to look at him, "some battle between good and evil, peace and violence?"

He grimaced. "You are losing your way in this. It is not a

thing where you can choose either peace or violence." He placed his hands on the floor in front of him and pivoted to face me. His spoke slowly, distinctly, concerned to drive home the import of what he was revealing.

"The sword that gives life, Burke, *is* also the sword that takes life. They are one and the same. Accept it. Accept yourself."

I felt a great weariness then, but simultaneously I had the sudden sensation of a yoke being lifted from around my neck. I bowed in obedience to my teacher, wondering what dark places this Way would take me to. "*Hai*," I said.

A few days later, an envelope with Sarah's handwriting on it. A letter.

> Dear Connor,
>
> Maybe it's me. Maybe it's you. Or us. I'm not sure anymore. But it's too much for me right now. I need time and space to heal.
>
> I'm not blaming you—I have so much to thank you for. But I can't stop thinking about what I saw and what I did. What we both did.
>
> It's your world, Burke. I thought it was something different, but it's not. I'm not sure I can be part of it. Time will tell.
>
> Some friends in the Berkshires need an office manager and marketer. It's a quiet place—part ashram, part B&B. I'm leaving tonight.
>
> I'll need some space Burke, so please give it to me.
> Write though.
> Be careful.
>
> Sarah

Days later, we sat by twilight in Yamashita's garden. Amid the meticulously tended bonsai, sparrows and chickadees fussed before bedding down for the night. A trickle of water ran through a bamboo tube onto rocks and a bell chime sounded faintly from a distant corner of the yard. Wood and water. Earth and metal. The thickening air of night.

"Will she be back?" I asked Yamashita.

His head swiveled slightly in my direction. "Perhaps. With time."

My hands fidgeted in my lap. "She feels— I don't know— somehow responsible. Guilty almost."

"It is not a logical thing," he sighed, "but it is not uncommon. Sarah Klein is a good woman, a compassionate person. All that violence revolts her—the realization that the world is, at heart, a dangerous place. It is a shock for someone as good hearted as she. She takes on a sense of responsibility—it is perhaps a last attempt at exerting control."

"She feels guilty," I repeated.

"Survivors often do," he answered.

I stared off into the garden for a time. Yamashita stirred. "Life is like the *katana*, Burke. A thing of beauty, certainly. But at heart dangerous."

"A weapon," I answered.

"Indeed. And how a person sees the sword is a reflection not so much of the thing itself as the state of mind of the viewer. For now, Sarah can only see the blade and its sharpness."

I turned my hands over and looked at them; thick things, grown through the years in imitation of my teacher. "What can I do?"

"She asked you to write, *neh?* So write her. Coax her into seeing beauty again."

"It's a tall order," I said.

"The fact that you have grown to be a warrior does not mean that you cannot also be a poet, Burke." He smiled slightly. "What was it I sometimes hear you say to trainees?" And then he broke into a pitch perfect imitation of my voice, its accent and cadence and tone: "Nobody said that the Way would be easy…" he left the statement hanging in the air for me to finish.

Only that the journey is worth the effort.

I smiled back and bowed.

"Yes, *sensei*."

We sat in silence together as night filled the world, two rocks in a garden.

ABOUT THE AUTHOR

John Donohue is a nationally known expert on the culture and practice of the martial arts and has been banging around the *dojo* for more than 30 years. He has trained in the martial disciplines of aikido, iaido, judo, karatedo, kendo, and taiji. He has *dan* (black belt) ranks in both karatedo and kendo.

John has a Ph.D. in Anthropology from the State University of New York at Stony Brook. His doctoral dissertation on the cultural aspects of the Japanese martial arts formed the basis for his first book, *The Forge of the Spirit*. Fiction became a way to combine his interests and *Sensei*, the first Connor Burke thriller was published in 2003. John Donohue resides in Hamden, CT.